Gunsight Trail

**Center Point
Large Print**

**This Large Print Book carries the
Seal of Approval of N.A.V.H.**

Gunsight Trail

Alan LeMay

CENTER POINT PUBLISHING
THORNDIKE, MAINE

This Center Point Large Print edition
is published in the year 2007 by arrangement with
Golden West Literary Agency.

The text of this Large Print edition is unabridged. In other
aspects, this book may vary from the original edition. Printed in
Thailand. Set in 16-point Times New Roman type.

ISBN: 1-58547-886-5
ISBN 13: 978-1-58547-886-6

Library of Congress Cataloging-in-Publication Data

Le May, Alan, 1899-1964.
    Gunsight trail / Alan Le May.--Center Point large print ed.
    p. cm.
    ISBN-13: 978-1-58547-886-6 (lib. bdg. : alk. paper)
    1. Large type books. I. Title.

PS3523.E513G86 2007
813'.52--dc22

2006021250

CHAPTER ONE

Clay Hughes, cowhand, awoke with the full knowledge that something was wrong. A glance at the slow wheel of the stars—very near and bright, there in the high Sweetwaters—told him that morning was only a couple of hours away; but the stars and the hour he noticed unconsciously, without attention, for all his faculties were concentrated upon the faint whisper of sound which had awakened him.

Something was moving slowly through the thick underbrush which overgrew the up-canyon trail. It was an old trail and disused, so that the unseen advance was made audible at every step by the scrape of twigs. And he knew at once that the approaching thing was neither horse nor cow, nor any other creature having any right there.

He listened to the slow approach with an impersonal curiosity modified by the high-keying which victimizes a man who is awakened by the unexplainable, the unknown. Nothing whatsoever had ever moved along a brushy trail by night in just the way this thing was moving toward him now.

He thought, "It sure sounds like a steer with web feet."

As he searched his mind for some commonplace explanation, the movements came close enough so that he thought he could distinguish beneath them the sound of short and curiously heavy breathing. At this

5

he leisurely chucked his blankets aside, tossed fresh tinder upon the coals of his fire, and stirred up a lazy new flame of light.

He remembered now something that he had heard earlier in the night. He had off saddled an hour before the quick dusk of the Sweetwaters, and thrown down his bedroll in the mouth of this timbered gash. It was called Crazy Mule Canyon, though, of course, being a stranger in the Sweetwaters, he did not know the name of the place at the time. When he had chucked his worn soft-leather chaps into his spread-out bedroll, out of the way of porcupines, he had made himself comfortable with bacon, bread, and coffee, all cooked in the same frying pan, one after the other; and after that he had sat for a long time smoking brown paper cigarettes, waiting for sleep.

He remembered thinking then, as he sat smoking, that the mountain night was uncommonly still. No least breeze stirred the stand of lodgepole and aspen in which he camped. The canyon's slender stream ran horizontally here, so that the rush of tumbling waters was soft and far away; and he had found himself listening for sounds a long way off.

Presently, far up the canyon, a mule had brayed with the preposterous distance-defying voice common to mules; and though the echoes were deceptive, he had estimated that his neighbor was perhaps four miles away. He speculated about this for a little while before the sharp air of the high country drove him into his blankets; for the range was not of the sort in which mules choose to run, and he had noticed no fresh tracks entering the Crazy Mule as he turned in.

It was a long time later, but he was only just dropping off to sleep, when the report of a gun—that queer, flat flutter of sound that is made by a gun fired within canyon walls—spoke abruptly far above; and Clay Hughes had raised himself upon one elbow, listening. A gun shot in the mountains is nothing to arouse comment by day, but—at night it is a different thing, uncommon enough to make him wonder what had happened, and what the explanation might be. A vague uneasiness made him reach for his rifle, with some notion of inspecting its action; but he had grinned at himself sardonically and drawn back his hand. In the end he had smoked another cigarette; and presently went to sleep.

Now, remembering that up-canyon shot, it was in his mind that his visitor might be some prowling bear that had been wounded at the camp of his unknown neighbor. A wounded bear can make trouble. Hughes pumped a shell into the chamber of his rifle and, cross-legged on his blankets, waited with sleepy interest.

The approach drew near slowly; for a long time he listened to it while it seemed, uncannily, to advance perpetually without getting closer. This lasted so long that he considered going out to meet the thing, to get it over with. Then at last, out of the shadows beyond the reach of his firelight, a dim tall form moved; and Hughes saw that his unaccountable visitor was a man.

"Howdy," said Hughes.

The man from up-canyon did not answer, but continued to advance, his steps slow and uncertain. The fire was between Hughes and his visitor, partly dazzling Hughes' eyes; but behind the slender, fire-tinted thread of smoke he could see the man's face clearly. It was expressionless, but strangely drawn. The upward striking light of the fire made the shadows upon the face unnatural, and gave the eyes a look of hard glaze. He came so close to the fire that Hughes thought he was going to walk directly over it; and the cowboy saw that the man's hands were locked upon his breast in a curious position, as if he carried something there.

"What do you say?" Hughes spoke again.

The stranger's lips moved grotesquely as he made an effort to speak, but no sound came, other than the rasp of his choking breath.

And now the little twisting thread of bright smoke from the fire swayed aside and Hughes saw that the man's shirt was so wet with a dark stain that it clung to his lower ribs and the lean muscles of his stomach, showing them in glinting relief.

Hughes sprang up. "What's the matter, pardner?"

As Hughes stepped toward him the man swayed; then suddenly crumpled forward, his body crushing out the blaze.

The sudden quenching of the light was followed by a moment of what seemed utter blackness, before the starlight came creeping back, faint and blue in contrast to the orange light of the vanished flame. Hughes dragged the fallen man clear of the fire, the movement sweeping the embers into a fan-shaped spread of broken coals that lay winking dimly beside the limp form of the stranger.

The cowboy picked up the long, sprawled body of the unknown man and carried him to the stream. Here he poured a couple of hand-scoops of water upon the stranger's face; then fumbled in his pocket for a match.

The stranger stirred and spoke audibly for the first time. "Who is it?"—a choking whisper.

"Easy," said Hughes. "You'll be all right in a minute."

He struck a match on his Levi overalls and crouched above the other.

"Listen," said the stranger's husky whisper. "Listen." He raised a heavy hand and clutched the shoulder of Hughes' shirt in a grip which, in spite of a hard grating tremor of the fingers, was surprisingly strong. By the flickering light of the match Clay Hughes saw a twisting contortion cross the features of the stranger, as if the face were a mask distorted by wires jerked from within. The man's eyes were starting from his head with his terrible effort to speak. Once more the colorless lips formed words, and though no sound came, Hughes, watching the stranger's lips, thought he made out the beginning of a sentence.

"Get—that damn—"

He almost heard the ghostly murmur of words unspoken, so plainly did he see the syllables form upon the stranger's silent lips. Then abruptly the tiny flame of the match went out.

The stranger's convulsive grip upon his shoulder tightened, and for a moment more Hughes, fumbling for a fresh match, knew that the man was trying to speak. Then the hand fell away, and the new match showed Hughes only a face from which all expression had gone.

With quick hands he sought to do whatever might be done for this man. Against the stranger's breast still clung the wad of moss which he had clutched with both hands against his wound, but the bleeding had stopped. His visitor was dead.

Hughes stood up, a sudden weariness upon him; and with that weariness was fused a strange, bottomless sense of loneliness, an unaccustomed sense of hopeless desolation. It was the first time in his life that a man had died in his very hands.

He went to the stream and washed. Afterward he covered the body of the stranger with one of his own blankets, leaving him in the spot where he had died; then with practiced hands assembled his meager cook outfit and his bedroll. For a few moments he considered the advisability of catching up his horse at once; but the long-legged blue roan which he rode could hide like a deer, and to try to catch the horse in the dark was hopeless. He rolled a cigarette and waited for the near dawn.

• • •

The millions of bawling white-faced cattle which fill the stockyards of the world still have to be calved some place. Not-withstanding the heavy motor traffic upon a couple of transcontinental highways, the west still has whole states where range horses outnumber the human population by five to one; where ranchers in need of supplies drive fifty miles to the nearest store; where roads are few and poor, and the herds which graze the vast quadrants of mountain and plain can be worked by the cow pony alone.

Clay Hughes, single man in saddle, was one of those who keep the ponies at work. He turned to the long lonelinesses of the horse trails with an instinct inherited from men drawn irresistibly to the frontier in a day when the frontier could offer no desirable thing. He had been working stock since his first memory; he supposed he would be running cattle—though he hoped it would be his own cattle—when he died. At twenty-five, Hughes owned the horse and saddle he rode, and the clothes he stood in; and little more. But the long horse-and-rope labors of mountain and plain had given him other things less easily detached.

The quick strength of his hands and his easy endurance in the saddle were perhaps the least of his heritages from the trails. More important, probably, was a certain essential attitude toward himself and the trails he rode; it had carved a deep curving grin line in one cheek, though not the other, and had put into his blue eyes a humor that was at once mild and keen. He was tall and long-legged, and though sufficiently slender, he lacked that notable gauntness common to most in a country where men grow as lean as the living rock; his physical ability was principally visible in a certain easy poised balance of movement, not only in the saddle, but on the ground as well. No one ever saw Clay Hughes look sprawling or unready; he was like some well-tuned animal, too close knit ever to take a wholly ungraceful position.

And he was a rolling stone. Young as he might be called, he had worked stock all the way from the Panhandle to Powder River, and westward through the Beaverhead country to the Divide, and beyond. He had never been able to take root. Sooner or later, wherever he might be, the old nagging question always returned to him: "Is this all there is?" And when that happened, all too frequently for his own good, nothing seemed possible to him but to move on.

He might be sleeping upon a far lonely prairie when the trail itch would come and wake him up, and he would sit up in his soogans staring at the stars, aware that this range could hold him no more. Or he might be foreman at a branding corral, or busting broncs at ten dollars a head, or running a pack train: anywhere or any time that irrational impatience might come upon him, and set him once more upon the weary, welcome trail to nowhere. Those long trails had made him at home everywhere, comfortable in any place, and almost any situation.

His circumstance now, however, was an unfamiliar

one, and he was at first uncertain what he had better do. Something was warning him that there were entanglements ahead; that he had better go over the hill now, leaving alone a situation in which he had no logical part. That sense of the impending, perhaps, took its source from a dimly incoherent note of warning apparent in the unschooled phrases of a letter now in his saddle bag. The presence of Clay Hughes in Crazy Mule Canyon was attributable to more than chance, if less than fortune. The letter in his saddle bag was from Bob Macumber, foreman of the Lazy M, now but a few hours' ride beyond. Those two, Hughes and Macumber, had crossed trails more than once; and though their meetings and partings were as casual as those of range horses, a strong tacit bond of friendship existed between them, made up of the exact understanding which each had of the other's ability. Lately, word having reached Hughes that Bob Macumber had become foreman of the Lazy M, the big outfit at the head of Buckhorn Valley, Hughes had written to ask if Macumber had a job for him there. The reply was the first written communication he had ever had from Bob Macumber.

"Friend Clay" [the letter said]: "I am glad to hear they haven't hung you yet.

"Yes, you can have a job at the Lazy M if you want to come, but I will be honest with you, if I was you, you had better stay where you are.

"Conditions is very funny here in the Buckhorn. I

would not be surprised if something would bust wide open any time now, and anybody can have my job that wants it.

"Take my advice and stay where you are at. Whatever become of them half-blood colts?

"Yours truly,

"ROBERT MACUMBER."

That peculiarly reticent letter had reached Clay Hughes during one of those periodic lapses of his when his bedroll was as good as on his horse, and his horse as good as on the move. With the long-dust mood upon him, he had taken Bob Macumber's unenthusiastic letter in the only way he could possibly take it—as an irresistible invitation: an invitation, he was wondering now, to what?

Tonight just before dusk, obedient to his instinct to take a look around before turning in, Hughes had climbed to a high point on the rocky rim which rose sheer above the Crazy Mule. A little way beyond, the Gunsight Pass trail which he had followed plunged downward sharply into the valley of the Buckhorn itself. From his high lookout point he had seen the valley spread out below him, a hundred mile reach, mountain-hemmed, but broad and level, stretching into distances lost in the purples of approaching night. Hughes experienced a quick lift of the spirit.

Below him, not five miles from the foot of the mountain trail, lay a broad patch of green, where acequias carried the waters of the river to long stands of

14

alfalfa, or some other hay. In the heart of this green carpet, backed by the quarter-mile shadows of evening, there nested a stand of cottonwood and willow, half screening a scatter of adobe buildings. This, he knew, must be the Lazy M, the ranch that commanded all the northern reaches of the Buckhorn.

By the color of the land he could judge the number of cows each reach of the valley could sustain. Here to the north a man could try twenty-five or thirty head to the section. Farther on, where cattle showed as ruddy specks, fifteen to the section would be enough; and farther yet, comprising the greater part of the valley, lay the desert, where a man would run what cattle he could. Assuredly the Lazy M, at the head of the water, held the present and the future of the Buckhorn in its own hands.

He realized suddenly that he was looking upon a vast dominion. Gazing down upon the Buckhorn he could envision the achievement of the coming years: the year by year advance of ditch and dam, conserving the spring rush of the high snows, until at last the Buckhorn should blossom with the full use of its water. With the great reserve of feed which could be raised upon the watered land, the day would come when the Buckhorn herds would be numbered in hundreds of thousands of head. That was the domain which a man of strength and vision could build for himself, and for the world, in Buckhorn Valley; the unborn sovereignty whose future rested in the master of the Lazy M. It was a good stand, a great stand; the best he had ever seen.

Then, before the death of this stranger in his camp had added grim reality to the vague warning in Bob Macumber's letter, it had been hard to believe that some hidden struggle was rising to the surface in that valley, that the Lazy M was waiting in the shadow of some impending disaster.

Even yet the mystery of that shadow gave the vast reach of Buckhorn Valley the irresistible allure of the unknown. As his mind returned to it, he grinned at himself wryly for ever supposing that he had any choice as to what he must do now. With the first light, when he had caught up and saddled, he turned the roan's head onward and downward—toward the Lazy M.

The sun was hardly above the jagged black outline of the Finger Peaks to eastward when Clay Hughes came out upon the hanging bench at the foot of Gunsight Pass. Once more, nearer this time, he saw the hundred mile valley of the Buckhorn spread below him, sometimes broad and flat, sometimes broken by thrusting spurs of mountains whose long barriers seemed to guard a chosen range. The Lazy M seemed to have its own way here, a practical monopoly of the water. He was wondering what disaster could threaten any one who held such a grand range for running stock.

Suddenly the rider conveyed to his pony the faintest flexure of his fingers upon the reins; and the blue roan stopped, and stood with that motionless disinterest of a horse very far away from the feed bins behind and with no special hope of feed bins ahead—literally a horse balanced in space and time. For a moment it had seemed to Hughes that the desert was trying to give him an answer to the question in his mind; an answer which he could not read.

Far down the valley of the Buckhorn—fifty miles it must have been—the early mirage parted and drew aside like the sudden draining away of false waters, so that for a few moments, by a trick of the desert, there became visible to the man on the hanging trail the minute huddled outline of adobe houses, naked and sun-whipped in the empty plain. That would be Adobe Wells, parched but clinging stubbornly to life in the desert.

Through the dry air of the Buckhorn he could make out every detail of that flat, sprawling cluster, microscopic, but surprisingly distinct. He could see the steely glint of the spur railway which ended at Adobe Wells, and the sketchy outline of loading corrals, covering a much greater area than the town itself. Even at first glance, Hughes thought that town was ugly. Adobe Wells looked like the worthless fragments of something smashed to bits by the hammering of half a century of sun. And those fragments somehow had a look of insensate stubbornness; as if they forever waited a malignant destiny, unable to yield their place until that destiny was fulfilled.

Turning over in his mind his experience of the night, together with Macumber's cryptic letter, Hughes was suddenly aware that he was looking down upon the true materials of war. If one man lived who controlled the desert—as in truth one man controlled the Buckhorn water—the man of the desert would hate the man of the grasslands with a hatred dry as the forage of an August prairie. Only the least spark would be needed to sweep all the Valley of the Buckhorn with a consuming feud. . . .

Hughes tightened his legs almost imperceptibly upon the barrel of the roan, and horse and rider jogged downward into Buckhorn Valley.

CHAPTER TWO

Bob Macumber, Hughes was glad to find, was almost the first man in sight when Clay coon-trotted into the layout of the Lazy M an hour later. Macumber shook hands with a strong wrenching grip, but almost no words at all.

"Why, hello, Clay."

"Howdy, Bob."

They stepped back and regarded each other with mild satisfaction; Macumber might have been looking over a favorite cow pony, pleased that the animal seemed to have wintered fairly well.

"Got your letter all right," said Hughes.

Bob Macumber searched the ground for a straw, found one, and chewed it reflectively. An uneasy melancholy seemed to be upon the man, resting heavily upon his blocky shoulders. His short legs, bowed and powerful, seemed planted with an unusual solidity, giving him a look of baffled stubbornness.

"I don't suppose," Macumber grunted, "you sighted anybody, coming over the Gunsight." His face was expressionless, a rugged irregular face such as a man might chop out of wood with a hatchet.

"Well, yes," said Hughes. "There's a dead man up there, Bob."

Macumber turned like a wheeling bear and took half a step toward a cow pony that stood saddled beside the nearest corral; but checked, and turned back to Hughes.

"What did he look like?"

Hughes told him, reeling off details. "A kind of easygoing, cowhand-looking feller, maybe four years older than me," he finished.

"How'd they get him?"

"One shot, drilled clear through, from behind and to the left. Got his left lung, I'd say. He checked in at about quarter after two this morning."

"Real close guessing."

"I was with him when he died, Bob."

Macumber's mild eyes jerked back to Hughes' face.

"He come stumbling into my camp," Hughes explained.

"Talk any?" asked Macumber, very low.

"Few words, Bob."

"Come here," Macumber growled. He gave Clay's arm a quick haul, as if the cowboy had to be started by hand, and went striding ahead toward the largest adobe.

The ranch house of the Lazy M was built in the

shape of a commodious square about an open patio. Its batten-shuttered windows were deeply recessed in walls the least of which was four feet thick, after the old southwestern fashion. Long gritty winds had sanded off the harsh corners, weathering the massive adobe until it seemed integral with the land.

The half-dozen outbuildings were of the same stuff, thick-walled and solid, with the heavy butt ends of timbers sticking out of the adobe at the line of their flat roofs. And all through the layout of the Lazy M stood the tall cottonwoods, scattered in random clumps. They rattled dryly in the hot wind of the valley, and threw shifting mottles of shade upon the sunny walls of the adobes. Their height and vigor suggested plainly that their roots were finding plenty of water, deep under the hot ground.

Following Macumber into the ranch house, Hughes found himself in a great shadowy hallway. Beyond, the patio opened; in the contrasting smash of its sunlight Hughes saw with visual shock the bright green of clipped grass, and the astounding scarlet mass of a bougainvillea, which climbed the posts of an inner veranda beyond. Macumber, turning aside, knocked upon a heavy door, and entered without awaiting the growl of acknowledgment from within.

An old man, dressed like a common cowhand, sat at a safe-like desk of old-fashioned design. The gaunt, big-boned frame of old man Major looked little at home in a swivel chair. His face was that of an old cow foreman, deeply furrowed, heavily weathered, but scrupulously shaved. Only his grey mustache, clipped short and straight at the line of the thin lips, suggested any compromise with modern ways.

But it was the presence of the other person in the room which appeared to dumbfound Macumber, who started to speak, failed, and stood turning his big hat in his hands. A girl was sitting near the old man's desk, and Hughes grinned, remembering that Bob Macumber was always tongue-tied by girls. She wore belted overalls and flannel shirt such as riders wear; but her fine faintly wavy hair, looking dust-colored in the shadowy light, altered the effect to something supremely feminine, supremely young—and Macumber was put out of working order.

"Mr. Major," Bob got out, "this here is a good rider, Clay Hughes."

The old man nodded, watching Macumber, as if he sensed—or expected—more here than the advent of a hand. The range foreman turned and made a curious, inarticulate gesture with his hat toward the girl; but no words came out of him.

"What the devil's the matter with you?" Major demanded testily.

"Mr. Major," said Macumber in a thick voice, "there's a man been killed."

Glancing at the girl, Hughes saw that she did not appear to have moved. Her lower lip was caught between her teeth, and she was watching her father with unreadable eyes. Suddenly Clay Hughes was struck by the fact that the faces of the men were rough and ugly, and that a cow camp, however elaborate, was made to seem crude and makeshift by the presence of this girl. Her casual stock-working clothes, of which only the boots were beautiful, could not conceal the slim strong grace of her body, any more than the deep golden tan of her skin could conceal that her face was delicately and beautifully made. It seemed strange to find her here in what, without her, would have been after all, just another cattle range. But this room, this range, could never be ordinary while she sat there among them, anomalously belted and spurred—but very much a girl.

An odd stillness seemed to come upon old man Major while, for a long moment, the cattleman and his foreman held each other's eyes. Then Major got up and walked to the wooden-barred recess of the window. He stood looking out for some moments; and as he stood there much of the weight of his years seemed to drop away from him, so that the silhouette against the outer glare of the sun might have been that of a young man. When he spoke, however, his voice was very old.

"You'd better chase along, Sally."

The girl looked astonished. After a moment she said, "You're sure you want that?" The low pitch of her voice surprised Hughes, it made her seem so much more mature than she had looked. It occurred to Hughes that the trail which had led him here was different from all those others he had traveled. He had followed a thousand long horse trails, drawn on by an unidentified allure of things supposedly waiting beyond; but until now none of them had ever brought him to anything at all extraordinary at the end.

"Chase along, I said," Major repeated. "Go see how that mare is getting along."

She hesitated a moment more, then left them silently. Hughes prevented his eyes from following her as she went out. Something more than a slim belted figure seemed to have left the room when she was gone. The space she left remained definitely vacant, and the place lost its meaning.

The old man waited a long minute more before he turned to face them. "Who is it?"

"Hugo Donnan!"

Oliver Major smothered an oath. "Who knows about it besides you?"

"Clay Hughes, here, is the only one knows anything about it. He just swung down, and I hazed him right in."

"Let him tell it, then."

The eyes of old man Major bored into Clay as he repeated briefly what he had told Macumber of the death of the stranger. Major's questions were few, and had to do chiefly with the description of the wounded man.

"There's no doubt of it, Bob," he said at last.

"No sir; that's Donnan all right."

Major swung upon Hughes. "Did Donnan say anything before he died?"

A hard, speculative quality came into Hughes' blue

eyes, altering their mildness. He answered Major as he had answered Macumber. "Few words."

"And what were those words?"

Hughes hesitated a moment more. "Maybe," he said slowly, "you don't want to know what those words were."

The old man's voice rose to a harsh thunder. "You mean to stand there and hold out on me?"

"I haven't decided yet," Clay answered. "Set easy."

The surprise that swept the old man's face was followed immediately by the narrowing of a swift suspicion. Hughes smiled faintly, and, flicking his tobacco sack from the pocket of his shirt, began the rolling of a cigarette.

Oliver Major's voice crackled and thundered. "So that's the tune, is it? Well, get this, young man: if I start to have what you know out of you, I'll have it out of you, all right! If you aim to come in here and—"

"You'll get no place that way," Macumber grunted at Major.

Major checked, and turned upon Macumber with the quick anger of a man—any man—who is told that the road he is passionately pursuing leads no place. A silence came into the room, strained and electric, to last while a man might count fifty. "Who is this rider?" Major demanded.

"I've sided him through more roundups than one," Macumber answered. "You can bank on him in every way. But if he sees reason to keep his mouth shut, *you'll* never get it open."

24

Major turned away abruptly, and once more stood looking out the window, his hands thrust deep into his pockets. When he spoke again his voice was mild.

"Just what do you aim to do, Hughes?"

Hughes spoke slowly. "When this feller died in my camp, I didn't know but what it could have been an accidental shooting. But it's pretty plain that you people here know it's something more. I can see where I'm getting picked up in a stampede that's no job of mine. Now suppose I tell I've seen enough of this, and aim to go out and fork my horse, and ride on?"

"*I* guess not! For all we know—"

"And there you are! I didn't ask to sit in this game. But if I'm in it, I'll hold my own cards. I'd like to know what kind of angle the sheriff's going to take, for one thing."

Major said, "Hell, don't you even know who Donnan was?"

"I guess he doesn't know anybody around here, but me," said Macumber.

"Well," said Major, "after a fashion, and according to his damned poor lights, Donnan *was* the sheriff, himself . . . Bob, you lather that buckskin and see how many of the boys you can get together in a half hour. Especially, I want Bart Holt. Hump!"

When Macumber was gone, Major stood for some moments against the wall, his thumbs hooked in his heavy belt, studying Hughes personally.

"Man," said Major at last, "are you right sure you want to hold out on me?"

"No," said Hughes.

"I'll tell you straight," said Major, "I got my work cut out for me from here out. It's liable to make a whole lot shorter haul for me if you come out with what Donnan himself had to say, when he cashed!"

"You sure you want to know?"

A dry, humorless smile crossed Major's face, and he shrugged. "I never turned my back on a fact yet," he said slowly. "I'm sorry I jumped down your throat like I done. You got no reason to side in with me."

"It isn't that," said Hughes.

Old Major waited.

"Let's suppose a couple of things for a minute," Hughes suggested. "Donnan only had time for just a word or two. Maybe, being a stranger, I don't understand what he meant. But when I do—how's the killer to know but what those few words mean the rope?"

The old man said, "You mean—"

"What if I keep my mouth shut? Does it look to you like somebody is going to begin to worry pretty soon? Sometimes, a man gets to worrying, and worrying, until after a while he overcrowds his hand."

Major looked at Hughes for a long time. As they stared at each other their eyes looked hard, and their faces expressionless; yet there was a feeling in the air that these two were very near an understanding.

"Just what are you after, Hughes?"

"I don't know much about this," Hughes said. "This looks like your fight, in some way."

"God knows it is," said Major.

26

"But I'm hooked into it; and now if I keep my mouth shut—"

"You might live a week," said Oliver Major slowly, watching him.

"Might live to force somebody's hand," Hughes amended.

"And for what?" said Major curiously.

"How should I know for what?" said Hughes. "Only,—'Never throw away the key to a door—'"

"'—until you know what's on the other side,'" Major finished. "Lord, how many years is it since I've heard that! There may be some awful pressure on you, boy. You think you can stand pat against them all?"

"You saw me stand pat, just a minute ago."

"Yes," Major admitted, "you stood out on Bob Macumber."

"Even Bob Macumber," Hughes agreed.

"And you know what this may bring down on you?"

"Does anyone know that?"

Major walked forward, his eyes looking deep into those of the cowboy, and slowly raised bony, gnarled hands to grip Hughes' shoulders. He opened his mouth as if he were going to speak, but shut it again, and stood looking at Hughes so long that Clay became confused. But at last Major only dropped his hands, and turned away to the window again.

"I'm guessing," said Clay Hughes, "that you pretty well know who downed Donnan?"

"God knows I do," Major mumbled. "I guess I always knew—"

The cattleman's voice trailed off, and as he turned away from the window his face was grey. He began a cigarette, and Hughes saw that the tobacco chattered in its paper as the practiced old fingers tried to twirl it into a smoke. When presently Major looked up his eyes were dark and bleak: the eyes of a man who has stubbornly made up his mind in the face of an uncounted cost.

"There's just one chance in the world," he said; and beneath the bitterness of his voice Hughes thought he detected a deep, repressed uncertainty—"one chance that I might be wrong."

"And if you are?" said Hughes.

"God help us all."

As Hughes walked out into the sunlight he was asking himself why he had foolhardily let it be thought that he knew more than he would tell. A quixotic instinct had led him to deal himself a hand in a game he knew nothing about. At the moment the favorite words of his father, old Pony Hughes, known on a wide frontier when the frontier was young, had seemed sufficient justification: "Never throw away the key to a door, until you know what's on the other side." This was plausible enough; but second thought was telling Clay that his play was all too likely to turn into a cross between a buzzsaw and a boomerang.

No one appeared to be watching him. Even now he could probably mount his long-legged blue roan and catfoot unnoticed out of the Lazy M, out of the Buckhorn, out of a situation which certainly promised no advantage to himself. If he was ever going to pull out, this was the time. But though he knew he ought to be sorry that he had so definitely involved himself in a rising cloud of trouble, he found that he was not. For once in his life, Clay Hughes had puzzled himself.

Then, out by a corral which stood hard against the Buckhorn water, he again sighted Sally Major. The girl looked almost fragilely slender; yet in her quick nervous stride there was the suggestion of the pliant strength of riders, so that she seemed at once intensely feminine and as competent as a man. Now as he watched her walk out of shadow into sunlight, and saw the brilliant southwestern sun turn her fine dust-colored hair to a mist of gold, he suddenly understood why he had chosen to draw cards, when he might more safely have remained a passive figure, meaningless and disregarded. A faint smile deepened the grin line in his cheek as he told himself, "I'll—play—these."

After Hughes had breakfasted it seemed for a little while as if he was to be ignored. Old Major was interviewing one after another of the riders sent in by Bob Macumber. Seven or eight of these Lazy M hands came in during the first three hours, dusty, leather-faced men in worn range-riding clothes; they came in at a high lope, sweat lathering like shaving soap at the edges of their saddle blankets. Most of them promptly departed again, more hastily than they had come, on errands the nature of which Hughes could only guess. Evidently, Oliver Major conceived certain immediate necessities to be implied by the death of Donnan. The stir which had come upon the Lazy M had all the look of a hurried gathering of the clans. Meantime Hughes, left to his own devices, strolled about the extensive layout, smoked, sat on the top rails of corrals.

Then presently an element was provided which told Hughes that he could no longer leave here if he chose. This was the continual dogging presence of a Mexican youth—slender, Indian-faced, and inexpressive—named José, who accompanied him like his shadow wherever he walked. Plainly, this boy had been set to watch him. It was the first time in his life that he had been reduced to the surveillance of a lowly horse-wrangler. The time for voluntary removal of himself had passed. Hughes was a potential prisoner, unable to withdraw even if he so desired.

Bob Macumber did not return until eleven o'clock, and it was later still when he came out, saturnine and uneasy, to talk to Hughes.

"I thought you'd want to know the lay," Macumber started. He spat apologetically, and began the making of a cigarette. "The old man wants you to stay here while we go up to the Crazy Mule." He was not looking at Hughes; having let fall his surprise, he tried to hurry on. "Art French has come in from the Dog Creek sand hills; and he'll—"

"What's the idea of this?" Hughes wanted to know. "I supposed naturally he'd want me to go back up with you all."

"Aw, I don't know," Macumber mumbled. "That

30

feller walking toward the far corral is Tom Ireland." He indicated a big, rawboned, bald-headed figure which was moving, hat still in hand, toward a saddle-hung fence. "The old man sent Tom with a car to Adobe Wells to bring back Jim Crawford. Jim was first deputy—he'll be acting sheriff now. Crawford wasn't there, but Tom left word, and Jim's expected to show before night. Jim Crawford's about the only good thing in this business. He's on our side."

"Our side of what?"

"That feller coming in now is Bart Holt," said Macumber, ignoring his question. "I'm right relieved. I signaled him in as best I could, but I didn't know if he'd seen. Bart Holt is the old school. He'd be foreman here, only he's got more sense. He'll do the tracking, up Crazy Mule; he's about the best we've got, until we get hold of Grasshopper Tanner. The stoop-shouldered feller going out to speak him is Art French. I bet—"

"You look here, Bob," said Hughes. Macumber tried to hurry on, but Hughes overrode him. "I've got roped into this, and I can't get out if I want to. And I want to know what the war is about. Major hasn't even sent a man up there to tally my story, or see what happened. But already he's rounding in every rider he's got; and some of the fellers has been cleaning their guns. I want to know where's the fight; and I want to know now!"

"Clay," said Macumber, after a long moment of baffled silence, "this is a bad thing." There was a ciga-

31

rette glued to his lower lip, but he started the making of another; then saw his mistake and let the makings drift down wind from indifferent fingers. "Earl Shaw, he'll be at the bottom of this, you can bet; and God knows what that means to us here. Earl Shaw, and Adobe Wells . . . It looks awful bad."

"And who is Earl Shaw?"

"Earl Shaw?" repeated Bob Macumber absently. "You never heard of Earl Shaw?" He seemed at a loss for an answer. Then another line of thought seemed to strike him, and he turned to Clay Hughes with a sudden, confidential attitude. "The old man would give a thousand dollars to know where his boy is right now, I'll bet!"

"His boy?"

"Old man Major has one son, name of Dick Major. He's been out on long circle for three days. Some of the remarks Dick has bust out with about Hugo Donnan from time to time— Say, if Earl Shaw sets out to hang the killing on Dick Major, he can drum up a case against him that will look awful bad."

"You mean, this Earl Shaw will try to hang the shooting on Dick Major?"

"Well—we don't know Dick's alibi yet . . . That girl talking to Sally Major over in the doorway is her sister. Her name is Mona."

The two didn't look very much alike, Hughes thought; though perhaps the white linen that Mona wore, in contrast to Sally's cow pony clothes, exaggerated the difference. Mona was taller and darker

32

than her sister; she walked with the leisurely grace of the Spanish, something very different from Sally's clean-limbed, impatient stride. It was Mona whom most of these lonely-lived, cattle-working men would go crazy over, Hughes guessed. Yet, to him, Sally in her dusty clothes was by far the more vivid figure.

"Sally give me a message for you," Macumber mumbled disconsolately. "It's a mistake; I wouldn't even pass it on, I suppose, if it was anybody else. But maybe I'd better tell you. She says she's real anxious to talk to you if there should come a good chance."

"Chance? I'll walk over and talk to her now."

"No, you won't, Clay. My advice is don't talk to her at all. You'll only get her in trouble with the old man."

"Looks like who she talks to is her business," said Hughes.

"Yeah; the old man has always handled his girls that way. But just lately, seems like a couple of things has happened to make him take a new twist. I never seen anybody change like the old man has changed, just the past week. He's sure gone tough, and touchy. I wouldn't monkey with him if I was you."

"To hell with him," said Hughes. "If Sally Major wants to talk to me she can."

"I wouldn't take that slant, Clay. I—"

Old Major himself now came striding out of the house, shouting for Macumber as he came. The foreman climbed down from his seat on the top rail.

"One thing I forgot, Clay," he said. "They're giving you a room in the house for a few days, instead of a bunk with common folks. José will show you where your stuff has been moved at. And I'll be seeing you, tonight." Hughes watched him curiously as he turned, and ran for his horse at a lumbering trot.

Clay found his assigned quarters, now shown him by José, to be small and cool, midway of the house on the stable side. The room opened from a narrow dark hallway, which led to the outdoors, and had a single window with bars of two-inch oak. A rusty padlock dangled from a hasp on the outside of the door, suggesting that the room might have been a storeroom once; but now a queer sensation stirred Hughes as it occurred to him that this room was mighty suitable for a jail.

Another objectionable surprise was waiting for him there. Unstrapping his bedroll, to get out more tobacco, he instantly saw that someone had been before him. His gun belt and his holstered Colt were gone; and a glance at his saddle, near by on the floor, revealed that whoever had got his gun belt had rustled his rifle, too.

An impulse to rush out and demand an instant showdown from Bob Macumber turned him savagely toward the door, but the muffled drum-roll of receding hoofs told him that the Crazy Mule party was gone. With a sudden suspicion he tested the door, but found it unlocked; and when he had cooled himself to a semblance of indifference he returned once more to the outer air.

The man who had been pointed out to him as Art

French strolled forward to meet him. The features of Art French were distinguished only by the battered twist put upon some riders by the adversities of the range; but his eyes were unusual. They were opaque eyes, so dark as to appear black; commonly they sought the distance, and they were almost dreamy now as they lay, apparently unseeing, upon the far peaks of the Sweetwaters. Hughes got an odd impression that French, while dissimulating with unseeing eyes, was attentively listening.

"I don't suppose you want to play a game of seven up?" said French, his eyes drifting.

"Might as well," Hughes agreed.

Slowly a faint smile, ironic but not unfriendly, showed itself in the weather-hardened features of Art French, and Hughes answered it in kind. Neither of them ever alluded to the fact that from that hour Hughes was a prisoner in truth, and Art French his jailer. It was a curious arrangement, tacitly recognized by them both, and warily accepted.

That was one of those days that seem to hang forever in mid-air. All day long riders came and went; but by supper time most of them had drifted back, and when, shortly before dusk, three more cowboys came in, hazing a cavvy of nearly fifty head of stock from Twelve Mile Corral, there were almost a dozen at the ranch which that morning Hughes had found so nearly deserted. In the presence of Hughes they were mostly silent; casual men, not unfriendly, and not notably curious; but he knew that they covertly studied him.

They argued among themselves in little groups, their voices low. Over and over Clay Hughes overheard the repeated names of Earl Shaw, Adobe Wells, until those names began to represent shadowy mysteries, definitely malignant.

Bob Macumber had not returned when Hughes, weary of the surveillance of Art French and the heavy constraint which the situation imposed, at last decided to turn in.

A light hung from the ceiling of the hallway from which opened the small room assigned Hughes. Even so, as Hughes, an unlighted lamp in his hand, preceded the silent and expressionless Art French down the hallway, he was of the opinion that he could have surprised French in time to down him with the lamp, arm himself from the belt of the fallen man, and make his get-away. But the conviction was strong in his mind that he not only himself held an interesting hand in a game that stirred his poker instinct, but that he as yet had little to worry about. "I'll play these," he assured himself again; and the door of his lightless room closed behind him.

He groped for the table and set down his lamp. As he did so a cautious metallic click from the door behind him once more brought a sharp turn of anger through him. The sound he had heard had been the snap of the padlock in its hasp.

Hughes hesitated a moment, then grinned one-sidedly in the dark. "I'll still play these," he thought again. He removed the lamp chimney and struck a match.

Then as the small flame flared he perceived, with a sense of almost physical impact, that he was not alone. And, immediately, a second amazement swept him as he saw that the slender figure which stood, back to the wall next to the window, was that of Sally Major.

She watched him, her grave eyes at once startled and recklessly resolute; perhaps she also had heard the click of the lock. One of her hands fluttered in a quick gesture urging him to silence. A dozen questions raced through his mind, but what occurred to him instantly was that his window was undoubtedly watched from without. They would not take pains to disarm him and lock him behind bars of ordinary wood without mounting a guard. He lowered the flame of the match, abruptly, so that it went out.

Immediately her whisper came to him across the waiting dark: "Go ahead—you must light the lamp."

He knew that she was right. If he was to simulate that he was alone, as Sally Major evidently wished, he must light the lamp, move aimlessly about the room, and so make his way to her side, where they might perhaps talk in whispers without being heard. The next match broke in his fingers, but the third flooded the room with its sharp yellow flare.

The lamp was never lighted. Something like an angry hornet zinged past him, so closely that he imagined he felt the breath of its flight against his ribs, to spatter into the adobe wall behind him in a manner not hornet-like at all. Simultaneously with this phenomenon the crash of a gun came to them from somewhere in the darkness beyond the barred window.

The match went out as Hughes dropped to his hands and knees. Somehow the lamp chimney slipped from his grasp and crashed upon the floor, adding to the sense of instant confused disaster in the dark. He heard the girl gasp; and then he felt the quick grip of her hand upon his shoulder as she dropped to her knees beside him.

"Are you hit?" a tense whisper in the dark.

"No," he answered, whispering also. "What in the world are you doing here?"

"I had to talk to you. The only chance seemed to be to wait for you here."

There was an instant's pause, and then she added—and he would have sworn that she smiled quizzically in the dark—"it begins to look as if that might have been a mistake."

"It begins to look that way," he agreed.

Hurrying boots sounded in the hallway outside like a sudden scurry of rising wind. Then the latch jerked and somebody flung his weight against the locked door. "Clay! Clay Hughes!" It was the voice of Tom Ireland. "Are you there?"

And another voice said, "I heard his lamp bust on the floor. Smash in the door."

CHAPTER THREE

To Hughes it seemed that his irrational situation had now become completely incredible—the more so because he was acutely conscious of the nearness of Sally Major, kneeling beside him in the dark. All day long his eyes had followed her whenever she was in sight. Her quick clean-limbed stride, the live warmth of her grey eyes—the least tones of her voice, the least movements of her hands—had held his acute attention from the first moment he had seen her. And whenever his eyes were upon her he had been aware of an unaccustomed sense of humbleness, as if the distance between them was very great and would take a long time to cross—if it were ever to be crossed at all. Yet this was the girl whom the unpredictable turn of events had now imprisoned beside him.

The voice that was raised beyond the door was hard with the pressure of an imagined quick necessity. "That feller may be dying in there!" came the voice of Tom Ireland. "What you waiting for? Set your shoulder to this here door! We got to smash it!"

"What with, you damn fool?" demanded a younger voice, high-keyed with excitement. There was a heavy thud as somebody charged his weight against the planking of the door. The hasp rattled violently, but the door did not appear to strain.

There was an electric tremor in the quick pressure of the girl's hand upon his arm. Reassuringly he covered her hand with his own. "Set easy," he whispered. He raised his voice, putting a tone of impatience into an unexcited drawl. "What's the matter with you blame fools out there?"

"Hughes, you all right?"

39

"Hell, yes," Hughes growled back. "But it's no fault of yours if I am. What kind of a rat trap are you running here, anyhow?"

"Well, heck," said a voice outside, "if he's all right, I suppose we may as well leave him in there."

"Leave him in there, hell! I've got to find out what's going on here, don't I?" said Ireland's voice. "Where's Art French with that key? Go out and find him." There was a sound of departing footsteps, and a shouting for Art French.

"Wait a minute, Hughes!" Ireland called, unnecessarily; "we got to get the key."

Hughes chuckled as he answered, "I won't go away."

Sally Major leaned against Hughes' shoulder to whisper intensely in his ear. "Listen!" Her fingers pressed his arm sharply. "Can you hear what I'm saying? They mustn't know I've been here—do you understand?"

"Why, of course—"

"It isn't for me. You can't possibly understand! But"—her words, tumbling over each other nervously, were no louder than the faintest breath, close to his ear, yet they were distinct and clear—"you have to do what I ask you—right away—tonight—do you hear? You must believe me: I know what is happening here better than you—maybe better than anyone else. I—"

"Then, this shot they just took at me—"

"I don't know—I don't know anything about that. There's no time to think of it now." The whisper

40

became suddenly impassioned. "I can only tell you what I came here to tell you: you must get away from here at once, without talking to anyone. I'll help you get your horse out; and then you must break clear, and get out of this valley, and lose yourself, until this whole thing is over and forgotten. Will you?"

"You're the first person," he whispered slowly, "who hasn't asked me what I heard Donnan say in Crazy Mule Canyon."

"Have you told anyone?" she demanded.

"No."

"Then I don't want to hear! God knows, I know too much of this already. They're saying that you won't tell what you heard because you don't know yet what it meant. I hope you'll never know. Promise me that you'll tell no one, not now nor ever!"

"I'll promise this:" he answered, "that I'll tell no one until I tell you."

"Good boy." She paused, and he turned his face toward her. She was so near that he was aware of the faint fragrance of her hair, but he could see nothing. Then her whispered words came tumbling over each other again. "Here, I brought you a gun." She found his hands in the dark and pressed the weapon into them. "Now you'll try to get away? Now—tonight? You'll do your best to—"

He knew that he could not do as she asked; but so intense was her urgency that he was uncertain what to say. "Did it ever occur to you," he asked her, "that you might need me here?"

41

"No, no!" Her words were breathless with a quick panic. "You—"

Her sentence was not finished. Now there were voices again beyond the padlocked door, and he could hear a key chattering its way into the padlock.

"Where the devil have you been?" Tom Ireland was demanding of French.

French mumbled something unintelligible as they heard the padlock snap. Hughes flung an arm about the girl and lifted her to her feet as he rose. "Behind the door," he whispered, guiding her. Silently she obeyed. He jammed the six-gun she had given him into his waistband, and with his fingers made sure that his open canvas vest concealed the butt. Then the door swung open, and a tall shaft of yellow light flooded his prison.

Hughes lost no time in stepping out. "You're a fine bunch," he told them; and shut the door behind him with an exasperated slam.

That was a bad moment. It was in his mind that if Sally Major wanted her presence in that room to remain unknown, he was going to keep it so, at whatever cost. Right now if one of them should decide to probe the darkness within—

"I don't know what goes on here any more than you do," said Tom Ireland. The big man seemed at once angry and at a loss. He turned to the cowboys who filled the narrow hall. "Anybody know who thrun that shot?"

A bow-legged man with a square muscular face

started toward the outer door. "I bet if I go out and look around by the—"

"Come back here, Dusty! There's enough fellers trampling around out there now." In the absence of the old man and of Bob Macumber, Ireland seemed to be straw boss. "Now the whole passel of you fellers go on in the mess hall, and stay there! Go on, now! You too, Hughes."

Dusty Rivers led the way down the hall toward the inside of the house, the others trailing after him uncertainly. Hughes followed last of all, except for Art French, who stood aside for Clay to precede him.

Outside they could hear Ireland and a couple of others shouting back and forth. There is a hollow-sounding strangeness in the voices of men who seek the unknown in the night; their voices carry a necessity for action oddly frustrated by the deceptive emptiness of the dark. Hughes heard some one call out: "I seen the flash of the gun, somewheres here!" Then Tom Ireland's answering bellow, "Then stay away from there, you damn fool, and get hold of a light!"

The random shouting became fainter, muffled by the massive walls.

The mess hall was in the main adobe house, a long trestle-tabled room which seated forty riders, during roundup time. Peeled twelve-inch logs supported the flat roof, and the floor was of ten-inch plank, worn hollow in the doorways by a generation of high heels. The nine or ten cowhands now gathered here kept questioning each other, and repeating details of scanty information. "I was just turning in when I hears the shot—"

Those were not men who would have waited indoors for long; but now the big straw boss came clumping in after them, his chunky face as red as a peck of apples.

"Harry's casting for sign with a pump-gas lantern. I don't want no more of you busting out there and milling around on top of what little sign he's got. Hell's fire! I wish the old man would get back."

"What busted, Tom?"

"Somebody let fly at this feller," Ireland jerked a thumb at Clay Hughes perfunctorily, as if this phase of the matter were the least of his troubles.

"Miss him?" demanded a stripling called Rowdy Lee.

"No—they killed me," Hughes answered.

"When the gun spoke," Ireland went on, "I seen his light snuff out and heard his lamp fall down and bust. That's all I know."

"Where was you, Art? I thought you was on lookout."

"I know it," said French. The unusual opaque eyes in the undistinguished face stared dreamily through the wall. "But I figured that he wouldn't whittle out of them oak bars in two minutes, nor five. I was in the kitchen bumming a cup coffee when the gun blew."

"That is so," said a thick-tongued voice from the kitchen door. The Lazy M cook was standing there, a tall, lank Mexican in a filthy apron. "He was drinking coffee by my stove."

44

"Of course it's so," said Tom Ireland testily, "if he says it is. I'm asking simple questions, and I don't want anybody to think I'm doing anything any different."

"I didn't think nothing of it," Art French added; "I drunk my coffee."

"Anybody else see anything?" Ireland asked.

There was a silence. "I heard the shot, and the lamp bust," said the stripling called Rowdy Lee at last.

"I guess we all heard that," said Ireland. His eyes were watching his hands on the table before him as they tore the butt of a cigarette into minute fragments. "Now I expect there's a couple of things I ought to ask you fellers. I'm not prodding anybody about this. We all know each other here."

It occurred to Hughes that he, alone, was the unknown factor here, a stranger to them all. Yet none seemed to question the logic of the attempt upon Hughes' life by parties unknown. He had told his story to none of them, but information sifts rapidly through a close-knit group. Apparently there was no one there who did not know already why he was here, and how he had come, and that he was believed to conceal the single essential fragment of information which was the key to the fate of Hugo Donnan.

"But the old man is going to want to know a couple of things when he gets in," Tom Ireland went on. "One thing, he'll want to know where all of us was. Art was in the kitchen. Dusty was sitting by the bunkhouse door. I was coming round the corner of the stable.

45

Harry Canfield was in the old man's office squaring up his calf tally." He looked around at the others, waiting.

"Me and José was turning in, or fixing to," volunteered Rowdy Lee.

Two Mexican wranglers, looking more worried than seemed necessary, now stated that they had been in one of the more remote stables together, fussing over a couple of thoroughbred colts. A big blunt-faced Norwegian admitted with evident reluctance that he hadn't been any particular place; that he had been on his way to the bunkhouse from one of the corrals when he heard the shot, and had just stood around waiting to see what would come off.

This left only one, a wiry, hawk-nosed man, so dark of skin as to suggest Indian blood. He smoked slowly, studying his cigarette with an intimate interest; apparently unaware that all eyes had turned to him. "Well, Walk?" said Ireland at last.

The man called Walk looked up and Hughes saw that in his dark face his eyes were a startlingly light grey, like bits of shell, making him look lynx-eyed. It was a curious effect.

"Me?" he drawled. His eyes dropped to study his cigarette for a moment more but rose again to meet those of Ireland. "I reckon I was in the nigh corral. It's in line," he added, the words slow and distinct. There was a silence.

"I don't suppose you seen nothing, Walk?" said Ireland at last.

"No."

Once more silence seemed to close upon the group in the mess hall, while slow curls of smoke rose from half a dozen cigarettes, and from somewhere outside in the night came one of those brief scuffling tramples of hoofs that forever keep the night awake, wherever many head of saddle stock are held.

Tom Ireland stirred uneasily, his big bald head dully reflecting the gleam of the overhead lamp. His eyes were still on his hands as he spoke. "You've took this mighty well, Hughes, I think," he said. "You got plenty right to holler, you being locked up and your guns rustled, and then shot at from outside. I ain't saying I would have tooken it so quiet as you've done." His words sounded idle, as if his mind was really hunting for a clue as to what he ought to do next.

"The old man," he went on, "isn't going to take it so quiet, I'm afraid. What you fellers don't realize," he accused his slow, restive hands, "is that we've come pretty close to being made a damn fool of around here. When it gets so that anybody can come pounding into the layout, and pretty near kill a man, and high-tail again without anybody hardly knowing the difference—that's a hell of a note, that's all I've got to say. I only wish to hell—"

Whatever it was he wished to hell was interrupted as Harry Canfield came in. Canfield's gasoline pressure lantern filled the whole room with a blaze of white light until he turned it out, leaving the mess hall dimly yellow and smoky again.

"It beats me," said Canfield grumpily, sitting down on the edge of the table.

"Nothing out there, Harry?"

"Hell, I was a fool even to look," said Canfield. "Everybody and his damn brother has boot tracks over every foot of this place, and their horses too."

"If once we get Grasshopper Tanner and his lion dogs—" began Rowdy Lee.

"Yeah, that'll fix everything," said Canfield. "Them hounds will jump that trail, and foller it twice around the barn, and three times into the kitchen, and out again, and down a well, and up a tree, and end up by biting the old man."

Chris Gustafson, the man who had been no special place when the shot was fired, now opened a suggestion. "I been figgerin'," he said in his slow, deep voice. "If you want to know exactly where that shot come from, we can narrer it down by lookin' at the place the bullet went in the wall."

"It came from right in the window," said Hughes.

"Maybe you just thought that."

"I'll go take a line on that bullet hole now, if you want," said Canfield, getting to his feet.

"No hurry, Harry," Ireland answered disconsolately. "We can just as easy wait for daylight."

"Well, it won't take but a minute to get a general idee," Canfield insisted. He moved toward the door.

"Wait a minute, Harry," said Ireland again. "You can't get in there anyway."

"Can't get in?"

48

"I padlocked the door again," Ireland explained, "after Hughes come out."

Some turned their eyes to Ireland, mildly curious over what seemed a reasonless act. But to Hughes the information had the stunning effect of a thunderbolt. If this was true, it meant that Sally Major was still imprisoned in the room in which she had so astonishingly waited for him.

Red anger exploded in Clay's head. He could picture her sitting on the window ledge in that little room; and he knew that she would be resting there passively, relaxed, her hands folded in her lap, and her head leaned back against the white-washed adobe as she watched the stars. She would never be the one to fret or fuss, or storm against the actual. It was hard to imagine her under restraint, unable to come or go as she pleased; but probably there would be a quizzical smile on her lips, half mocking, half rueful, for that would be like her, too. The lifted poise of her head would always be dignified, and sweet, somehow above the ugliness of common things; and there would be humor in her smile, and the suggestion of something warm and human beneath, whatever situation the bungling of iron-headed cow-men might bring her to.

Hughes blamed himself—without knowing exactly why—for her position now. At best it was awkward, surely; but her warning suggested that more might hang in the balance than he could know.

"You locked it up?" Harry Canfield repeated. His

long horse face was pitying as he stared at Ireland. "Well, for the—love of—"

Ireland did not rally. He was studiously marking slow, laborious squares upon the table with a burnt match. "I've read too many detective stories, I guess," he mumbled sheepishly, without looking up. "It seemed like a good idee at the time."

"He was scared somebody would get in there and move the bullet hole," Dusty suggested.

"'Never raise hell with the scene of no crime until the coroner blows in,'" quoted Canfield, facetiously. "Oh, good lord, Tom!"

"It'll be all right," Hughes assured them. "I reckon when you come down to it, I'm the scene of the crime myself. Say—I guess it's all right if I go and get some tobacco out of my bedroll, isn't it?"

Silently Tom Ireland tossed his own tobacco sack down the table to where Clay Hughes sat. Hughes let it lie. "I'm much obliged," he said, "but if you'd just as lief, I'll smoke my own."

"I don't see no objection," Ireland mumbled. He dug a key out of his pocket and tossed it to Harry Canfield. "Let him get into his things, Harry."

Hughes rose slowly. Canfield was waiting for him at the door. Hughes knew that somehow he must get rid of Canfield—once the door was unlocked. Then as Hughes moved leisurely around the end of the long table, the voice of Rowdy Lee was raised again.

"What's that coming?" he wanted to know.

"Horses," said Harry Canfield, helpfully. "You

know—horses? They make that noise putting their feet down."

"Wait a minute, Harry," said Tom Ireland. "That'll be the old man coming back. There's no call to do anything more until he gets in."

"Give me your key," said Hughes, "and I'll get my tobacco."

"To hell with your tobacco!" said Tom Ireland, looking at him square and hard for the first time that night. "It can wait."

The silence that followed seemed to last for a long time while Clay Hughes and Tom Ireland held each other's eyes; yet long as it was, it seemed longer to Hughes. The particular and immediate object of the game seemed to have become the opening of a door. If he slipped his chance now, he could not tell what further delays might follow.

"I don't know what to make of you people," he drawled at last. "You act a whole lot like a bunch of old women in some ways. What do you think I aim to do with my bedroll—hit somebody with it? Hide it out on me if you want to, like you've already hid out my guns!"

"No call to jump the fence," mumbled Ireland, dropping his eyes again.

"I've ridden the cow country for a long time," Hughes went on, "but I guess maybe I've always ridden on a different kind of range than this. After this sheriff of yours died on my hands I rode on down here, open and above board, and of my own free will.

51

What do you do? You sneak-thieve my guns out of my bedroll behind my back, and you set a Mexican horse-wrangler to watch what I do. Then you show me my bed, and when I go to it you padlock the door. Maybe I was wrong in thinking that I'm still in the cow country. Some of your ways of doing business here strikes me a whole lot less like cattle than like sheep."

Nobody moved. Only Tom Ireland's hands became suddenly quiet upon the table before him, as if he were listening to something beyond.

"Now," Hughes went on, "I tell you I'm through. From here out I'm taking full charge of myself, and my war bags too. Those that don't like it, speak up! Because that's the law according to Hughes. To begin with," he said to Harry Canfield, "I'll take that key!"

Canfield turned alert, faintly entertained eyes to Tom Ireland and waited.

"You talk pretty big," said Ireland; "but I wouldn't jump into no trouble if I was you. In the first place, you got nothing to jump with."

"Haven't I?" said Hughes.

Ireland's head came up with a curious widening of his eyes, as if he were just coming awake. "Have you?" he said.

Hughes showed his teeth in a peculiarly personal, humorless grin. "That," he said, "puts a different light on it, does it?"

He saw Tom Ireland anger; but it was the curbed anger of a man old in the saddle, old in the man-killing work of the range. It was the uncertainty of his own position that was troubling Ireland now. He was a man who found himself under sudden responsibilities without knowing where he stood, or much about the undercurrents of his situation. It was the uncertainty of Ireland's position that Hughes had counted on, sure that the straw boss would concede a minor point, in order to delay a definite breach until he could turn the whole thing into the hands of Oliver Major himself.

But now the dusty drum of hoofs was very close. Hughes saw Tom Ireland hesitate; then rise and shoulder his way toward the door. "Just a minute," he said. "I got to see the old man."

Without exception the others got up to follow him; but at the door Ireland turned on them savagely. "Stay there, will you! All of you! By God, this is going to be one time you fellers can be found when you're wanted. Come on, Harry." He went out, a huge lurching figure on his high heels, accompanied by Harry Canfield. Hughes, uninvited, followed them out.

CHAPTER FOUR

The three from Crazy Mule Canyon and the Gunsight trail were already swinging down from the saddle as Hughes and Canfield followed Tom Ireland outside.

"Have someone corral these horses," Oliver Major told Ireland. The old man looked very grim. "Is that you, Hughes?" he asked, peering against the light from the doorway. "I want to talk to you."

"Mr. Major," said Ireland, "a funny thing happened here a little while ago."

The old man waited, watching him sharply.

"This feller, Hughes, had just gone into that room we give him, and we'd locked him up like you told us to; and somebody throwed down on him through the window."

A faint smile, very weary but very hard, crossed the old man's face as he slowly turned his eyes to Clay Hughes. The two exchanged a slow glance; to Hughes it almost seemed as if the old man's brief stare were saying, "Yes, you were right. I thought you were a fool, and I was wrong." Then Major turned hard eyes upon Tom Ireland again.

"Well, what did you do?"

"We let him out," said Ireland nervously.

"Naturally, man!" Oliver Major exploded. "What then?"

"We got all of the hands into the mess hall and asked them where they was, but seems like nobody knowed anything. All the boys back up each other, except two of 'em that was alone."

"Who were they?"

"Chris Gustafson and Walk Ross."

"Uh huh." Oliver Major seemed to be puzzled.

"After that," Tom Ireland went on, "Harry looked over the ground with a gas lantern, but he didn't find nothing; and we was just talking it over when you come up. I told all the fellers to stay in the mess hall where they'd be handy if you should want 'em."

"Keep 'em there," said Major, stalking into the house. "You go on to the mess hall, Bob, and see they set tight. Me and Bart Holt is going to talk to Hughes; and then maybe I'll call the whole crowd in. I ain't decided."

Hughes and the man called Bart Holt followed old Major into the room in which Hughes had first met the boss of the Lazy M.

"Mr. Major," said Hughes, "before we talk I'd like to take a minute and get a couple of things that I want from the room where they've got my stuff locked up. Harry Canfield has the key, and I—"

"Just a minute," said Oliver Major. "We want to ask you a couple of things here, and after that—"

"All the same," said Hughes, "I'm getting good and tired of having everybody on this place paw through my stuff, and I—"

"You got something in your stuff you're right anxious to get rid of?" Bart Holt demanded, unexpectedly.

"Certainly not," said Hughes.

"I guess your stuff is safe enough for the next five minutes," said Major, grumpily. "I told 'em to stay in the mess hall, and I'm used to having what I say acted out around this dump. Come on in here."

So again the unlocking of the door was delayed; and once more Clay Hughes found himself standing before old Oliver Major, in the room in which he had first been questioned. Major's big-boned frame was relaxed, as if he might be weary; but in the light of the kerosene lamp which lit the room his eyes were

55

glowing coals. Bart Holt, gaunt and weather-scarred, stood square planted beside the table in the middle of the room; his thin mustache was grey against a face of deep-carved leather, and his deep-set eyes were faded blue gleams which seemed to have squinted into ten thousand suns. The fact that Holt had not sat down gave a sense of imminence to that meeting, as if the old range wolf smelled action—perhaps had the makings of action already in his own hands.

"This is Hughes, is it?" said Holt.

"Yes," said Oliver Major. Hughes waited.

Major slowly rubbed his eyes with thumb and forefinger. "That was a kind of a lucky shot for you, boy," he said to Hughes.

"Lucky it was punk shooting," Hughes agreed.

"Luckier than that," Major said. "Lucky in other ways."

"What do you mean?"

"Bart Holt wants to ask you a few questions," said Major. "You'll see what I mean when he's done."

Bart Holt turned his deep-set eyes upon Clay Hughes. "You own a forty-five six-gun?" he began, his voice bleak and lifeless as winter rock.

"I did own a forty-five six-gun," Hughes challenged him. "Where it is now, you people know better than I do, I expect."

"When you load that gun, do you load it with six shells or five?"

"I carry my hammer on an empty cylinder, same as anybody else," Hughes said, his voice unpropitiatory.

"After a shot, do you reload that cylinder right off; or do you maybe leave it go?"

"Sometimes one way is handier, and sometimes the other," said Hughes, "as anybody who put his mind to it ought to be able to figure out for himself."

"Did you throw down on anything this morning or last night?" Bart Holt asked quietly.

"No."

"Nor the day before?"

"My gun hasn't been out of its bedroll for a week."

Bart Holt leaned forward, and for the first time his voice took on an edge. "And yet you carried an empty shell in your gun all that time, and didn't reload until you bedded down in Crazy Mule?"

"I made no reload in Crazy Mule, and I fired no shot," said Hughes definitely. "The six-gun wasn't out of its leather."

Bart Holt turned to Major with a brief, conclusive gesture. "There you are," he said, his low voice ironic.

"No, go on, Bart," said Oliver Major.

Bart Holt hesitated, then turned to Hughes again. "Then, just how," he said slowly, "does it come there was an empty U M C shell, forty-five caliber, in the ashes of your fire?"

There was a silence while Hughes studied old Holt. The inescapable intimation that he had lied made him suddenly wary. He knew, however, that he must not bend to this man. "I don't so much mind," he said, his voice low, "being taken for a liar; but it sure riles me to be taken for a fool."

Bart Holt swayed forward to toss the empty shell of a forty-five cartridge onto the table in the light of the lamp. "There it is, just like I took it out of your ashes," he declared, his voice rising a little. "The ash dust still sticks to its grease. You claim you never chucked it there?"

Hughes also leaned forward as he answered. "I give the flat lie," he said, "to the man who says he found the cartridge there at all."

Both Oliver Major and Holt stirred. "No, you're wrong, Hughes," said old Major. "I've known Bart near all my life, and I know that he'd no more back a lie than he'd twist a brand." He paused. "It ain't hardly necessary to put in, seeing that it's Bart, that I seen him sift that cartridge out myself; but I so done."

Hughes stared. "I'll take back that last," he decided. "In place of it I'll say this: if that cartridge was in the ashes of my, fire, someone else put it there."

Bart Holt's voice turned abrupt and gruff, as if he was eager to be done with words. "I don't claim to be no long tracker," he said, "but I guess I can read plain sign. I'd say by the ground it was a month, anyway, since any man come into Crazy Mule from the Gunsight side except you, as you say, last night. And only one man came into that part of Crazy Mule from up above—and that man was Hugo Donnan. You and Sheriff Donnan were the only ones there last night—and the only ones since!"

"You sure you want to lay that down flat?" said Hughes.

"It's one of them things that can't be got around," said Bart Holt. "No half-way tracker could have read that canyon any other way, not in a hundred years!"

Hughes considered. When he spoke again it was directly to Holt. "Then," he said, "if you back-trailed Donnan to where he was shot you know that I wasn't there."

"No," said Holt, "but you went up on the rim rock! Hugo Donnan was shot from the rock of the rim!"

"Wait a minute,—pull in, Bart!" old Major intervened. Evidently he had not foreseen the potential turbulence of Clay Hughes, who, in his own resentment, had stirred Bart Holt to an active and virulent antagonism.

"If you mean to—" began Hughes hotly.

"I can read plain sign as good as any man," said Holt angrily; "and when I've read it I don't want to see my word bucked, nor my horse sense neither!"

That he had climbed the long flank of naked rock which these men called the rim, Hughes could not deny. A blind instinct had made him do that; an instinct perhaps inherited from men before him, who had penetrated these far places in a day when the man who hunted beaver and the man who searched for gold forever had to think about keeping his scalp on, if he wasn't going to be rubbed out. Now, in a tamer west, that lonely look-around ritual had become as meaningless as the revolving of a dog in lying down—but remained equally automatic. Hughes had gone through it a thousand times without ever questioning why he did so, or thinking about it at all. But now it seemed to him that he had been drawn up onto that rim by an impelling fate. He knew that he probably might have followed the rock a long way, if he had been careful, without leaving any visible trail.

"I don't dodge that, Holt," he said slowly. "I was up on the rim all right."

"And there you are," said Holt again, turning to Major. "There we was an hour ago, Bart," Major said. "But we're no place now. You see that, don't you?"

"I don't see nothing of the sort," Bart answered harshly.

"This morning," said Major, "Hughes stood where he's standing now, and stood pat when we asked him what Hugo Donnan spoke before he died. I've told you that. And I've told you I judged he was making a fool play. But now I'm ready to back down on that. Bart, I swear, we'll come to find out that half the Buckhorn already knows about Hughes holding out the word that's going to hang a man. It's a game, gutty play this boy's making: and it's already drawn fire tonight. It's only by the grace o' God he stands there alive right now. Only one man could have wanted to down Hughes out of the dark—and that's the man who wants to keep Hughes from telling what he heard Donnan say before he died. Find that man, and you'll be right close to finding the man that downed Hugo Donnan."

"You can't get around the shell in the ashes, Ol'ver," Bart Holt insisted, stubbornly.

60

"Hughes," said Major, "don't you reckon you might have chucked that shell in there and forgot about it?"

"No," said Hughes.

Major banged a fist upon the desk beside him. "There you are, Bart. No man would pass up his chance for an out unless he was telling the truth."

"I don't know nothing about that," said Holt. "Donnan had friends that were mighty bitter against us here, as well you know. How do you know it wasn't one of them that took a shot at Hughes, knowing that he was the man who put down Donnan?"

"For that matter—" Major began.

"For that matter," said Holt, "I'm not afeared to say that I was never no friend of Donnan's, and more power to the man that downed him. But I don't figure to have it throwed in my face that I'm a liar and a fool. By God, I know what I'm talking about, and I aim to prove I do!"

"Nobody would make a point of coming in here and taking a chance of a night shot with all hands in except for some reason a lot more pressing than evening up a killing," said Major.

"Maybe that's hard to swallow," Holt agreed, "but if you're going to take his story you're going to have to believe that somebody stood on the rim and threw that empty shell a hundred and fifty yards through the trees and it lit in the ashes of his fire."

"Until we know more about it," said Major, "we'll have to take our choice between the two impossibilities."

"Well, I've made mine," said Bart Holt.

"And I mine," said Major, "but it's a different one from yours."

As Major met Clay's eyes, Hughes thought that for the present, at least, he could count on the old man of the Lazy M to back his play. Yet, the inexplicable appearance of the cartridge in his camp fire gave him a new sense of hazard, as if he no longer could be sure that the impossible would not rise against him. And the stubborn and virulent Bart Holt was a man whom Clay Hughes would far rather have had on his side. It was too late for that; it had already been too late when Bart Holt, sifting the ashes of the Crazy Mule fire, had made up his mind.

"Bart," said old Major, "I'm going to call the hands in here. I've got a couple of things I want to say to them all. And I want you to hold your cards close to your belly, Bart. Until I get new light, this boy stands on a par with anybody else around here, or maybe a half notch higher. I kind of like the way he stands up and spits in a man's eye . . . Go sing out for the hands."

"One way or the other," said Holt, moving slowly towards the door, "the harm's done now. We're against a finish fight this time, Ol'ver. The time for turning back's past."

Old Oliver Major answered him with a slow, hard grin. "I thought the fight was gone out of me. I thought I was too old and tired to care about standing off Adobe Wells any more. But today when I stood on the rim, and looked down at the Buckhorn spread out below—something always kind of happens to me when I stand on the rim. And there's a fight in the Lazy M yet! I tell you, Bart, I may be broken down and old, but by the Almighty, I'm still boss of the Buckhorn water! I've taught 'em that twice before. This time, so help me God, I aim to teach 'em so they'll never forget!"

Holt said, "I'm glad it's come . . ."

"Call in the boys."

For a moment, as if there had been an Indian magic in the old man's words, a deep stirring eagerness came into Hughes to know who "they" were, who had come against the Buckhorn water twice before, and twice been turned back; it was as if for a moment, he, like these old men, caught the scent of an approaching battle. Over the waiting Lazy M hung a sense of grim fatalism; everyone there seemed moving warily under the threat which hung over the Buckhorn, awaiting the impact.

And now there were drifting through Clay Hughes' head the names of old feuds, savage, bitter wars of the range which had taken heavy toll of men who could never give in until the last of their factions were dead. Tonto Basin—Lincoln County—Black Plains—Doghead Flats . . . Each of those names had its bloody history; some of them men spoke of only circumspectly, as if the embers of those hatreds might not yet be entirely dead. A somber history can lend thunder to a once commonplace and unconsidered name. Buckhorn Valley— what would that name mean tomorrow, next year?

But there was a more immediate necessity pressing upon him now. He was haunted by the face of Sally Major. He was seeing it in profile against stars as she sat, head leaned back against the adobe, in the recessed window of the dark gun room. There was gallantry in that girl, and stamina; but also something else indefinable that got to him, called out to him, as no one else ever had. And he blamed himself unreasonably for her present position. Once more he took up his stubborn effort to get possession of the key to the padlocked door.

"And now," he said, "if you'll just ask Canfield to give me the key to my stuff——"

The cowboys of the Lazy M were trailing into the room now, quiet, stiffly unhurried, their hats in their hands. "Give Hughes the key to the old gun room, Harry," said Oliver Major. "From here out, Hughes is hired on for as long as he wants to stay. And while we're on that, I want to say this: we didn't have call to ride herd on him, nor to lift his guns. He gets his guns back, and he's got free run. Give him his key. What's the matter, Harry? Ain't you got it?"

"Yes, but," said Canfield, embarrassed, "leave me say something, will you?"

"Well?"

"Something kind of funny come up, just since you've been back and talking in here. We all thought that we'd go and take a look at the bullet hole in the wall of that room, to see if we could make out just where the shot come from; and——"

64

"I thought I said you all was to stay in the chuck hall," Major growled at him.

Canfield looked confused. "Why, Mr. Major, we reckoned you just meant you wanted us on hand, in case there was call for us."

"All right."

"So we went and unlocked that door—" Canfield hesitated, and Hughes held his breath—"but—darn it, this sounds funny—"

"Well, well, come out with it!" Major snapped impatiently.

"Well—we couldn't get in."

"*How* couldn't get in?"

"Mr. Major," said Canfield with conviction, "that door is barred from the inside."

"Fiddlesticks!" grunted Major.

"That door," Hughes put in, "has been locked ever since they let me out of there."

"It sure has," Canfield admitted. "But all the same, that door's barred!"

"You act like a lot of kids," growled old Major. "What's the matter with you fellers? You shy like a bunch of near-sighted fuzztails. That door's swelled and jammed, is what's the matter with that. Go on, take your key, Hughes, and if the door sticks, I hope you'll have the sense to kick it in!"

"I ain't so sure—" began Dusty Rivers.

Major turned his eyes to Dusty sharply. "You too, Dusty? What's eating you, boy?"

"Oh, I don't know, but I thought—it just seemed

65

like to me for a minute while we was letting Hughes out of there—oh, well—"

"Spit it out, man!"

"Well," said Dusty sheepishly, "I thought I heard talking in there."

"I'm sick of this nonsense," Major exploded. "Are you going to pass over that key? You, Art, go along and get Hughes his guns. We shouldn't never have disarmed him to begin with."

Tom Ireland allowed himself a humorless chuckle. "He kind of fooled us, at that, I guess. Seems like he held a gun out on us after all."

"He sure did," French grinned. With good-natured impudence Art French jerked up the corner of Clay Hughes' vest, so that for a moment all eyes saw the black butt of the gun that Sally Major had given him. It was the first time that Hughes had actually seen the gun himself, and now, glancing downward, he saw that its black butt was marked by a white star the size of a dime, apparently inlaid in bone: the sort of nonsense a cowboy works on sometimes, during the long winter layups.

And now as he looked up he saw that the faces of the men in that room had changed. Art French had drawn back his hand, but some of them still looked at the line of Hughes' belt as if they could not believe that they had seen there, a moment before, the star-marked black butt of the gun; and he read in the eyes of one or two that they found what they had seen impossible to believe.

He shifted his eyes to Oliver Major's face and for a

moment he thought that of them all, old Oliver Major was the only one who had not seen or, at least, had found no special significance in the white star upon the black butt; but as he watched he saw the old man's face slowly change. The light went out of it, leaving it as harsh and ugly as cold lava slag, with only the eyes, which somehow now seemed deeper set in the rugged old head, burning with the light of a slow, dark fire behind. Hughes had never seen a man looking into the face of black ruin, but as he watched the transformation of Oliver Major's face it seemed to him that the old man was looking through him and beyond into dark vistas of irrevocable disaster.

Harry Canfield had been moving around behind the other cowboys, bringing the key to Clay Hughes as Major had directed him. He, with two or three others in the background, had failed to glimpse the momentarily revealed mark of the star upon the gun which Hughes wore. Close behind him Hughes heard Canfield whisper, "What's up?" and Walk Ross turned to answer from the corner of his mouth, "Dick Major's gun!"

"Canfield," said Oliver Major, slowly, without seeming to move his eyes from the thing they were seeing far beyond the walls, "I'll take that key myself."

Obediently, Harry Canfield gave the long disputed key into the old man's hands, and Oliver Major arose, stiff and slow.

Bart Holt said, "Ollie, what you aim to do?"

And Major answered, "I'm going to open that door."

The room was motionless, silent, while Oliver

Major moved slowly across it. Then Bart Holt called out to Major in a queer voice, "You sure you want to do that, Ollie?"

For just a moment the lord of the Buckhorn water hesitated. Hughes, looking about him, thought that while all seemed to feel that something extraordinary had happened, something mysterious and strange, only Bart Holt and old Oliver Major seemed to think that they knew both the question and the answer.

"Yes," said Oliver Major at last, in an almost sound-less voice; and he moved toward the door. "I've never hid anything yet. I'm too old to start it now." He turned down the hallway toward the courtyard, his slow stride uneven. Here and there, in the room he had left, cowboys looked at each other; then, one by one, moved to follow.

"Stay back," Bart Holt snarled at them.

"Let them come," said old Major in the contemptuous voice of a man to whom small things no longer matter.

Half furtively, yet apparently drawn by an irresistible curiosity, the cowboys of the Lazy M began to trail after old Oliver Major and Bart Holt, their boot-heels unaccustomedly quiet upon the tiles.

CHAPTER FIVE

That was a strangely silent procession which followed at the spurred heels of old Oliver Major and Bart Holt. The dozen cowboys who trailed down the unlighted hallway seemed abruptly subdued, so that even the click of their high heels sounded lightly, slow and uncertain, upon the tiles. All of them had seen in those strained moments in Major's office that the black butt of the gun Clay Hughes wore was marked with an inlaid star. But if any of them understood why this discovery should knock the wind out of Oliver Major as definitely as if a horse had been shot from under him, he kept it to himself.

And Clay Hughes, who wore the marked gun, knew least of all the significance of what had happened. He had seen black ruin come into the face of Oliver Major at the sight of the inlaid star; but Hughes himself knew nothing about the history of the weapon. It had been pressed into his hands by Sally Major, in place of the guns which had been taken from him. In Major's office Hughes had heard someone behind him whisper that this was Dick Major's gun, a fact which hinted at much; how much he could not tell in the sparse state of his present knowledge.

Nor did he have any time on his hands now to figure it out. Above all else, now, he wanted to postpone the opening of the gun room door. Various futile means occurred to him. He could turn upon Art French, whose casual hand had revealed to Major and the rest the star-marked butt of the gun, and, in an explosion of belated resentment, smash the man down. But he knew that when this diversion was over, old Oliver Major would once more turn his implacable attention to the padlocked door of the old gun room; and nothing would have been accomplished except that Major would have the definite knowledge that Hughes had attempted a desperate concealment. All Hughes could do, he decided, was to wait, casual and cool, for the developments which the next few moments would bring forth.

They crossed the corner of the patio, the brilliant moonlight of the desert country striking cold sparks from the polished steel of Bart Holt's spurs; and turned into the dimly lit hallway from which the old gun room opened. Old Major was in front of the gun room door at last, and a long moment seemed to pass while his unsteady hands fumbled at padlock and key. Dusty Rivers said in a low voice, "Shall I get something to smash the door?" and Major answered, his voice lower still, "We'll try it, first. By God, it'll open for me—I think."

Then abruptly the door swung back. Once more a tall shaft of yellow light from the hallway was flooding into the narrow room; and Oliver Major went in with the slow, grim step of a man who leans against the steel. Bart Holt planted himself in the doorway, facing the rest, as if he would bar them out. This was unnecessary, for the Lazy M hands, burning with curiosity as they obviously were, were yet holding aloof now, unwilling to intrude too far upon these old men. Clay Hughes, who was nearest, turned away his eyes. Fruitless as his efforts had been to obtain the key, they had yet been the best that he could do; and he did not wish to see the accusing glance of the girl as she faced at last that grim old man.

There was silence when Oliver Major had entered the old gun room; a silence that held them all in a curiously motionless grip. For there was mystery here, and the shadow of bitter defeat, which they had seen in the face of old Oliver Major, had given it immediacy and unknown weight. As moment after moment that silence continued, the sense of strain increased until something in the air was taut as winter wire. Hughes, without moving his head, turned his eyes to the face of Art French, and saw that a dew of perspiration had come to the man's forehead. French's eyes were fixed upon distances beyond the wall, and, as once before, Hughes knew that French was listening, listening . . .

Oliver Major's voice, coming very low from within, must have startled them all as sharply as the sound of a shot would have done. "Bring a light." Something in that voice was hair-raising and very cold.

A curious terror swept Clay Hughes. What had happened in this room since he had been released from it, and the door had been locked again behind him? That that room was not empty he alone knew best of all; yet, the long silence, ended finally by the request for a light—

It was Tom Ireland who, straining his gigantic height, unhooked the lantern from the beams above and handed it to Bart Holt. In the sudden darkness of the hallway the silent men watched the bar of light from the doorway of the old gun room waver and

71

shift, casting Bart Holt's shadow as a strange, swaying grotesque upon the opposite wall. Then at last Oliver Major came out, his face puzzled, and looking unfamiliar in the up-striking light of the lantern in his hand.

"Bart—Tom Ireland—was there ever another key made to this lock?"

"Mr. Major," said Ireland slowly, "I'm dead certain there never was."

There was a short silence before the voice of Bob Macumber said, "Just the same, if ever a door was barred, that door was, as I threw my weight against it tonight!"

"And yet you claim the door has been shut all the time?" Major said.

"That padlock," said Tom Ireland, "has been closed every minute since Hughes came out—except when we was trying to force it, and it held."

"Well, it's empty now. I think you're a bunch of fools," said Major, without conviction. He tossed the key aside so that it rang upon the tiles, and, leaving the door of the gun room wide open behind him, took a couple of long strides forward, as if he would walk through them all, unseeing.

Hughes had never been more mystified in his life. But before he could muster his wits to an explanation, Oliver Major suddenly turned upon him, his voice exploding. "Where did you get that gun?"

"I—"

He had started to say that he had borrowed it, or that he had stolen it, or that it was none of the old man's business. He never knew exactly what his answer would have been, for it remained unfinished.

Sally Major's voice came from the patio end of the hallway, startling them all. "I gave it to him," she said.

Everyone's eyes jumped to the slender figure—she was wearing a white dress now—which had stepped into the hallway from the moonlight of the patio. The cowboys moved closer to the wall, so that a lane was opened between father and daughter, down which they faced each other for a long moment. Hughes saw that Sally Major's face looked very white, even in the yellow light of the lantern; and her slim figure was very straight and uncompromising—defiant almost. Oliver Major's face he could not read.

Old Major spoke at last. "Go hit your blankets, all of you," he told the cowboys wearily. "Get some sleep while you can. For all I know we may be out of here long before sun-up. I haven't decided yet." For a moment or two nobody moved; and Major's voice rose in anger. "Go on! Turn in, I said!"

Those were not men accustomed to jump when they were spoken to. But now they began to drift slowly out into the night, sidling past old Major, who stood aside to let them go.

"Macumber—Hughes," said old Major, "you two stay back a minute. I want to talk to you. No, Bart, you get some sleep with the rest."

When the rest were gone, Major moved slowly down the hallway toward the patio, followed by Hughes and Macumber. "You too, Sally," he said, as he passed the waiting girl at the end of the hall. Thumbs in belt, he led the way toward his office again, his boots slow and heavy upon the tile.

Hughes, trailing behind, found that Sally Major was walking beside him, seeming light-footed and ephemeral in the moonlight of the patio. He turned toward her, but though the moonlight shimmered in the fine mist of her hair, he could not see her face. Then as they entered the shadows of the great hallway, her fingers closed upon his hand and she leaned close to whisper in his ear.

"I take back everything I said: I don't want you to leave! I want you to stay and help me—help us, here." Hughes drew a deep breath. Perhaps until now he had remained a factor in the Lazy M situation less by necessity than by his own stubbornness. Now all matter of decision on that score was over with. He knew that whatever might follow, he was in this game to stay. "Count on it," he answered.

"Sally—" Oliver Major turned from the deep recessed window at which he liked to stand looking out at nothing—"bring Dick here."

Hughes did not miss Macumber's start of surprise at this first open acknowledgment that Dick Major was anywhere on the place. Macumber had told Hughes that Dick Major was riding long circle, and Clay had neither noticed nor heard anything to the contrary. For a moment Sally Major hesitated, a slim, cool, poised figure, with vivid eyes that met her father's squarely;

then she acquiesced and went out. Major turned upon Clay Hughes.

"How many of the boys did you talk to about this business up at Gunsight?" he demanded.

"None of them, to amount to anything."

"How many of them asked you if Donnan had said anything before he died?"

"Not one," said Hughes. "We didn't get to talking together much."

Major turned upon Macumber. "Bob, nobody but you and me and Bart Holt knew that Hughes wasn't telling all he knew. Yet, somebody tried to kill this man tonight while he was unarmed and shut up, here in my own house!"

Macumber's shoulders dropped, as if something had suddenly crumpled inside of him. The mild eyes were troubled in his blunt, hatchet-chopped face. "I reckon it's my fault, Mr. Major. I told Tom Ireland when we was talking it over. Naturally we all thought Tom—"

"What's that got to do with it? Did you tell anybody else?"

"Tom told Art French, I think, when he picked Art to ride herd on Clay. I don't know who-all Art's told."

"And there you are," said Major. "There's not a man on the ranch tonight that don't know all about it!"

"I know, I expect so. If Clay had been killed, it would have been nobody's fault but my own." That was a man who forever blamed himself for everything that went wrong. He never passed the buck, nor let himself off of anything in his life. There was a massive self-accusation in the set of his shoulders now.

Major sighed. "That's all, Bob." He turned to the empty window again.

"Clay, I'm sorry," said Macumber. "If you get it in the neck you can blame me."

Hughes smiled faintly. "I wouldn't have it any different, Bob." He could say no more than that; he couldn't tell the chunky foreman that the strength of his position—if it had any strength—rested entirely upon just such spreading of the news as Macumber had begun. He watched Macumber affectionately as the foreman wandered drearily to the door and let himself out.

"It's a great night for trouble," growled Major wearily, turning away from the window. Then, sheepishly, he turned back to close the shutters. "After all," he explained himself, "they've took a shot at you once tonight. Seems like most fellers that get shot do all they can to lay themselves wide open for it. Did you ever notice that?"

"Yes," said Hughes.

Major went to his desk and cut himself a chew of tobacco. "I don't know what I ought to do about you, Hughes," he said. "The only fair thing to do is to tell you to take your horse and get out of here, as far as you can, and as quick as you can. Way things stand, you're awful likely to get gunned."

"Probably," Clay agreed.

"Do you realize," Major insisted, "that even if you want to back down now, and admit Donnan never said anything before he died—do you realize it's too late for that? From here out, no matter what you do or say, them that are against us are going to have to go ahead on the idea that you know something almighty dangerous. Do you realize that?"

"I don't even know who's against us, yet," Hughes reminded him.

"If anybody in the world's got a right to know, you have," Major admitted. "We all have lived under the shadow of this feud for so long that it's hard for us to realize that there's folks that never even heard of it. Us that's lived here a long time—we can't look any direction without seeing the marks of old trouble, and the makings of new. It's in the set of the hills, and the lay of the land; it's in the run of the Buckhorn melts. . . ."

"If I'm going to play this hand out," said Hughes with determination, "I'm going to have to know something, at least. Over and over, all day long, I've been hearing the name of Earl Shaw and Adobe Wells, Adobe Wells and Earl Shaw. Now I'd like to know who is this important cuss? He sure sounds like part rain-maker and part haunt-up-a-canyon. And I want to know what ails Adobe Wells—ants in the pants, or a set-to of the water-gimmes?"

"You can't savvy—nobody but us here can understand it—what it means to us here to hang onto this range." The old range wolf drew a deep breath, and the slow red glow came into his eyes again. "You first set eyes on this valley today, did you? Yesterday? Seems hard to remember when I first rode in from the

Gunsight, like you done this morning, it's so long ago. But this I remember plain: as soon as I saw the Buckhorn, spread out below, I knew that this here was the range that I'd come a long way to find. My brother and me—his name was Sol—we'd scraped together nigh two thousand head, and I went back, and we carried 'em here. Only a little over half of 'em made it all the long way—but they was enough for seed. It was hard going those first few years, but every once in a while we'd make a little beef drive—for the government usually—and get enough out of it to piece along a little while more.

"Then, while we was still in our beginnings, was when Earl Shaw put in his appearance for the first time. Well, it's no wonder if you've heard that name!

"Well, this Earl Shaw come riding through, and we put him up at the ranch and made him at home; and he took an almighty interest in our range. Then he rode on.

"But a year later he was back. He come in the lower end of the valley this time—and he was driving with him five thousand head. Five thousand head! I thought that was a lot of cattle then. Earl Shaw built his main ranch at Adobe Wells, and that was all right; though I could see that his cattle was going to run mighty gaunt, down on that desert land. But the next year, come grass, the Shaw herd come trailing north."

The old man's hands were restless, as if his mind was only partly on the story he was telling, while the rest of him listened for the step outside the door,

78

which still did not come; yet the part of him that was speaking was reliving old battles. It was a story old on the ranges; a story that Clay Hughes could understand as vividly as if those early scenes of stubborn struggle were being relived before his eyes.

Even in that first year many a trailing bunch of cattle bearing Shaw's Bar S brand wandered northward into Lazy M territory. The longhorn blood, still very strong in the range cattle of those days, could carry the herds so far that only the great distance between water holes held most of the Bar S stock upon the lower desert. Then, in the second year Earl Shaw made a drive of it from roundup, moving his herds bodily into the better territory of the Lazy M.

Shaw began his drive northward without serving the Major brothers any notice of his purpose. Not until the drive was on the way did Oliver Major realize that their grasslands were about to be flooded with Bar S stock.

In those days it was not always practical for two brands to run intermingled as one. The cow country was still too close to the days of the wild cattle, when unbranded stock was free to the man who would go out and make it his own. The Majors looked their choice squarely in the face. They could give up, now and forever, before superior numbers; or they could fight, turning to the only court of appeal the west then had—the six-shooter and the buffalo gun.

There was nothing timorous in the Major blood. The brothers swung into the saddle and rode out to meet the first of the Bar S herds.

Earl Shaw was not outriding that first herd; he was somewhere in the background, many miles to the rear—as, it seemed, he was always to be thereafter. As the Major brothers came up, the Bar S range boss, who was himself riding point, was joined by three or four more cowboys who came up at a high lope to back their brand in whatever play was to be made. They were expecting trouble all right—and it came.

The Bar S range boss laughed in Sol Major's face when Sol warned him they could not let the northward drive go on. This was very much to be expected; and as was to be expected too, one word led to another, and before either side knew exactly how it had begun, the guns were out of their leather. It was the beginning of the Buckhorn feud.

Sol Major went down in that first crashing volley. Oliver Major caught his brother as he swayed from the saddle, dragged him clear of his stampeded pony, and held him upon the withers of his own horse. Firing across the body of his brother, Major downed the Bar S range boss; and another cowboy was downed, and a third wounded, before they let him ride clear.

That night, beside his brother's grave, Oliver Major raised clenched hands to the stars, and pledged his last cowhide, his last ounce of powder, to the wiping out of Earl Shaw and the Bar S brand.

It was a hard, bitter struggle before the Bar S gave up. At one time the little Lazy M was carrying no less than fifteen riders, competent gun fighters brought at

80

any cost from far away. Young Oliver Major, saddle-raised and trail-hardened, turned into an avenging fury; irresistibly he swept the valley of the Buckhorn clear. Many an unremembered rider went down before that first war was done. If it had happened a few years later it would have become one of the famous range wars of the west. But such feuds were common then.

Yet, Oliver Major never accomplished quite all he had meant to do. He broke the Bar S brand, and sent the remnants of it back to the Adobe Wells desert, where it stayed; but Earl Shaw himself he did not meet. The riders with whom the Lazy M men repeatedly clashed were only the employees of Earl Shaw, good tough men who fought gamely for their brand, but who had had no more connection with the death of Oliver Major's brother than the ponies they rode. So Oliver Major sickened of it at last, and let peace return to the Buckhorn, while Earl Shaw himself still lived and retained the remnants of an outfit at Adobe Wells.

And there at Adobe Wells Earl Shaw had hung on stubbornly. It was Shaw who had got the spur track which eventually ended at the loading corrals of Adobe Wells. Starting with this frustrated railhead and the Buckhorn's first saloon, Shaw had managed to gather about him the beginnings of a desert town. It had even boomed a little, once, as the gold fever swept southward. And it remained a thorn in the side of Oliver Major that every head of his annual calf shipments paid a profit into the pocket of Earl Shaw.

The Buckhorn was still free range when Earl Shaw

came up the valley the second time. This time the herds that crept northward into the Lazy M land were neither long-horned nor white-faced—but instead a broad, slow-flowing river of sheep. The blatting grey tide came onto the grasslands, its dust clouds drawing nearer week by week; it left a new belt of desert behind it, as if it carried the curse of the dry land. The sheep cropped to the level of the soil, and their sharp hoofs cut to pieces the very roots of the feed. Long after the grass returned, the soil remained impregnated with the hated odor of the woolies, so that no horse or cow would graze where they had fed.

Earl Shaw had counted upon the law this time; but he learned that he had counted upon it too soon. The law of that country was still cattle law. Once more, unimpeded by outside interference, the cowboys of the Lazy M swept down upon the encroachers, and the coyotes grew fat on fresh-killed mutton. It was a hard thing, this ruthless destruction of the blatting herds, and the manhandling of dismounted men; but for the lord of the upper Buckhorn there was no other way, except to fold up and quit altogether. Once more Earl Shaw was driven back to Adobe Wells, hating the boss of the Buckhorn water as only a stubborn and defeated man can hate.

After that Oliver Major thought he had learned his lesson. He scoured the southwest for government land scrip, railroad scrip, any scrip; he bought it high and low, or at any price at all. Into it he poured all the gains of the past, and mortgaged his future as deep as the faith of money can go. He nearly broke himself; but in the end he made the upper Buckhorn his own.

He had thought the battle was over then, that nothing remained except to develop the future of the Buckhorn Valley. And the whole of the Buckhorn Valley was embraced in his far-seeing dreams. Looking into the future, Oliver Major saw the ultimate impounding of the Buckhorn's annual spring torrent, and the final bringing to full fruition of the possibilities inherent in the Buckhorn water.

And now, after all this time, Earl Shaw had turned his guns upon the Lazy M once more. This time they were a different sort of guns, treacherous and subtle; Earl Shaw at last was not only backed by the law, but was using the fabric of the law itself as an entrapping net. The new attack was from the rear; it struck at the very source of the Buckhorn water.

Oliver Major, ready at last to sink a fortune in the impounding of the Buckhorn's surplus flow—the project toward which the whole of his life had been built—had suddenly found his plans blocked on every side, and his project lost in an entanglement of legal complications as intricate as a snarled roll of barbed wire. Shaw had in truth made good the vacant desert years. Working steadily, always in the shadows, Earl Shaw had made himself the political boss of first a county, then a region; until presently he became a cog in the machine which governed the state. Being a cog in that machine was worth something, for when the machine was running smoothly it pulled strong wires in certain departments of the national government itself. It was running smoothly now. Earl Shaw, the defeated, the man sentenced by his own stubbornness to the desert land, was now able to clamp Oliver Major's project in an iron grip.

Nor was this all. It was Shaw's plan now to seize the Buckhorn water in the hills at its source, and by a practicable engineering project divert the Buckhorn River from its own valley entirely, carrying it across a range to water the Silverado desert on the other side!

As an engineering feat it was well within reason; and unexpectedly, the legal obstacles had proved surmountable too. Only a nominal trickle of water was to be left to the vast holdings of the Lazy M. The watering of the Silverado would enrich by many a million the instigators of this extraordinary scheme; while in the deprived valley of the Buckhorn the old cattleman would be left broken and hopeless in the dust of a withered domain.

It was a stupendous scheme, resolute and daring; and Earl Shaw had waited until all was ready before he made his play. Once started, his movements had been swift and sure. Almost before the first rumors of the Silverado project were out, the thing had gathered a momentum almost impossible to stop. Every technical blockade dissolved before the political influence of the machine of which Earl Shaw was a part. At the last only Oliver Major himself, the fighting old lord of the Buckhorn water, stood in the way.

Yet, Oliver Major, once aroused and aware of his

danger, was a formidable opponent still. That state was shot through with the drivers of the old trails, to whom Oliver Major's name had meant something since the earlies. Almost overnight Major brought to bear such a thrust of luridly expressed opinion that Shaw's allies were checked by a new fear for their own strength.

Thus the old man of the Buckhorn water now stood as stubbornly back to the wall as a run down bear. Once Major's personal influence in the southwest was broken down, ruin would roll over the Buckhorn like the herds of sheep which he had once turned back in another way.

As one scene after another fitted itself into the story, the great sweep and thrust of the Buckhorn feud seemed to loom before Hughes suddenly, as a gaunt mountain becomes visible behind fog, monstrous and terrible, yet with an elemental grandeur. Certainly the forces of war which shadowed the Buckhorn had their roots very deep, deeper than the roots of the cottonwoods which drew a prodigious strength from sources deep under the hot surface of the ground.

The exact significance of the death of Hugo Donnan, which had led to his own involvement, he did not at once see so clearly; but certainly old Oliver Major seemed to fear that the final fate of the Buckhorn water would turn upon this one killing. And though the feud was old, this much was new: Clay Hughes was now committed to it as a new factor. Overnight he had become a new card in Major's hand, another gun, a fresh impact of stubborn youth in this last conclusive chapter of the Buckhorn struggle. He found himself eager for the half-understood conflict ahead; for with the face of Sally Major in his mind it seemed to him a privilege to bring horse, gun, and wit unreservedly to the support of her people, careless of cost. He half smiled as he recalled again the words of old Pony Hughes: "Never throw away the key to a door . . ."

Oliver Major got out a pipe and lighted it. The blue smoke poured from his nostrils in a prodigious blast. He leaned forward through the smoke and his face twisted wryly as he gimleted Hughes with his acute old eyes.

"I ought to hustle you out of this; but I don't dast overlook the least bet. It'll come very hard," he said, "if it turns out that you, a youngster, a stranger in the Buckhorn, should turn out to be the only hope of the Buckhorn water." The old man raised a shaking fist above his head. "I tell you—"

The awaited step in the hallway was approaching the door at last. Oliver Major lowered his fist to the desk top, and the flame in his eyes burned lower as Sally Major came into the room, followed by a young man who Hughes knew must be old Major's son.

CHAPTER SIX

"Hughes," said Major, "this is my boy, Dick."

Hughes thought that there was a dry irony in his

voice as he spoke the words, "my boy." The two nodded without shaking hands, and waited while the old man seemed to study his son.

"But I guess you know each other already," Major added, slowly.

"What do you mean by that?" Dick Major flared. He met his father's eyes squarely. Father and son were alike, and yet not alike. In Dick Major's face was no suggestion of any shrewdness of judgment, nor perhaps even any notable quickness of wit. Instead, it showed the marks of a reckless boldness, a fiery temper and an explosive defiance of all restraint. Still, the qualities that were lacking in the young man's face might perhaps have been those which age can bring; Hughes thought it quite possible that he was looking at a good duplicate of the old man in his young days. If so, the similarity had incurred no bond of sympathy between the two. Hughes knew that if he had ever seen a father and son who had behind them a lifetime of misunderstanding, he was looking at them now.

"If you two don't know each other," said old Major to his son, "what's your gun doing in this man's belt?"

Dick Major opened his mouth, but shut it again, as if momentarily at a loss. Sally spoke. "I got the gun from Dick and took it to Hughes. I gave it to him just after he was shot at. If he's going to be shot at here in your own house, I say he has the right to something to defend himself with."

The glance that Sally shot at Clay was unreadable, but it was sufficient to stir Hughes acutely. Sally, out

87

of her cowpony clothes, was like something unexpectedly delicate and lovely out of a cocoon. Her presence in the heart of this ugly tangle of male lusts and
hatreds was the most extraordinary thing he had ever
seen; yet she gave a soul of urgent necessity to the
Lazy M's impending battles. She was at once the heart
of all action and an all but unattainable anomaly. That
they were mutually concealing even a meaningless
circumstance created a tenuous bond between them,
which to him was a welcome one.

Old Major hesitated, looking balked; then took a
new angle. "Where have you been for the last couple
of days?" he demanded of Dick.

"I told you I was going to ride long circle," Dick
Major answered him.

Father and son held each other's eyes as intently as
prairie wolves facing each other across the carcass of
a winter-killed elk. "Looking for what?" said Major.
There was a moment of silence, but Dick's stubborn
arrogant eyes did not waver from the old man's face.
"A man," he said at last.

Sally Major seized her brother's arm, but it was her
father to whom she spoke. "Dad, be careful what you
say! Can't you two ever use any sense?"

Old Major's face had turned a shade more grim, if
that were possible; but his words were quiet and slow.
"Where were you hunting, son?"

"On the upper rim," Dick snapped.

Old Major drew a deep breath and dropped his eyes
to his hands upon the desk before him. "All my life,"

he said, "I've worked toward one thing. And now in the end it had to be you to knock it out from under me. Oh, I'll get you off all right," he went on as Dick made a move to speak. "I'll get you out of it, and you'll ride clear, and be proud of your work too, I've got no doubt."

"But, Dad," Sally Major insisted, "he didn't do it."

The old man tossed her a glance. "You always took his part, Sally, in the face of everything."

Sally said hotly, "That isn't true, Dad, and you know it; but if Dick says—"

"I'm not asking him what he says. I suppose that's the last thing I want to know."

"If you won't even believe what we say any more," Sally rushed ahead, "then at least use your own reason! The only gun Dick ever carries is that thirty-eight—" she pointed to the star-marked black butt at Clay's belt—"and the empty shell that was found in the ashes up at Crazy Mule was a forty-five."

"How do you know that?" Major demanded instantly.

"You could hear Bart Holt shouting his story from any place in the house," Sally answered. "He sounded like he was rounding stock."

"We don't even know that that shell was connected with the killing, yet," said Major.

"It's a doggone funny thing, just the same," Sally insisted. "But if you aren't going to believe what Dick says—"

"I didn't say I didn't believe him. He's never lied

89

yet, so far as I know. Well, I've noticed that the plain truth can generally do more damned clumsy damage than anybody's cooked-up lies; I suppose that's why he's always stuck to it."

"Do you aim to believe me or not?" Dick demanded.

"Oh, I believe you all right."

"Then," said Dick Major, "I tell you I never killed Hugo Donnan. I heard he was somewhere up on the rim, but I couldn't even find him."

Old Major sat up, his eyes opening. "You mean to tell me that after you've let everybody hear you threaten to kill Donnan, you set out to get him, and went where he was—and failed?"

"Yes," said Dick.

A strange spasm of laughter contorted old man Major's face. He bowed his head, his shoulders shaking. "This is good," he gasped, half strangled by his extraordinary laughter. "This takes the cake! You do all the damage you can possibly do, and raise hell and high water by just letting your purpose be known; and then you go out and turn in just one more high grade, hundred per cent failure!"

He raised his head and the laughter disappeared from his face like a snatched mask. "You might just as well have killed him as to have stacked the cards against us like you have. I was hoping you'd been some place else, any place else but on the rim, so that you'd have an alibi. But as it is—" He made a gesture of futility.

"I—" began Dick.

"Why did you come sneaking in here without letting me know you were back?"

"I didn't come sneaking in here," Dick answered hotly.

"I talked him into staying out of your way for an hour, till you cooled off, was all," said Sally. "Enough things have gone wrong here already because you two always blow up at each other."

"What were you doing in the old gun room where we had Hughes locked up?" Major pressed his son relentlessly.

"Now just a minute," Hughes put in sharply; but Sally signaled him to be silent, and he obeyed.

"I don't know what you're talking about," Dick answered. "I haven't been in any locked-up gun room, with this man nor anybody else."

"Then who was in it?" Major insisted.

"I tell you I don't know anything about it. I never set eyes on this man before tonight, in this room."

"What do you say to that, Hughes?" Major demanded.

Hughes had been listening for something that would tell him why Sally had first urged him to leave the ranch, and then within an hour or two had changed her mind; and how it was that she had disappeared from the gun room. Now, however, he was sorry that the question of the gun room had come up.

"He's answered," said Clay flatly. "I wouldn't go against what he says, even if I knew different, which I don't."

91

"I didn't ask you to go against what he says. I'm putting it to you straight: who was in that room? If you mean to—"

He checked. The door had opened softly, and Mona Major had stepped into the room. She started as she saw Hughes; and immediately turned to withdraw again.

"Wait a minute, Mona! Come here," Oliver Major ordered; and once more Hughes was struck with the inept harshness of manner which the old man used toward his children. Perhaps he loved them so deeply that he tried to regulate every detail of their lives as he did his own, and unconsciously fell victim to a bitter resentment that they each insisted upon being as distinctly individual as himself. Certainly he took angry liberties with their pride which no cowhand would have stood for.

Mona hesitated, then closed the door and came forward listlessly. Her eyelids were inflamed, but the pale beauty of her face was apparent still; and Hughes noticed again the lazy grace of her walk.

"I hope you're satisfied," the old man told her brutally. "Dick's got no alibi."

"If you aim to jump her in front of this stranger,—" Dick Major began, the red color coming into the bronze of his face again.

"If you want me to get out, say so," Hughes said.

"Stay here," Major tossed at him. "This here is Clay Hughes," Major told Mona. "He's got hooked into this along with the rest of us through no fault of his own.

You may as well know who he is, because it may be he'll turn out the only living man that can pull the Lazy M out of its box."

"Well, I know who he is."

"I'm *generally* the last one to find out anything around here," Major commented. "I suppose you know that your brother did not kill Donnan."

Mona's voice was very low and lifeless as she answered: "He meant to; it's the same thing."

"It's very far from the same thing. It pitches us into the same kind of trouble exactly; but maybe since somebody else done it, we can turn the tables by locating the *hombre* that did do it."

Mona's eyes tightened, and a note of interest came into her voice for the first time. "You think you can do that?"

"By God," said Major, his voice rising again, "we've got to! But first we've got to find out a little something about Donnan; and you, God help you, are the only one of us who had anything to do with him!"

"Now you be careful what you say," his son flamed at him. "What's past is past, and you've got no right to air it in front of a stranger. I tell you, I won't—"

"What difference does it make?" said Mona in her lifeless voice. "I would have gone to the ends of the earth for Hugo Donnan—or with him. And I would have, too, if you hadn't stopped it. It doesn't make any difference who knows that now; for all I care the world can know it."

So that, thought Hughes, was the reason that Dick

Major went gunning for Hugo Donnan. . . . It seemed to him suddenly, as if the lives of these people lay open before him in brutal cross-sections. Especially it seemed as if the emotions of this girl had been laid bare before him in an exposure more stark and more unkind than if her clothing had been stripped from her. He stirred restively; and Sally Major turned her clear grey eyes upon him in a look of apology, under-standing, and companionship in difficulty. It made him grateful to her, as if Sally and himself were the only ones there who remained clear-headed and real-istic in the welter of blind loves and hates which had brought war back to the Buckhorn.

"Who would have been out gunning for Donnan except your brother?" Major demanded.

Mona shrugged faintly. "Anybody. I don't think he had a friend in the world except me. All the Earl Shaw people had turned against him because they thought he'd come over to our side, because—because of me."

"But who in particular?"

"I don't know."

"I suppose you realize," said Major, "that you're giving us no help at all?"

"I don't see that it matters," said Mona.

"You don't see that it matters!" Oliver Major exploded. "Good lord, girl, do you realize that your brother may never come out of this alive?"

"They can't convict him," said Mona, listlessly.

"Convict him? I doubt if they ever try. Once in the hands of an Earl Shaw posse, do you suppose he'll ever live to see the jail?"

"These aren't the old gun fighting days, Dad," said Mona without interest. "There's the law. . . ."

"The law," repeated Major, staring at her with an ironic hopelessness. "The law!" He seemed despairing of words with which to tell these youngsters that the machinery of the law itself, when owned and subverted to private ends, could become a weapon more ruthless than the six-gun had ever been; and so, in the end, clamp down so relentlessly upon a brand as to bring the six-gun back.

"I don't doubt he'll get out of it," said Mona.

"I mean that he shall," said Major, "but where do you think the Buckhorn water will be when we're done?"

"The Buckhorn water—?"

"Who do you think has been standing off Earl Shaw's Silverado project, that'll leave the Buckhorn dry as a last year's horned toad? What stands in the way of it but me, and me alone?" He crashed a fist upon the desk. "Once I'm discredited, once I'm shown as a renegade old gun fighter bucking the law, who's going to block the water steal then? What stand will I be in to buck the politics of a state when Earl Shaw gets his own sheriff in again, and his posse is swarming up the valley trail to rope in Dick, and Clay Hughes, and who knows how many of us more, on a charge of being mixed up in shooting a man from behind? What becomes of the Buckhorn water then? This is the time that Earl Shaw's been waiting for all his life—and my own flesh and blood has played me into his hands!"

Even the arrogant Dick Major seemed shaken to uncertainty by the old man's fury; but he spoke up briskly, "If you mean to quit without a fight—"

"Quit, hell!" said Major. "Bell that telephone! Get me the telegraph operator at Adobe Wells. They'll find there's a buck in the old longhorn yet!"

Dick Major stepped to the wall phone and twirled the handle. "Sally, go to the storeroom and get Clay Hughes' gun belt for him. What's the matter, Dick?"

"There's no connection. The line's busted again some place."

"I expected that. It wasn't cattle that busted it this time, you can bet your bottom cent. Go get out the—"

He was interrupted by the squeal of brakes, as a car slid to a stop close outside. Major flung open the shutter. "Who's that?" he hailed.

"Jim Crawford," came the answer from the dark.

Old Major snapped his fingers with a pop like an exploding firecracker. "That does it! I was beginning to think they got him. Dick, rout out Bob Macumber and Bart Holt. Tell 'em gun belts and six-guns—no rifles this time. Hughes, Sally's gone to get you your gun—give Dick back his own. The rest of the boys are to stay in their bunks, Dick. Hump!"

Jim Crawford came clumping into the room, clean-shaved and competent looking, but with an active worry in his green-grey eyes.

"Jim," Major told him without preface, "we're going

back with you to Adobe Wells. Is Earl Shaw in town?"

"Yeah, I'm sure he is, Mr. Major. I—"

"Then, if he's still to be found, I mean to have him in jail by sun-up, and his brother with him, and Dutch Pete too, if we can lay hands on him!"

"On what charge?" said Jim Crawford.

"Conspiracy to murder."

"You got any proof?" said Jim Crawford, uncertainly.

"Not a nickel's worth," said Major.

"Then how can we—" began Crawford.

"You were first deputy, weren't you? That leaves you acting sheriff now, doesn't it?"

"Yes, but—"

"We'll try to grill something out of some of them or their gang, and little enough we'll get; but if we can bluff Shaw's weak-kneed board of supervisors into leaving you in office for a few days—even a few hours—that'll be something."

An anticipatory gleam came into Jim Crawford's eye. "I don't think," he said slowly, "that those fellers are going to leave us put 'em in the jail. Not if they see any kind of a break at all, Mr. Major. There's going to be gun talk before morning, I wouldn't be surprised."

"We'll soon know; and boy, I'm praying to God you're right!" The old man was strapping on his gun as he went striding out.

"Is Hughes going?" Sally called after him.

He grinned down at her as he took his gun belt from her hands. "Don't you think I'm good for anything at all, child?"

97

The surprising night chill of the desert freshened them as they stepped outside. Dick Major had not yet brought around the car his father had sent him for. Oliver Major went striding off around the corner of the house, mumbling something about "infernal delays," and Crawford followed him. Hughes loitered, buckling his gun belt; and in a moment or two Sally Major joined him at the door. When he had belted on the weapon she walked with him a few paces into the cool light of the stars.

The moon had set; but as Sally turned her face to the night sky the light of the near dry country stars gave it a dim and lovely radiance. So still she stood for a moment that Hughes, watching her with his hat in his hands, thought that she had turned her face to the skies in prayer. When she spoke, however, her voice was prosaic and practical.

"Look here. Do you realize that you're the only one in this posse that seems to have his right sense left to him?"

"I don't get that, exactly," he drawled after a moment.

She made a gesture of impatience. "Dad is tied up, body and soul, with his dream of the Buckhorn water. It's bigger than he is, bigger than anything else in his life. If he's put to the wall, there'll be no chance too desperate for him to try."

"Yes, I see that all right."

"Dick—he's just a wild, crazy kid. He has all the courage in the world; but you never can tell which way he'll jump. Bart Holt sometimes gets pig-headed notions of his own, but mainly he's just a shadow of Dad. Jim Crawford will stand by Dad, but he'll never stop to think for himself. Bob Macumber—but I guess you know Bob better than I."

"Bob will play a game, steady hand," said Clay. "I don't know as I'd look to him to put in many new ideas of his own."

"But you," Sally went on, her words coming quickly now, "you're different. You've just come here. You're dragged into this thing almost accidentally, and with nothing in the world at stake. You can see things clearer than these others, and judge them for yourself."

"I don't know if—" Hughes began to protest.

"You do," she insisted. "You do know it, and you must make the most of it. I have no right to say it, but it's true: I'm counting on you for that."

"You're counting on me for—?"

"You're one of the hot-head posse that's going to jump down onto Adobe Wells from the outside, and try to make a roundup of some of the hardest men to handle in the country—men who hate us all from a long way back. There won't be a single lick of reason nor common sense in the whole affair, and it'll turn into a shoot-out at a second's notice. The only hope that both sides won't stampede into something crazy and terrible is that you put a cool head into it."

"It's a big order," said Hughes.

"Sometimes a word, an interruption, will turn aside a shoot-out. If a chance comes will you do whatever you can to keep the guns out of it?"

"I'll do what I can," Hughes told her. "I expect it won't be much."

"This is a dreadful thing," said Sally, her voice sounding dim and far away. He waited, watching her in the starlight. "You have your whole life ahead of you. When I think of that—I wish you hadn't ever come here at all."

"I don't," he said. "I don't wish anything like that."

She turned her face upward, and for a moment seemed to study him curiously. The starlight was insufficient to tell him what was in her eyes; but it made her face a delicate thing, like a flower, or like something half-seen, half-dreamed, in the mountain mist. She was no longer the spurred and belted cowgirl she had been that morning, but something unfamiliar, and new. Her hair—it seemed the color of starlight now—was swept back from her face, dramatizing the fine lift of her head so that, delicate as she appeared, there was about her something of the look of conquerors. He was thinking, "This is a thoroughbred, if ever there was one in the world."

"Mostly," she said, an uncertainty in her voice that he had not heard there before, "I think I'm glad you came."

He suddenly felt very humble. "I want to tell you

100

something else," he said. "I want you to know—"

The roar of an engine swept around the corner of the house and Dick Major skidded to a half-turn stop, reckless of his tires. It was a long touring car, topless, grease-streaked, and in wretched condition as to paint, but its voice was a deep, smooth drone. Jim Crawford dropped from the running board, ran to his own car, and stepped over the door to the wheel.

Oliver Major sung out from Dick's car, "Jump in with Crawford, Hughes! Bring Macumber. We're taking Bart Holt." Dick's engine roared; there was an angry smash of gears, and earth jumped from under the driving wheels as the car careened into the road.

Hughes swung aboard Crawford's car as it turned, and let himself be thrown into the back seat by the lurch. A light in the bunkhouse door showed them Bob Macumber running toward them, still trying to manipulate the buckle of his gun belt. Macumber made a final sprint and was with them as Crawford's car swung into the dust kicked up by Dick Major.

Looking back, Hughes caught a glimpse of Sally's white dress; she stood where he had left her, watching them go. It occurred to him that she wasn't going to see some of them again if things broke wrong at sunrise. Any particular danger to himself had not occurred to him until then—nothing fatal had ever happened to him before—but it seemed to him now that if the unexpected happened, he was lucky to wolf-trot into eternity with so clear a memory of Sally's face upturned in the starlight, and her low, faintly husky voice.

"What's the hurry?" yelled Macumber as he sprawled into the seat again after a lift that had nearly bucked them out.

"Dick always drives that way," Jim Crawford answered in a sort of plaintive yell. "It's dangerous, too!"

Hughes grinned; Crawford was a cowboy, all right, always ready to complain bitterly of such dangers as that of sitting down on a cactus, or getting slapped by a scorpion, but never seeming aware of the real dangers at all. Side-swinging crazily, they rushed booming through the night, hanging tenaciously to the dust-muffled gleam of Dick Major's tail light a quarter of a mile ahead.

At twelve miles they roared past the dim outlines of the Lazy M's southernmost corral; and a little beyond this Hughes sensed that the country was changing rapidly. The dry, dust-baked smell of barren ground replaced that of sun-cured grass, and the vast levels, dotted by black clumps of yucca and stunted greasewood, took on a paler color under the light of the stars.

The light of dawn was edging up cool and clear behind the black divide, dimming their headlights upon the road, as they neared Adobe Wells. Dick Major had pulled up and was waiting for them a mile outside. Close together now, the two cars rolled more slowly into the gaunt desolation of a desert town at dawn.

Dick Major led the way on through, past the long loading corrals and the head of the single track spur;

and the sprawled buildings of Earl Shaw's Bar S lay ahead of them at last. The headquarters of the Bar S were very close upon the town; no doubt what little there was of Adobe Wells would have been directly adjoining the ranch corrals, had not an idiosyncrasy of the railroad engineers dropped their railhead a scant half mile away.

And now as the two cars wheeled into the stronghold of Earl Shaw, they saw that as far as the Bar S was concerned at least, Adobe Wells was not asleep. Broad-hatted figures, grey and shadowy in the early light, were visible here and there among the outbuildings and the corrals. A group of two or three sat like crows along the top of a pole gate; a couple more stopped pitching hay over a fence to watch the cars come in; and there were others moving about the place by ones and twos. A group of three or four leaned or squatted on their heels against the wall of Earl Shaw's house itself, before which Dick Major pulled up now. "They're ready for us, all right," Jim Crawford grunted.

Apparently no less than fifteen or twenty men were on that place, an extraordinary number for a ranch supposedly as poverty stricken as the Bar S. It was the time of summer when work was slack; all these men, had they been needed here at all, should at this hour be only sleepily struggling into their boots, or making their way grumpily toward the mess shack. Instead, they stood about picking their teeth, loafing, as if they had been routed out and fed long ago; nor did they seem to be either working or getting ready to work. The Bar S, thought Hughes, certainly had the look of waiting for something very definite, of which it had full advance information.

What struck Hughes most sharply, and gave the entrance the look of an anticipated and hostilely awaited invasion, was that no one walked forward to speak them, and none flung up an arm, or raised a hail. That silently waiting reception was different from anything Hughes had even seen; it was the sort of thing that puts a sarcastic jauntiness into a man's walk, and makes him glad of the heavy swing of the gun at his thigh. Hughes jerked his disreputable hat over one eye, and humorously returned the expressionless stares of a couple of the lounging cowboys, as Jim Crawford, now taking the lead, walked stiffly to the door.

"Shaw here?" Crawford demanded.

No one answered him. Crawford made a sound in his throat like a snarl, thrust open the door without knocking, and went in, followed by the others.

A tall square-set man sat sideways at a table in the middle of the room, lean legs crossed, a steaming cup of coffee in one hand.

He was not alone. At first it seemed that the room was full of men, but that was because of the confusion of movement which was occasioned by the opening of the door; in reality only four men were there beside Earl Shaw. They had got to their feet as the posse thrust its way in, but at a word from the man at the

104

table they drifted into the background, lounging against the wall.

Shaw alone had made no move at all. Setting eyes on him as he sat there, relaxed and waiting, no one would ever have needed to be told that this man was the boss here, master of everything within his ranch. He was sallower than the others, as if for a long time it had been no part of his work to ride the range; his clothes were better, and he looked in every way better kept, as if he had never known defeat at all, but had only chosen to direct his efforts in new and more profitable ways.

Yet there was great strength in that face: strength in the blunt bony nose, and in the wide heavy jaws; and the prominent eyes were very hard and keen. Those eyes were very wide apart, giving the man an extraordinarily bulldog look; and there was in them—this was the amazing thing—the marks of a sense of humor, harsh and rugged perhaps, but humor just the same. A formidable man certainly, and a bad man for an enemy: for no one could look at him and picture his ever letting go.

But it was only as Hughes remembered the story of this man—of how he had always chosen to work in the background, preferring devious ways—that he sensed this man's full strength. Add the cunning that prowls warily in shadows to the bulldog grip, and the result is a combination that better men may break their hearts against, and never put it down. This was the man who would make barren dust of the Buckhorn

Valley itself rather than see it brought to fruition by an enemy whom he could not dislodge.

The keen bulbous eyes were upon Oliver Major now, disregarding the rest; and there was a grim irony in the eyes of both as they met. Compared to that of Earl Shaw, the face of Oliver Major was very gaunt and weathered, the face of a man still tirelessly active in the saddle in spite of his years. It seemed to Hughes that now the whole story of these two men was visible in the look of them as they faced each other here: one the old wolf of the ranges, who, driven to the wall, could fight with a slashing cold fury of destruction not to be withstood; the other the bulldog who would always return to the attack, seeking a new angle perhaps, trying a new way, but never once considering that there was such a thing as giving up! Certainly the war between these two could have no definite end while both lived. If those two could have shot it out back in the beginning, so that one or the other was put out of the way forever, it would have been a far less expensive, and perhaps a kindlier thing, than the long struggle which still prevailed, unassuaged, in their later years.

The lamp at Earl Shaw's elbow, still burning in opposition to the advance of the grey light outside, was backed by a tin reflector. Shaw reached out a deliberate hand and turned that reflector so that the light shone upon the faces of his visitors but not upon his own. "Mr. Shaw," said Jim Crawford, "I'm afraid I am going to have to ask you to come along with me."

Earl Shaw glanced at him then, and each of the others in turn, but his eyes returned to Major, and it was Major to whom he spoke. "You've got guts all right," he said, a touch of ugly humor in his eyes. His voice was hard and heavy, but had the quality characteristic of men who speak readily and well. "You certainly have got all the guts in the world."

The boss of the Buckhorn water permitted himself a faint ironic smile. "That oughtn't be any news to you," he answered.

"Not exactly," Shaw admitted without expression. He turned his eyes to Clay Hughes. With the glare of the reflector against him, Hughes saw the face of Shaw only as a shadow in shadows, with an obscure dull gleam of eyes. "I take this to be the feller named Hughes," said Shaw.

"Right," said Clay.

"And just what is your look-in in this?"

"Cowhand," said Hughes promptly.

"And what else? Riders don't blow in here from outside and jump the gun like you're doing, without some pretty unusual hook-up. What's your game, boy?"

"My game?" Hughes repeated. It seemed to him that Oliver Major's enemy knew a whole lot more about the affair than was to be expected in the normal course of events. He even knew Clay's name; and he had not so much as asked Crawford what had happened, or why he was wanted now. "Why, I reckon," Hughes answered, "my game is just to horn in freely where I'm not wanted. Where I come from it seems like there's been an awful shortage of trouble."

"You'll find it here all right," said Shaw. "Yes, I think you will."

Such a conscious menace had come into his tone that Hughes grinned.

Dick Major stirred restively, and Jim Crawford cleared his throat. "Maybe you didn't hear me," he said. "It begins to look like you already know what we're here for, Shaw. I was first deputy under Hugo Donnan. It's plain to see you know a whole lot more. Anyway, I'm going to take you, and I'm going to hold you, until I find out."

There was a moment's silence. Clay Hughes stepped forward and gently turned the lamp so that the reflector shone directly into Shaw's face. Shaw half rose, and out of the corner of his eye Hughes saw the nervous jump of Dick Major's hand; but Shaw only leaned over to blow out the light and sat down again. The cool grey dreariness of early morning flowed in to fill the room with a new cold actuality, replacing the golden light of the lamp.

At this point a movement beyond the window caught Hughes' attention, and stepping close to the squared pane he saw that every man on the place seemed to have gathered in front of the house. They lounged against the wall, or stood in groups that covertly watched the door.

Shaw was talking as he turned back. "What makes you think you're acting sheriff?" he was demanding of Crawford. "What have you got to show for it? What have any of these fellers with you got to go on, except hearsay and your own fool notions?"

"It's registered," said Jim Crawford. "I—"

"Is it?" said Shaw, a one-sided smile twisting his mouth. "Is it?"

He paused to let this suggestion soak in for a moment. In the brief silence Oliver Major was heard to say from the side of his mouth, "Watch Dutch Pete, Dick."

"It's a good, game bluff you fellers are making," Shaw went on. "I'll grant you that. But it's an almighty thin one. Now you want to ask yourselves a couple of things. How do you know you've got an acting sheriff with you? What have you got to show that Crawford was even a deputy at all when the sheriff, Hugo Donnan, met with his mishap? Suppose you start trouble here, and something happens that has to be investigated later. Ask yourselves what proof you're going to be able to show that you were acting for the law, or had any authority to act for it? What good are the suppositions of half a dozen cowboys, forty miles away, as against the board of county supervisors?"

"You know that I was first deputy as well as I do," said Jim Crawford. "I stand as sheriff until somebody else is picked."

"You can prove that, can you?" said Shaw.

There was a brief silence. "I won't quibble with you," said old Major, stepping forward abruptly. "Crawford has full say until a successor is named, and

109

I'm going ahead on that basis."

"And I," said Shaw, "don't accept him as acting sheriff, nor you as deputy—and I'm going ahead on *that* basis!"

"You know me well enough," said Major, his voice very hard, "to know that if I come here to take you, I'll take you all right, if it's my last act."

Shaw locked his hands behind his head, tilting back his chair. "If you fellers want to come in here as private citizens and start a shoot-out, I suppose all hell can't stop you, and you'll have to take the consequences. You're here on nerve, and nothing else in the world, and you know it—but it won't stick. As for taking me, that's ridiculous. If I give the word, not one of you will ever get off the place."

"If it breaks that way," said Major, "I guess you know well enough that you'll be the first to drop."

"Ask yourself," said Shaw, "what would be your own answer to a proposition like that?"

"I'm not going to speak but once," said Major, his voice very low and hard: "stand up and give over your belt."

There was a short silence while Shaw, teetering back and forth on the hind legs of his chair, made no move to obey. Already, in the exchange of a few sentences, they had reached a point from which there was no going back. Hughes knew that it was not within possibility for Oliver Major to back down and turn tail now, however great the odds; any more than it was possible to Earl Shaw to recede from the stand he had taken, and submit to his enemy before his own men. The two old men had exchanged words enough, more words perhaps than they had used to each other in years; the next move could only be something else, in which action would take the place of words. It seemed that the smoke of guns was about to fill that room that was now so deadly silent with the strain of impending disaster. In the taut stillness a clock somewhere in the room clicked slowly five times.

"Just a minute," said Hughes. "Hold your horses, Major!" Behind Shaw one or two men stirred.

"Keep back," Major ordered him. "By God, I'll—"

"Be still, Major!" Hughes strolled casually between Major and Earl Shaw so that he stood by the table. He hunted about among the litter on the table. "You got a pencil here some place? Yeah, here's one."

No one moved nor spoke now as he scribbled something on the margin of an old newspaper, tore off the scrap, and handed it to Shaw.

Earl Shaw looked at the scrap of paper for a long moment; then raised calculating eyes to Clay Hughes, and the silence held while the two regarded each other. Clay's eyes were sober, but there was a grim self-assurance in the faint smile that twisted his mouth as he stared back at Shaw across the cigarette he had begun to roll.

"I don't see it, exactly," said Shaw at last.

"That's funny. I hardly supposed I would be suggesting anything new," said Hughes, "considering the question you just asked me, a little while ago." He took the scrap of paper from Shaw's relaxed fingers, slowly tore it to tiny bits, and thrust the fragments into a pocket of his vest.

"What do you want here?" said Shaw.

"Naturally," said Hughes, "you can't hardly expect me to answer that, can you?"

The others in that room, listening, waiting—there was not one of them who could know what was happening here. Shaw himself seemed only partly to understand with what he was confronted now. Their voices, as they spoke again, were low and confidential. It was as if some sort of an understanding had sprung up between them, based on something to which no one else there had any clue.

"If you want to walk out of this," said Shaw, "you have my leave."

"Hell," Hughes answered contemptuously, "that's no good."

"It puts me in a very funny place," said Shaw, studying him.

"You must be crazy," Clay told him. "Look at your cards, man! You know what's the only reasonable thing to do." Then while Shaw hesitated, Hughes added cryptically, "After all, it's probably for the last time."

"Yes," said Shaw, slowly, "it's probably the last time." He turned his eyes to Oliver Major, hard and expressionless. Then slowly he got to his feet, unbuckled his gun belt, and flung it on the table in a gesture of surrender.

CHAPTER EIGHT

Dick Major's car, with Bob Macumber at the wheel, plugged homeward a good deal more slowly than it had come, clinging to the twisted ruts. Hughes and Macumber were alone. The rest had remained in Adobe Wells, where Oliver Major was working hard to make the most of the short span of power provided him by Jim Crawford's temporary authority.

Macumber's face was worried and puzzled; repeatedly he seemed about to speak, but when he at last was able to formulate what he wanted to say, his well considered words were something of a disappointment.

"This is certainly a funny thing, Clay," he got out at last.

"Yes," said Hughes, sleepily.

"I suppose you realize," said Macumber, "that you are kind of being rid' herd on again?"

"Yeah—and you're the rider this time," said Hughes.

"Oh, it ain't exactly that," said Macumber, uncomfortably. "You know I'd never raise hand to your comings and goings, Clay. But I guess you realize you got the old man ten miles in the air?"

"People sure do go up easy around here," Clay agreed.

"Why wouldn't they? You coming in with some private understanding with Shaw kind of took the wind out of everybody, I guess."

"There isn't any special understanding, Bob."

"I suppose not, but what do you expect everybody to think? You sure have got yourself mixed up in this about as deep as anybody ever I see. I don't know you like I thought I did, Clay. Just as all hell is about to blow up in a general shoot-up, you scribble a little note to Shaw, and he does like you say. And when the old man asks you what was in that note, you tell him it wasn't anything, and you stick to that, too. Damned if I understand what you're working up to, Clay."

"I didn't see a thing in that shoot-out," said Clay doggedly, "but a good chance to get hurt."

"Oh, sure," Macumber said. "We was all glad to see him give in. The queer looking thing is how you done it. You've got the old man wondering what your inside hook-up is, with Earl Shaw."

"That's ridiculous, Bob."

"I suppose it is, Clay."

"I have a good reason for not telling the old man what was in that note, nor anybody else either; and the reason is that I have a fine chance to be misunderstood, and get into more trouble than I'm in already."

"I'll be damned if you don't beat me," said Macumber.

"It'll come out in the course of time, I expect," said Hughes, "and you sure are going to be disappointed when you hear what it was. All I've got to say is that it was the damnedest fool thing you can imagine, and nobody was more surprised than I was when it worked. But the old man is making a bad mistake in

114

sending me back to the ranch. And it's pretty plain that he's sent you with me to see that I don't jump the range or something."

"I know," admitted Macumber, disconsolately. "You ought to realize that as long as you hold back what Donnan said, everybody's going to handle you like you was dynamite. I'm beginning to think you don't know what you're doing very good, Clay."

"You don't realize how close to the truth that is," said Hughes.

"What you aim to do, Clay?"

"I aim to go to sleep." He pulled his hat over his eyes and settled himself in the seat.

"Hold out on me if you want to," said Macumber at last. "I'm going to keep on thinking you're on the up and up, no matter what the others say."

A gentle snore answered him from under Clay's disreputable hat.

Back at the Lazy M Hughes found that he was not so much in need of sleep as he had supposed. He had fully expected to sleep until the following day; but the morning was hardly gone when he found himself broad awake again, cool and clear-headed.

Grasshopper Tanner had come and gone while Clay slept. Hughes remembered dimly having half waked to listen to the mouthing and wailing of Tanner's dogs, that curiously stirring noise of casual voicings which forever follows a lion pack. Clay wished now that he had roused to talk to the old hunter, but Grasshopper had left for the Crazy Mule almost as abruptly as he had come, and as yet Hughes had not seen the old man at all.

As the afternoon wore on, and no word came from Adobe Wells, Hughes began to chafe at the turn of the luck which seemed to have shunted him out of the center of action. Then as he prowled the premises he came upon an ancient banjo, forgotten in a dusty corner, and he appropriated it lovingly. It had been a long time since he had had a banjo in his hands; but he found that his fingers were still practiced and sure as he tuned the slack strings.

His first instinct was to seek a lonely spot on the top rail of a corral behind some barn. Then a speculative smile crossed his lips as an alternative occurred to him. He turned back, and sought a shadowed bench in the patio of the house itself. Slowly, at first, but with sure, unhesitant rhythm, his fingers sought out the old familiar chords; and presently he began to croon to the beat of the strings.

His voice was husky and low, but deep and sure in its tone, as he drifted into the lilting, swaying strains of romantic Mexican *versos*.

"—Que toda la vida es sueño
Y los sueños sueño son . . ."

He was singing in the manner of the vaqueros, the dark, reckless-riding cowboys who sometimes drifted into the northern ranges from old Mexico. To the Spanish a place with no song in it is a place with no soul. Those Spanish-Indian vaqueros were mostly horse killers, and Hughes did not think much of their work; but they knew how to strum and sing. The passion of old Spain, sometimes flamboyant, sometimes melancholy, was tempered in those songs by the vast emptiness of long prairies and the implacable hush of night skies. Under swaggering mockery could sometimes be heard an echo of all the yearning loneliness the world has ever known.

Only the vaqueros could sing with just that combination of plaintive effect, and Clay Hughes had got some of the trick of it from them.

"Ya se va, para donde ira,
Voy a buscar un fino amor—"

He was singing to Sally Major, whom he knew to be somewhere in the roomy ramifications of that great sprawling adobe. The syncopating plunk of the strings was gentle and his voice low; yet he was certain that she was listening somewhere within those cool adobe walls. Thus he boldly made love to her by broad daylight in the very heart of the layout which held him a virtual prisoner.

The fact that she was a daughter of wealth and power, as that country understood it, bothered him not at all. Hughes came from a line of men schooled to think that one man was as good as another, if not a damn sight better, and that no one knew what changes the turn of a year might make in the relative fortunes of men. In the west the wheel of fortune had always been on the spin; it was turning yet. Old Pony Hughes and the men before him—as far back as word of mouth history could reach—each made his fortune and each had lost it again: some of them not once, but many times. And as for Hughes himself, he had plans which—

From the Spanish songs Hughes drifted to others, cowboy songs that many a weary rider had sung through the long hours of night circle, quieting bedded herds. Mostly they were songs that hinted at stories, and the words were simple, bordering upon nonsense sometimes: the words of long-riding men who didn't know how to express themselves very well. But they were the heart of the west, unmistakable for anything else, and Hughes and his banjo knew how to make those songs their own. He had an instinct for putting blue harmonies into plain old tunes that had originally grown out of the creak of saddle leather and the jog of hoofs. The musical lilt of the Spanish melodies was not in them, but in their own way they had all the meaning that the versos of the vaqueros had, and something else too that the Spanish never understood.

He played for a long time, absorbed in the banjo which he had not fingered for so long. Then as he let the last chords of "Twenty Miles From Carson" die away, he became aware of a sense of incompleteness. He had been kind of half hoping, he admitted to himself, that Sally Major would come into the patio, and that he would get a chance to talk to her again. She had not come, and this fact gave the singing business futility, as if he couldn't play the banjo after all. No one seemed to be moving anywhere in the layout. From the dry cottonwoods a locust droned metallically, like a coffee mill; and when this noise had ticked off into silence the place was as still as if it had been abandoned completely. Hughes snapped his thumb across the banjo in a discordant crash, and got up.

"Where are you going?" said Sally Major's voice, unexpectedly close behind him. He turned to find her sitting upon the inner ledge of one of those deep recessed windows, almost immediately behind his bench.

"How long have you been there?"

"About half an hour. Go ahead with the serenade. If you want to know what I think of it, I think it's pretty good."

"Of course it's good," said Hughes, sitting down on the outer ledge of the window. "If I'd known you were there it might have been even better."

She studied him enigmatically. "I've been talking to Bob Macumber."

"Yes? He told you what happened at Adobe Wells?"

"His version of it."

She waited, and he knew that she was inviting him to tell her his side of the affair. He was not, however, accustomed to explaining himself to people, and he resented the circumstances which had seemed constantly to demand explanation from him ever since he had crossed Gunsight Pass. "I couldn't improve on what Bob would tell you, I guess," he said slowly.

"According to him," said Sally Major, "it was the strangest thing. By Bob's story, nobody was ever closer to a shoot-out than you people were. And then, he said, you wrote something on a piece of paper and handed it to Earl Shaw, and Shaw folded right up."

"Well—the main drift sounds something like what happened," he admitted.

"So now you've gone and got yourself in trouble again?" said Sally.

"Have I ever been out of it?" Hughes grinned.

"Not since you've been here. And now Bob says Dad is all heated up. Very naturally, Dad would like to know what was in that note."

"Yes," said Hughes, "I expect he would." He tried to change the subject. "I've been wondering a couple of things myself. For instance, who ever let you out of that room I left you in last night?"

"Nobody."

"I'm surprised to hear it," he said. "In that case you must be in there yet."

"Not exactly. That room is the one Dad used to lock Dick up in when he was a boy. Those two are just exactly alike, but they've never understood each other, and Dad has always been awfully hard-boiled with Dick. Dick was just as rebellious and hard to handle as Dad was, and when Dick was a youngster, Dad used to punish him by locking him up, sometimes for a couple of days at a stretch. I always sided in with

120

Dick a little bit; and we found a way to work loose a couple of those oak bars, so that a couple of them slide out of place. That was how Dick used to get out and in; and that was the way I got out last night."

"I sure worried about it for a while," he told her.

"You were sweet to worry; but I can usually take care of myself."

They were silent for a moment. He was thinking that, in the difficult and complicated position in which he found himself, she was the only one in the Buckhorn who met him frankly and openly, seeming to assume that he was a friend and to be trusted as such. Not even Bob Macumber was sure of what to believe any more. Yet, this girl apparently wanted to believe in him, and was ready to give him credit for playing a square game, no matter how curious things might look. The directness of her next question took him unawares.

"Don't you think," she said, "you'd better tell me what was in the note you wrote Earl Shaw?" There was no least note of appeal in her voice; as she spoke it, it was a simple question, raising a question of expediency, nothing more.

He hesitated. "That was a funny thing," he said. "I was just trying to carry out your orders in a way."

"My orders?"

"Didn't you tell me to keep things from coming to a shoot-out, if I could?"

"Yes, I did that."

"I suppose you realize that an order like that puts me

121

in a kind of bad place? Like as if I was afraid of the shoot-out itself."

"It might look that way," she admitted, "to people who don't know the difference between a hard way and an easy one when they see it."

"I guess maybe," he told her, "you didn't expect me to take what you wanted as seriously as I did."

"Oh, yes, I did."

He looked at her curiously before he went on. "I couldn't think of any good way to do just that thing. I had to take a long chance, which took in the possibility of getting myself plenty misunderstood."

"Of course, it looks kind of funny to Dad as long as he doesn't know what was in that note," she suggested.

"Did you ever happen to think," he asked her slowly, "that it might look a whole lot funnier to him—to everybody—if they *did* know what was in that note? Sometimes it's better for things to look awfully queer for a man, rather than to have people dead certain of something else—something that isn't so."

"If a thing isn't so, you ought not to be afraid of it," she said, "at least—"

She left the sentence unfinished, and Hughes, letting his fingers wander idly upon the banjo's strings, tried to figure out what the rest of the sentence would have been. After a moment he thought he had it. "At least, with you," he guessed aloud.

She did not deny that his guess was right. For some obscure reason this girl believed in him, and expected him to believe in her. Suddenly he felt again that unaccustomed sense of humbleness to which she sometimes reduced him. He stuck a thumb and forefinger into the pocket of his vest and drew out the little scraps of paper which had been his note to Earl Shaw: insignificant pencil marked scraps—but they had prevented a shoot-out and caused the unexpected surrender, in his own stronghold, of the Bar S boss.

"Here," he said, handing them to her. "It can be pieced together easy enough, I guess."

She held the scraps in her open palm, studying him. He said, "Try to remember this: I was trying to do what you asked me to—and the means at hand were few and poor." He turned back to the banjo.

"What's the matter?" She was still looking at him across the fragments in her hand.

"Nothing."

"I think you don't want me to read this," she said.

"No," he answered, "I expect I don't."

She hesitated, puzzled. Then, "Here—take them back." She pressed the scraps into his hand.

He looked at her, but she had dropped her eyes. There was silence for a long moment. Then, "Thanks," he said, and slowly put the scraps of paper back in his pocket. He was acutely aware that he did not understand this girl as well as he had supposed. He stared at her wonderingly, but since she did not meet his eyes, he was unable to read her quiet face. He wanted to tell her that he was grateful, and that in returning to him, unread, the fragments of his note to

123

Earl Shaw she had done more than he had expected or asked. He thought that developments would justify him, in the end. But just now he angrily resented the circumstances which urged him to withhold anything from Sally. He felt suddenly lonely, as if there had been a new gulf struck between himself and this girl, just as they were beginning to draw near.

The unnatural strain upon the Lazy M distorted every relationship. What was happening in Adobe Wells—in Walkerton, the county seat? By what means had old Major chosen to carry the fight, and how was the scrap going? As they sat there, now, in this very hour, the fortune of the Buckhorn water might be swaying in the balance of finality. Whatever was happening today affected them all, yet they had no news, no means of communication. For all they knew the guns might be speaking in Adobe Wells by now. They could only wait, each with his own special hopes and doubts. It could not last long: when word next came from down-country they knew that it would be definite, at once significant and prophetic.

"It won't always be this way," he told her. "Pretty quick, now, all this stuff will be sifted down and shaken out, and everybody will stand out plain for just what they are."

She did not answer him. Momentarily at a loss for words with which to accomplish the impossible, he turned again to the sounding strings. The banjo spoke softly, its cadences true and sure; and in a moment or two he began to sing to her, his voice hardly more than

124

a whisper above the gentle minor thrum of the chords:

"De la Sierra Moreno,
Cielito Lindo, vienen bajando . . ."

He was looking at her as he sang. He and the banjo were talking to her as plainly as if he had found the words which had eluded him. "There are you and here am I, and that is all that matters," the throb of the banjo said. No vaquero had ever sung that sadly lilting song with a deeper appeal, nor with a plainer meaning to one listener alone; and there was the history of the world in the pulsation of the strings.

Looking up, Clay Hughes saw that Sally Major had covered her face with her hands. She faced him immediately, however, and he was rocked backwards as he saw that her face, lovely still, was perfectly expressionless, and her eyes, as they met his, were as cool and hard as grey eyes may be. He had not realized that for a little while her eyes had been gentle—tender almost—until he saw them once more unyielding and aloof.

"Look here," she said. "I've changed my mind again."

"You mean you—"

"I want you to get out and stay out: saddle and ride, and get out of this valley, and as far from it as you can; and if anyone follows to bring you back here—see that he doesn't succeed!"

"But—"

125

"It's Bob Macumber they've set to watch you now. I'll handle Macumber."

"Why?" said Hughes.

"Because I say so. I think you'll find out that that's reason enough!"

She turned abruptly to leave the window, but he caught her wrist. Someone was coming into the patio, but he was unwilling to let her go without one word more. "I suppose you know," he said, "that I won't do anything of the kind?"

"If you know what's good for you, you'll do exactly what I say."

The slow click of heels upon the patio tiles was very close upon them now. Reluctantly, Hughes released her wrist, and instantly she disappeared into the inner shadows.

He turned to face Bob Macumber.

CHAPTER NINE

"Singing! For gosh sakes!" said Bob Macumber. "Singing! What have you got to sing about?"

Hughes struck a final dissonant chord and laid the banjo down. "Maybe not so much as I thought," he answered. "What's the matter now?"

"I been looking all over the place for you. Didn't you hear the old man's car drive up?"

"Yes, I heard it."

"That was him come in the front of the house a little bit ago. He wants to see you."

"All right."

As Hughes turned away, Macumber gripped his arm with a heavy hand. "Listen," he said. "Listen! Use your head. I'm going to help you. I don't care what comes of it, I'm going to help you. I'll get out your horse for you, and I'll give you one of my own. I'll give you the lay of the land—how you can get out of here without being followed very good. I'll fake it out here some way so as to give you all the start I can. I don't know what's going on here—not even as well as you do I guess—but you and me have ridden together some awful long trails, and I'm not going back on you now. If you know what's good for you, you'll get out, and get out quick! I'll—"

"To hell with that," said Hughes.

"You won't clear out?" Bob demanded, nonplussed. Hughes shook his head. "I think," said Macumber, "you must be crazy."

"If you bet on it," said Hughes, "try to get odds. Is the old man in his office?"

Macumber nodded. "What am I going to say to the old fire-eater when he wants to know why I let you keep your gun?"

"I'll handle that," Hughes said. Again he found himself in familiar circumstances—one man in a wilderness, with no one to depend upon but himself. He went striding off toward the hallway that led to the front of the house and the old man's office. Once more his disreputable hat was jerked over one eye, and that saddle-bound swagger was in his walk. Macumber, a

127

disconsolate figure in the dusk, stood motionless, watching him go.

Oliver Major, sprawled deep in his chair beside that ancient ornate desk, regarded Hughes morosely from deep-set eyes as the cowboy let himself into the office unannounced. Hughes saw at once that the old man had changed notably since he had last seen him, that morning in Adobe Wells. He appeared younger, but at the same time the creases in his leathery face were very hard and deep; and a look of battle was upon the whole man, so that he resembled more than ever an old wolf, an old war eagle.

If Major's battle for the Buckhorn water was going to force him to spend the last energies of his declining years in bitter war, apparently he was reconciled to it. Now that it had come, it seemed that the old man was something more than willing to throw the last of his resources into one final, irresistible raid of destruction upon his enemies. Apparently, also, he was more than half convinced that one of his enemies stood before him now.

"I see you're still wearing your gun," said Major noncommittally.

"That I am," Hughes said. They faced each other across the ancient desk. Unexpectedly the old man began to chuckle, but it was a strictly private chuckle, for it ceased immediately as soon as Hughes permitted a faint, one-sided grin to come into his own face.

"I was kind of hoping," said Oliver Major, "that you'd be gone."

"Gone?" said Hughes. "Where?"

"Anywhere," said the old man. "Don't tell me you couldn't have out-smarted Bob Macumber and got away."

"It never come into my head to try."

Oliver Major sighed deeply. "You're one too many for me," he admitted. "I've been watching you awful close, but I'm darned if I know where you stand. Bart Holt is dead certain—but you know what Bart Holt thinks. You certainly have got no friend in Bart Holt. It's a mystery to me why, with nothing to gain and everything to lose, you didn't go over the hill while you had the chance."

Hughes admitted to himself that that was certainly something hard to explain. He couldn't very well tell the old man that the grey eyes of Sally Major made it impossible for him to turn tail, even if he wished to. He had watched vaqueros make their horses stamp and rear when a girl was watching, and he had held them in contempt for that; but he had to admit to himself that the presence of Sally Major at the Lazy M gave him an entirely different view of expediency than that which he would have considered reasonable a week before. There was still a chance—slender though it was—that such circumstances would arise as would enable him to throw the balance between right and wrong. But how could he explain all that to Oliver Major?

"Of course, what Bart Holt hangs to," Oliver Major went on, studying him, "is that empty shell that was

129

found in the ashes of your fire in Crazy Mule; though I must say I take less stock in that particular thing than some do. But, considering that nobody understands exactly what your game is here—it looks mighty funny, even to me, when you crop up with an understanding with Earl Shaw that makes it possible for you to fold him up and back him down."

"Ask yourself what would have happened if I hadn't backed him down," said Hughes.

"I haven't any pipe dreams about that," Major assured him. "There ain't the least doubt in my mind but what Earl Shaw would have made a fight of it, right there, the way things was going. We was awful close to fight—and we would have got licked too. I've heard of cases where five men stood up to twenty and beat 'em, but the Buckhorn is no place to get together twenty such nincompoops as *that* takes!"

"Then just what's your complaint?"

"What Bart Holt keeps asking me is just what's your connection with Earl Shaw. The way he puts it, when we know what your connection with Earl Shaw is, we'll know why you haven't gone over the hill before now—and some other things too, maybe, that he only hints at, probably because he doesn't know what he means himself."

Hughes swung one leg onto Major's desk and helped himself to the old man's tobacco. "I've sure worked myself into a funny position," he admitted. "Almost anything I say seems to be taken for a lie; and the more I try to side you fellows, the worse I look.

I'm plenty tired of this everlasting dodging around the bush. If you want to know what backed down Earl Shaw, there it is." He tossed the torn fragments of his note to Earl Shaw upon the desk.

Major stared at him for a long moment. "How do we know this is the same note you wrote Shaw?" he asked.

"There's a good sample of it," said Hughes. "Nobody's going to trust the least thing I say. I suppose you can call it a sample of the thanks a man gets now days in the cow country. Well, this time I'm ahead of you, Mr. Major. I tore that piece of paper off a newspaper that was lying on Earl Shaw's desk. You'll find the date line of the paper on it, which'll show you that it came in no earlier than yesterday— and also you'll notice that his name is printed on the margin, where they put his address when they mailed it to him! I took special notice of those things when I tore that piece of paper off."

"By golly," said Major, "I guess you thought of everything, all right." With slow fingers he began arranging the fragments of the paper before him. Yet, when this was achieved he seemed mystified, and slowly turned the whole assortment of scraps over to see if there were anything on the other side. "Is this all?" he said at last.

"It was enough, wasn't it?"

Major read aloud, " 'Did you ever shoot a United States Marshal?' Just that one line," he said wonderingly. Then abruptly he demanded, "Are you a federal man?"

"No," said Hughes.

"Then how—"

"It was just a kind of a hint," said Hughes, "sort of rigged up to side-track Earl Shaw's mind, and maybe confuse him, some."

"But why should he—"

"Put yourself in his boots. That stand of his, that Crawford had no authority to act as sheriff, was all right as a bluff—as long as he controlled the county, and the general machinery of the law, but if one of us had been a United States Marshal—down here to look around for some wanted man, for example—and Shaw's outfit had gunned him down, look what a different breed of investigation Shaw would have been up against then! Shaw isn't wanting any investigation of a shoot-out from the federal government. He's been wondering, same as you, why I'm putting into this thing. When I made that suggestion; it came to him all of a sudden, I guess, that there was some outside reason—and he guessed the shoot-out better be postponed."

"I can hardly believe it," said Major slowly. "I'll never forget you standing there grinning at Shaw, and him sizing you up, and wondering. I'll swear if ever a man looked like he knew what he was talking about, you did then."

Hughes shrugged. "Well, anyway," he said, "it looks as if he didn't want to take the chance."

"But you actually ain't a marshal at all?"

"No. It's easily looked up if you've got any doubts."

"Then why didn't you show me this when I first asked you in Adobe Wells?"

"It's a queer thing," said Hughes reluctantly, "to dodge out of a shoot-out on the basis of a lie. It isn't a place that a man wants to put himself in, Mr. Major, if it can be got around; nor a thing he likes to talk about when it's done."

"Why did you do it then?" said Major abruptly.

There was weariness in Clay Hughes' smile. He was thinking of Sally Major with the starlight on her upturned face as she had told him that she counted on him to prevent a shoot-out if he could; counted on him because he was the only one in the Lazy M's posse who had his right sense about him, and a cool head. He couldn't very well tell Oliver Major that he had promised the old man's daughter to turn trouble aside if he could; nor could he explain, even to himself, why he had taken that promise literally and seriously, and would have felt he had to do his best to carry it out at whatever cost to himself.

And now, he thought dimly, all that move had got him was an imputation of cowardice. He had hoped that the thing could be slid over, withheld until circumstances had awarded him a better average of achievement. The ignoble concealment to which he had been impelled in withholding the Shaw note from Sally had done him no good. Her last words to him had voiced the suggestion to get out and stay out. Now that he had tossed concealment aside, he supposed that she would consider him yellow, as well as an undesirable

133

renegade. Yet he did not see how he could have done any differently, the way things had fallen out.

"I played it as I did because there wasn't any sense to a shoot-out," he told Major impatiently. "What would it have got us?"

"Nothing," Major admitted. "You mean you wasn't scared of a fight, if it come to that?"

"Sure I was scared," said Hughes. "I was scared stiff, and if there was anybody else there that had any sense, so was he!"

Oliver Major's face relaxed in a grin. "I guess there's not much danger of anybody accusing you of lack of nerve," he said. "I'm sorry I sent you back from Adobe Wells. Even then, I kind of thought maybe you was still with us—though for a little while it was pretty hard to see how, the way you made it look like you had a stand-in with Earl Shaw. You was a blame fool not to tell me at the jump-off what the game was."

"I suppose," said Hughes. What he couldn't tell the old man was that if Sally Major had not, only a few moments before, appeared to withdraw her moral support, he would have been holding out yet. The stiff brittle pride of youth was very strong in Hughes. Until Sally went back on him he could not have brought himself to expose the details of a device which had been forced upon him, but which he felt put him in an ugly light.

"Did you make out all right after I left?" Hughes asked.

Openly, but with a minimum of words, old Oliver Major now sketched over what had been accomplished—and what had not—since that morning. With Earl Shaw under lock and key, together with Dutch Pete and two more, the Lazy M had made a vigorous but hardly hopeful effort to wrangle some sort of information out of their prisoners. From Earl Shaw and his lieutenants they learned exactly nothing, however. Nor could Oliver Major find out the whereabouts of Alex Shaw, brother of the Adobe Wells boss, whom Major had hoped to seize along with the others.

Immediately Oliver Major and his son, leaving the Adobe Wells situation in the hands of Jim Crawford and Bart Holt, had driven the rough eighty miles southwestward to Walkerton, the little, dusty county seat far down below, where the main line of the railroad crossed the corner of the county. Major hunted out the supervisors there. With Earl Shaw in custody pending a capital charge—supposedly that of conspiracy to murder—Major had hoped to throw such a scare into Shaw's personally owned county supervisors as to make them confirm Jim Crawford as sheriff, successor to Hugo Donnan.

This attempt, bold as it was, had carried a certain promise. Two of the three county supervisors were characterless men, who, Major had hoped, would abandon Shaw's support in time of danger, like rabbits leaving fired brush.

And he had partly succeeded. Being of a type of men forever fearful of being with the loser, two of the three had been thrown into the air by the sudden turn of events which had lodged Earl Shaw in the Adobe Wells jail. To confirm Jim Crawford as sheriff in the face of the powerful Earl Shaw was beyond their courage; yet they were momentarily paralyzed by the apparent strength of Oliver Major. They sought cover, stalling for time, hoping to leave. themselves a loop-hole or two in case it should turn out that Earl Shaw was once more to be ridden down by the Lazy M tornado. They had expected the Lazy M to show no strength at all; and news that the great Shaw himself was in jail on a dangerous charge rendered them incapable of immediate action. For the present Jim Crawford was acting sheriff; how long this might endure, nobody knew. Unless the luck continued its swing toward the Lazy M, it could not last long.

"One thing," Oliver Major concluded, "is absolutely sure. The minute that Earl Shaw gets control of the county law again, he'll have a posse here to take Dick—and you too, Hughes. If that time comes—but it mustn't come, that's all—God knows how we'll hold it off, but we got to."

"But if it does?" Hughes asked.

"I never supposed," said Major in a clear voice, "that anything would ever come into this feud more important to me than holding onto the Buckhorn water. I'm not so much afraid of Dick being brought to trial; they'd never convict him, I'm certain. And I'm not afraid of what I know they'll hang on me either—the least of which would be accessory after the fact. Of course, you can see what would become of my influence in this state then. Once a trial for murder got to dragging out, I wouldn't have no more influence left than a banty rooster in a cyclone; and the machine that Shaw's a part of would bite down on the Buckhorn water like a trap, and this valley wouldn't ever be anything but desert again. But, I tell you, it isn't that that's worrying me now."

"What then?" said Hughes.

"Hughes," said Oliver Major, "I don't know as you'll believe. You young fellers don't understand the iron type of guts that goes with the old ways. Men have died before, in this long feud between me and Shaw; good men, some of 'em, too. I tell you Earl Shaw isn't the man to be afraid to add on a couple more to the string. If his posse ever rides down a long prairie after dark with you and Dick—" he raised a clenched fist above his desk but lowered it slowly—"I tell you neither one of you will ever be seen alive again."

"It don't hardly seem like—"

"And why not?" Major exploded at him. "It's happened in this valley before, and will again! It's too easy a thing for a crooked sheriff to do, if his case is uncertain, and there's a powerful lot at stake. 'The prisoners was trying to escape,' says he. He had to gun 'em when they tried to 'escape.'"

"I guess," Hughes said, "some of us has got kind of used to thinking that things like that don't happen any more."

"When we finally got the law established here in the west," said Major, "we kept it going good for quite a while, but once politics goes rotten on you, I tell you, you're a lot worse off than before there was any law at all! With the law you can gang up to crush a man so he hasn't got no chance. People didn't use to stand for that. If you read the papers, you know that law in the cities has been haywire for a long time, and as for killing off a helpless man in some lonely place at night, they've even got a special name for that in the towns, it happens so much. You can't pick up a paper without reading that somebody was 'took for a ride.'"

"I know," said Hughes.

"If ever you or Dick get into the hands of a Bar S posse, do you think Earl Shaw will be the man to pass up his easy chance, after all these years? It'll be a western style of 'ride,' maybe, and different in some ways, but you won't come back from it, just the same!"

"If you're sure of that—" Hughes began.

"I know my man!" declared Major. "I licked him when he come with cattle, and I licked him when come with sheep, but now if he comes with law—boy, I don't know! But this I do know: Dick Major never goes into the hands of Earl Shaw's men not if I have to fight the county and the state. I'll never surrender him, nor you neither."

"You mean you'd stand out against the law?"

"What choice would be left me?"

"Whatever could be the end to it?" Hughes wondered.

"Quien sabe?"

There was silence while they looked at each other, yet neither seemed to be seeing the other's face. Perhaps each was looking beyond into the shadows of a possible cataclysm so relentless and implacable as to offer no choice and no escape.

Oliver Major stirred himself. "But it must never come to that. If it does—but we've got to stave it off. Walkerton is buzzing like a bee tree; I never saw news spread so fast. Adobe Wells, and I guess Walkerton too, knew all about the death of Donnan before ever we rode in there. Within two days Shaw's lawyers will have him up before Judge Greer on a writ of habeas corpus. Greer is a Shaw man; he'll turn him loose if there's any possible way. Twelve hours after Shaw is out of jail he'll have his supervisors whipped into line, and the Buckhorn will have a new sheriff—Alex Shaw himself I wouldn't be surprised. Whatever the end will be, it'll come very quick after that. We've got to balk all that! I've wired for the best lawyer in the state. He'll have to come to Walkerton by plane to carry the law fight."

"Who's that?"

"Stephen Sessions—maybe you've heard of him. Old Judge Sessions that used to be on the state supreme bench. He's better than half way retired now; but he's still the man that can bulldog them all."

"Are you sure he'll come?"

"Steve never went back on me yet; he'll be here all right. And when he gets here we've got to have such a

139

case to lodge against Shaw as will hold him tighter than a drum, regardless of bail or anything else. Dear God, Hughes, if only you can figure out what Donnan was trying to say—"

"Whatever it was, he'll never add to it now," Hughes evaded.

"But there's another man who'll come close to telling us something," said Major. "I suppose you know Grasshopper Tanner's gone up to the Crazy Mule?"

"The old fellow with all the dogs?"

"Yeah, that's him. If there's a man in the world that can unravel sign, Grasshopper's the man. I wish now that I hadn't gone up there with Bart Holt before Tanner come. If he'd had a fair chance—I don't believe it's possible to kill a man and not leave sign of some kind that Tanner could nail onto."

"He's got little enough chance now after you four fellers have been all over it."

"I know," Major admitted wearily. "I know, but if only he'd find something, some one little thing— He promised to start down from the Crazy Mule as soon as it got too dark to work. He'll be trailing in some time tonight. Go get some sleep. I'll see you're called when he comes."

Out in the patio Clay Hughes picked up the banjo again and ran weary fingers over the strings: "De la Sierra Morena. . . ." The banjo did not answer the notes he hummed; there was no use trying to sing any more. Those last words of hers—"Get out and stay out—" took the assurance out of song. He no longer had the feeling that she was near and listening. He struck an angry thumb across the strings, and one of them broke with a shrill whine.

CHAPTER TEN

It was nearly morning, however, before Hughes was awakened by the noise of Grasshopper Tanner's lion pack.

Tanner had no less than fourteen dogs; his pack was one of the largest of its kind in the southwest, as well as one of the best. It was rumored that old man Major had recently raised his bounty on lions to a hundred and twenty-five dollars a head for the admitted purpose of holding Grasshopper Tanner at work in the hills flanking the Buckhorn. The western mountain lion prefers horse meat to any other, and the long-headed, cautious, and powerful breed which infested the rim rock took a heavy toll in the upper Buckhorn every year.

Men who could hunt those lions down were hard to get. There is entirely too much running on foot involved in following a hound pack to suit the average cowboy; and though every year a number took a shot at it, none of them lasted long. Nor can a crack lion pack be built in a week. The long-running, fox-hound type of dog used in hunting lions does not hunt properly of its own accord; long training, and often brutal punishment, is necessary before such faults as sight-running and the following of worthless game are min-imized—and the labor of months may be ruined in a day. Nor is a good pack leader easy to come by. Every famous lion pack is built upon the genius of a single dog, and a man's luck only grants him such a dog two or three times in the course of his life. But with a bounty of a hundred twenty-five dollars on lions, and a hundred dollars each on wolf and bear, Grasshopper Tanner made a good thing of his job. He was a good hunter, a long hunter from way back, who knew how to clean the varmints out of a range.

Yet, nobody seemed to have any particular affection for Tanner; and studying the man now, as the old lion hunter wolfed his breakfast in the mess hall of the Lazy M, Hughes could understand why. Tanner was as gaunt as the rawhide of a braided quirt. He had enor-mously long arms and legs, more suggestive of a spider than the insect after which he was called. His face was wizened, and deep-carved in hard weathered lines, but Hughes could see that its expression had been fundamentally brutal, once. And his manner was openly scornful, devoid of friendliness, as if he judged all men according to their lion hunting proficiency. Long use of this narrow and exacting standard seemed to have induced in Tanner a permanent contempt for all other men.

Nor did he seem to have any particular respect for the animals with which he worked. Perhaps he had a sort of repressed admiration for lions; but he admitted no liking for horses, which he regarded as simply a poor means of getting from one place to another, and his dogs—they forever kept a furtive eye upon the short blacksnake coiled at his belt—he referred to as "smelling machines."

In spite of his great proficiency and the scarcity of lion hunters, Grasshopper Tanner always managed, sooner or later, to get himself fired, in a tornado of black rage, from every range on which he worked. Like the time he had worked for old man Major three years hand running. On his very first hunt his dogs had found a she-wolf's den, and he had dug out an even dozen wolf whelps—at a hundred dollars a head. The next year he had got eleven whelps from the same wolf. The third spring, when Tanner brought in thirteen whelps more, old man Major paid down the thirteen hundred dollars only with severe pain.

"Tanner," he had complained, "the wolf crop is getting to be a darn sight more regular than the calf crop around here. Now I know darn well that the old wolf comes hanging around when you dig out these whelps. How come you never get a shot at her?"

"A shot at her?" Tanner repeated. "Sure I get a shot at her. Why, this last time, she come so close I could pretty near have brained her with a club!"

"Then why in all hell isn't her scalp here with the rest?"

"What?" Tanner yelped. "Destroy my brood bitch, that's bringing me in better than twelve hundred dollars a year?"

It had been years, and the lions had become very bad

in the Buckhorn, before old Major got over that sufficiently to send for Grasshopper Tanner again.

So there was no particular warmth of affection for the old hunter among those who attended that extra early breakfast which the cook had been routed out to prepare. Besides Hughes and old man Major, Bob Macumber was there; and by ones and twos the other cowboys of the Lazy M began to trail into the mess hall, grumpy and sleepy-eyed, in the darkness before dawn.

"For plain, dumb, swivel-brained monkey-shines," the lion hunter was saying, "I never see the equal of you fellers." Tanner, who thought people who had to have regular meals were all sissies, had had nothing to eat since yesterday morning. He now crammed himself mightily with hot cakes, syrup and salt pork, so that his words came as broken interjections between enormous knife-fulls. "You fellers have trampled up and down, and backwards and forwards and across the Crazy Mule until it looks like a passel of sheep's been through. What's the matter with you ninnies, anyway?"

Bob Macumber chuckled. "I'm sure glad Bart Holt ain't here."

"Bart Holt don't know a cow track from a dish of potaters," said Tanner.

"We wasn't hunting cows," growled old man Major.

"It's a good thing," Tanner grunted. "One of 'em would probably have come up behind you and hooked you. Like one time in the Mokelumne Basin. Bart Holt

144

swang a big circle and cut his own trail, and follered it round and round the Basin for upwards of a week. And he ain't figgered out to this day how come he never sighted hisself."

"I'm right sorry we made you fall down," Oliver Major came back at him. "Of course, if a feller gets so he can't tell one track from another no more, he has to be the first one to come up, or he's helpless."

"Who says I fell down?" Tanner demanded with his mouth full. "I can tell you every move anybody made in the Crazy Mule night before last." They waited, and after two more knife-loads of hot cakes and syrup Tanner went on. "This feller here—Hughes, did you say his name was ?—come riding over the Gunsight an hour and a half, and maybe two hours, before dark. He—"

"Was you there?" said Macumber.

"No, I wasn't there."

"How do you know it was an hour and a half before dark?"

"If you'll stop asking fool questions you'll see in a minute. Hughes built his fire"—he pronounced it "far"—"and et, and then he clumb up the rock of the rim to where he could set and look out, and there he smoked a cigarette. If it hadn't been still daylight, what would o' been his idee in climbin' up to look around? A child could see through that."

"How do you know it was me?" said Hughes.

"You're the only stranger around here, ain't you? And you're smoking brown papers; everybody else around here's smoking white papers. I found your brown paper butt up on the rim. Meantime," Tanner went on, "Hugo Donnan has come in the other end over Dog Ridge. He works along, fishin'. Finally he makes his camp. Two fellers is watchin' him from the rock of the rim as he makes his camp."

"How do you know that?" said old Major.

"Just keep on buttin' in," said Tanner testily, "if you want to keep from findin' out nothing. They've already made up their mind to gun Donnan, but now they see Hughes' smoke from down canyon. One of 'em walks along the rim in his stockin' feet to see who it is. He almost walks right onto Hughes where Hughes is settin' up on the rim. He sights him at twenty yards, and of course, Hughes is lookin' the other way. Wouldn't you know it. Also, I guess he don't hear very good, does he? At least, he doesn't listen very good. Well, this feller that's stalking him steps behind a clump of junipers not over twenty yards away and watches him."

Clay Hughes' hair rose at this suggestion. It is a queer thing to be told that hostile eyes have watched you from a distance of but twenty yards, while you were unconsciously going about your own affairs. He remembered the stillness of the night, and found himself unable to believe Tanner.

"I would have heard him," said Hughes.

"Just the same, he was there," said Tanner, "because there's a little dirt collected behind those junipers, and his track is there where he stood quite a while. All

146

right. Hughes goes down to his camp again. The other feller lies down on the rock behind the junipers, keeping Hughes in sight. He lies there between half an hour and an hour."

"And how do you know that?"

"He left the butts of three white paper cigarettes. Finally Hughes turns in and settles down for the night. The other feller works back along the rim."

"How do you know he did?"

"Because he ain't there no more," said Tanner with withering contempt. "The two fellers that's been watchin' Donnan has a hard time gettin' together in the dark, but finally the feller that's been watchin' Hughes finds his partner, and passes the word that to all intents and purposes Hughes is blind, deaf, and dumb. One of them two, probably the feller that's been watchin' Donnan, comes climbin' down the rock. His boots is hangin' from his belt. He—"

"Wait a minute, wait a minute," said Oliver Major. "You couldn't know what was hangin' on his belt! Unless—*you was him.*"

"I sure get sick of explaining plain, common things to you blockheads," said Tanner. "I know he was in his stocking feet, don't I? And he wasn't carrying his boots in his hands because he wanted both hands free. A child would know that. But pretty soon when he leaves there, he's got his boots on. I suppose you fellers would say his boots was just follering him along, jumping from twig to twig or something. Me, I know better. He had 'em hooked to his belt." Tanner forked another load of hot cakes to his plate.

"All right, go ahead."

"The feller that's stalking Donnan eases down onto the little low rock ledge. Donnan's camped right under him. There's a little brush on the ledge, givin' the feller cover. The feller snakes his gun out and pokes it through the brush. The brush rattles. Donnan turns around and sees the other feller and the gun. He makes a jump for his rifle that's standing against a tree. 'How do I know it was against the tree?' says you. Because that's what a feller does with his rifle—he don't sink it in the crick to cool. I get tired of these damn fool questions."

"Nobody asked you a question," said Major.

"Well, you was about to, wasn't you? Donnan makes a jump for his rifle—isn't there somebody wants to know how I know he jumped, instead of walking on his hands?"

The riders stirred restlessly. The slurs of the cantankerous old lion hunter were getting on their nerves. Hughes had known lion hunters before. Mostly they were aloof, self-sufficient men, very quiet except when in argument with others of their own profession; but easy to get along with, full of the generosity and hospitality of men who are much alone. Tanner was different, an aggravated case. Yet Hughes could understand how a lifetime of self-sufficient loneliness had warped the old man's views. Probably there were months at a time in which the old man spoke to no living beings except his dogs; while the signs of

148

obscure wilderness trails were his only newspapers, and the reading of those signs his only diversion.

Small wonder if he learned, after fifty or sixty years of that, to read and understand a thousand small indications that other men did not even see. In Tanner the long hunter's intuition was probably developed to a remarkable degree. More than any other men, perhaps, the lion hunters learned to depend upon a fifth sense that was probably partly imagination, but partly also a restored instinct for verity such as animals possess, and which becomes smothered in the world of men.

"Come on, come on, what happened then?"

"Why, you jugheads," said Tanner, "the feller shot him. Ain't you heard he was shot?" he demanded sarcastically. "Now somebody ask me was he hurt."

Nobody asked him anything, so Tanner was reduced to going ahead under his own power. "Donnan goes down, out of reach of his rifle. The feller that shot him stands tight, not moving. He's ready to pop him again if necessary. It ain't. Donnan lies quiet. After a minute or two, which seems like about an hour to the feller on the ledge, the feller cleans his gun. He has a nail on a string, with a rag on the end of the string. He drops the nail through the barrel of his gun and pulls the rag through three, four times. Why does he do that? He does it so that if anybody comes busting up and wants to know did he shoot Donnan, he can show them he never fired his gun—see, it's all clean. How do I know he done it? Because I found his cleanin' wad, nail, string, and all, hanging on the bush. It's a wonder you jiggers wouldn't have found it and took it for a fish hook, and put it in the crick, so's it would look more at home."

"Somebody's going to put you in the creek one of these days," Macumber grunted, "and I'll bet you'll look at home there too!"

Tanner devoted himself to concentrated eating for a moment or two. In the comparative silence, two or three of his dogs outside could be heard blooping mournfully in the loud pointless conversation that lion packs carry on incessantly.

"The feller that shot Donnan went away. After he's gone Donnan gets on his hands and knees and crawls over to his rifle, and pulls it down onto the ground. He lies restin' on top of it. Then he changes his mind. He don't need no rifle, the fellers is gone. He crawls over and puts a stick on the fire, leavin' the rifle lie. Next day when you fellers are wanderin' around up there, one of you picks up the rifle and lays it across his saddle. Now, if you fellers want to ask me somethin' I can't answer, there's the chance of a lifetime. What did you fellers do that for? I don't know. A man can figure out almost anything, except what is you fellers' theory when you do most of the things you do."

"I picked it up to see if it had been fired," said Macumber.

"He didn't know if it was loaded," said Tanner, sarcastically. "Well, anyway, Donnan now drags hisself up onto the ledge where the shot comes from. Somethin' flickers in the light from the fire. He picks up the shell from the gun of the feller that's dropped him."

"What makes you think so?"

"Because the shell ain't there any more. And I know that the feller that shot him ejected it, because he never would go to work and clean his gun without he reloaded it. Furthermore, and lastly, it looks to me like Donnan went up there and picked up something—and what else would be there for him to pick up?

"Maybe you fellers was hopin' that the killer would drop his gun—and you'd find his name carved on it. Well, it's too bad, but things don't work that way. If you fellers think that Donnan didn't go up there and pick up no empty shell, I'll just bet you two to one that proof will turn up he so done. 'Why is Donnan collecting empty shells?' says you. Because Donnan is dumb, he used to be a cowboy, didn't he? Sure. He's a game feller, though very easy done for, and he figgers he'll get a clue as to who knocked him over.

"The shell is nice and shiny so he picks it up and saves it, thinking it may mean something. Of course, all it means is that some feller reloaded his gun. If you fellers think that that was a nutty thing for Donnan to do, you're right. But what you want to hold in mind is that you master minds could of been counted on to do something different maybe, but just as crazy. I've worked around cow pokes for a long time, and all I ever found out is, you can't never tell what fool thing is liable to appeal to a cowhand as reasonable to do."

"Just the same," said Macumber, "he's telling a

good story for a man that's just making it up as he goes along."

"Leave him alone, Bob," said Major. "Grasshopper, go ahead."

"Donnan grabs up some moss and holds it on his wound, and starts down canyon, where he seen the smoke from Hughes' fire. Undoubtless, he figgers he's goin' for help. 'Help for what?' Don't ask me—I'll leave that to some of you that understands cowboy minds. He gets clear down to Hughes' camp. Well, down there you fellers played drop the handkerchief or something, and it's pretty hard to find out much, but it looked to me like Donnan walked right spang into camp and fell down on top of Hughes' fire. Hard to say. Some darn fool has sifted out them ashes and sprinkled 'em all around—probably noticed some-body fell in the ashes, and was sifting 'em out to see if he was still in 'em.

"Just the same, we found something," said Major. "We found the empty shell of a forty-five. Hughes claims he didn't put it there, and nobody else had been there up to the time we went up. So maybe you're right about that empty shell, Grasshopper. Maybe Donnan had it in his hand, and dropped it in the ashes himself!"

"And there you are!" said Tanner. "Who was it wanted to bet me about that shell?"

"Those two gun throwers," Major asked: "did you locate where they left their saddle stock?"

"No. If they had any sense, they left 'em a good

152

ways off, where saddle stock's got every right to be. There's plenty places in walking range of there where you can find hoof prints; and I s'pose there're ten thousand places where they could have come on and off the rock. Now, I've told you exactly what happened up there night before last. Take it or leave it, it's all one to me."

"Looks like," said Major grumpily, "you could have taken a look around for them hoof prints, while you was at it, just the same."

"My work's done," declared Tanner stubbornly. "And I'll tell you right now, I got no notion of chasing my pack all over the Sweetwaters trying to track down no mule. It's hard enough to get a bunch of smelling machines to follow—"

"Mule?" said Hughes.

Old Tanner's eyes struck upward at Hughes' face, but he hesitated only a fraction of a second. "Horse *or* mule," he corrected himself. "I've got enough trouble with this pack, teaching 'em not to go hollering off after every buck deer that jumps, without giving 'em the idee they can take out after every cow, horse or mule that crosses—"

"How did you know that one of those killers was riding a mule?"

"Riding a mule?" Tanner tried to put him off. "That's rich! A killer on a mule!"

Two or three of the cowboys snickered, but Hughes stuck to his point. "How did you know?" he insisted.

"I never said he rode no mule!"

"It came into your head, just the same! And that sure is the last thing that would come into any man's head, on this or any other range. I'm asking you flat—how did you know there was a mule in this?"

"A child could tell the sign of a—"

"You've already said you didn't know where they left their saddle stock. You tried to make us think you never cut their track after they went back onto the rock of the rim. *What told you about the mule?*"

Old Tanner let down his knife with a clatter, and came onto his feet to face Hughes with blazing eyes, like a lion treed. "How'd you know yourself?" he fired back.

CHAPTER ELEVEN

There was silence while Hughes and Tanner regarded each other, Hughes insistent, the old lion hunter angrily defiant. Perhaps there was no one there who was not convinced in that moment that Tanner had discovered something definite and revealing which he had not told. The tension in the old man's weathered features suggested more: that he had held back that one last item of his knowledge because he was afraid! It seemed that they were very near to an all-important disclosure—if Hughes, who had tripped him, could force the old hunter out.

Hughes waited; and to the surprise of every one, it was the old man who was first to break. His voice was shrill as he flared up. "You ask me how I know about a mule! I put the question back to you . . ."

"Because, about the time I turned in, on the night Donnan died, I heard a mule singing at the moon."

"Well, if you did," said Tanner viciously, "I suppose there was one there, but that's the first I've heard of it!"

"You as good as admitted you knew there was one there," Hughes insisted.

"I never said no such thing," declared Tanner. "I said I don't aim to chase my pack off onto the trail of no cow, horse, nor mule, and that's all I said." He sat down; but it was like the sitting down of a balking horse.

Major kicked Hughes under the table, and Clay, puzzled, nevertheless obeyed the signal, and pretended to back down. "All right."

"You got anything else, Grasshopper?" Major asked.

"What the hell more do you want?" Tanner demanded irascibly. "I went up there after your whole gang trampled backwards and forwards over the whole place; and I've told you everything that happened up there the night Donnan was killed. What do you want now? You expect me to go on and find out who done it, and arrest him too, and try him and convict him and pass sentence? I've done my work, I tell you, and the dogs has done theirs!"

"If those two fellers walked stocking footed along the upper rim, it looks like you could put your dogs on it and find out where they left the rim," suggested Major.

"You got a hell of a funny idee what dogs is for," Tanner sneered. "I can tell 'em to take lion, or I can tell 'em to take bear; and if they cut a trail of their own, I can tell by their yelling what's at the end of it— bear, lion, wolf, or something worthless, which it usually is. But they've never tracked men in their life; and even if I could put 'em to it, you fellers have put five or six fresher trails of man in there than the ones you want trailed now. If anybody thinks he knows more about hounds than I do, let him try it! Me, I've been made a fool of before."

"Yeah, that's so," Macumber agreed heartily.

"Dry up, Bob. I tell you what," said old Major. "I'd appreciate it, Grasshopper, if you'd take three, four of the boys up there and show 'em exactly what you found, step by step, so's they'll be able to stand witness to it. You do that much more, and I'll own up you've done your share. But I sure would like to have you do that."

"All right, all right," Tanner conceded. "I'll show 'em; but I got to get some sleep first. I was a long ways from the trail when night come on, and got a late start back. I ain't had no sleep since night before."

"How soon can you start?"

"I got to have anyway four hours' sleep," said Tanner dogmatically. "I don't aim to budge from here before half past eight o'clock this morning."

"Do you think four hours' sleep will be enough?"

"Do you think I'm a sissy?"

After Tanner had turned in, Oliver Major signaled

Hughes and Macumber to follow him to his office.

"I'm damned if that isn't the most extraordinary lie I ever heard in my life," said Oliver Major.

"It sure is," agreed Macumber; "but is it all lie?"

"No, it ain't," said Major. "But the old boy's imagination runs off with him. He sees some few things and gets 'em right; then on top of that he builds up a great long story of his own that he believes is of a piece with the rest. There was a pile of pipe smoke in that story Bob."

"Some of it is stuff that checks up," Macumber pointed out. "He explained pretty good how come that empty shell was in Clay's fire."

"Yes, and he checked Hughes' story on what he done when he rode in there that night. But, Bob, we don't know how much the boys told that old renegade before he went up there with his dogs."

"I don't expect anybody told him that I laid Donnan's rifle across his saddle," Macumber pointed out, "and I don't guess anybody told him there was a cleaning-rag hanging in a bush there. We never seen that ourselves. And if we want to check up his story about the cigarette butts, we only got to go look. It's kind of uncanny, it sure is. But you got to admit his story runs almighty smooth, just like anything could have happened; and whenever there is a fact, that fact fits right in."

"Oh, he's smart, all right," said Major. "Uncanny smart in some ways. But here's what worries me." Major leaned forward. "That old rooster hasn't told it

157

all. Hughes was right about that mule! I hope you understood me all right when I kicked you under the table, Hughes. He'd shut up like a trap, anyway; and if we'd pinned him down too tight, we'd have got him so worried we wouldn't have no more chances to trip him up again."

"I guess you're right," Hughes admitted dubiously.

"That's the next thing we've got to do—we got to trip up Grasshopper Tanner into telling what he knows. Maybe he can't tell who done it, and maybe he can't put his finger on 'em right now, today, if he wants to; but I'll bet you my bottom dollar Grasshopper *thinks* he can!"

"I'll tell you something more," said Hughes, "Grasshopper Tanner's scared."

"If he is, I didn't see it," said Macumber.

"By God, I saw it," Major said. "We don't know all about Tanner in this affair, not by any means. For one thing, assuming somebody did ride a mule into Crazy Mule Gulch; who in the Sweetwater mountains would be more liable to be riding a mule than anybody else?"

Macumber and Major exchanged a long stare, "Tanner," said Macumber softly, at last.

"A mule was in Tanner's mind this morning," said Major; and a mule was heard by Hughes that night."

There was a silence. "It gives a man the creeps," said Macumber. "A man don't know who to count on around here no more."

"And here's another thing," said Major. "When we left for Adobe Wells yesterday morning, I left instructions with Walk Ross as to what Grasshopper Tanner was to do if he got here. Tanner got here while I was gone and Walk Ross gave him his orders. One of 'em was that he was to start back as soon as night come on. He promised to do that. According to his own story, he did do it. But if he did, where was he that he had to ride from dark last night to four o'clock this morning to get here? Have you seen his horse?"

"Yes," said Macumber.

"A tuckered out horse if ever I saw one in my life," said Major.

"Of course," said Macumber, uncertainly, "that horse has been working ever since yesterday morning."

"Tanner does most of his work on foot," said Major scornfully. "That horse wasn't worn out by standing around Crazy Mule all day, Macumber. It was rid, and that good and plenty."

Once more there was a silence. "What do you think?" said Macumber at last.

"I think that what that old ridge-runner told us he saw, he saw, all right. But also he saw something else—something that he almighty wishes he hadn't never seen."

Macumber and Major held each other's eyes. "I guess you're right," Macumber agreed at last.

"I'm sending you and Hughes and Walk Ross and Art French up to Crazy Mule canyon with Grasshopper Tanner today," said Major, "as soon as he rolls out of his blankets. You look at what he shows

159

you, fair enough, but mostly, you'll look for what he isn't showing you: something that's in his mind and he doesn't want to come out. Do you understand?"

"Mr. Major," said Macumber, "I got the feeling we're awfully close to something here."

"See that it doesn't give you the slip," said Major.

Hughes walked out into the cool quiet of the sunrise. Behind the dry hills the sky was a vast welter of incredible oranges and reds. The air was cool and very clear, but perfectly still, as if in abeyance to the blaze of heat that the direct sunlight would presently bring. Some one was milking in one of the barns, and the rich warm fragrance of fresh milk came down breeze, mingling with the faint clean smell of the dew upon sun-curing alfalfa. Hughes realized suddenly that this was the prettiest spread he had ever seen; it had every-thing that a man could want. If only hate and anger and war could leave this valley alone, it would be the sort of place that a man could work in always, and be content. It had water and grass, and vast open range; it had immense herds and plenty of saddle stock. The home ranch even had shade. And it was the place where Sally Major lived, and had lived all her life.

It occurred to him suddenly that it would be a dark day for him when he took the trail again and left this place behind. Of course, he supposed that he would presently—if nothing worse occurred first—be sad-dling up to ride on. He had always done so before; it was not easy for him to picture himself as a steady fix-ture in any one place now. Yet, he knew that he had never been in a place which suited him so well, and which he would leave so reluctantly.

Looking about him in the cool clear light of the fresh morning he found it very hard to believe that this spread was in a real and definite danger; that an imminent disaster could destroy it past all recognition, leaving only crumbling walls, the gaunt skeletons of dead trees, and dust. That was unthinkable; yet, if Oliver Major knew his valley, that was what they were fighting now. The difficulty from a rider's point of view, thought Hughes, was that the opening stages of the fight were so vague and complicated that a man hardly knew what he was up against at all. The old free-range, no-law, gun-fighting days, when a man had simply saddled and gone out to shoot it out, certainly had had their points of advantage. Altogether too much of a sense of creeping hidden things, shadowy suspicion, and threatening mystery was upon the outfit much too much to suit Hughes.

He went and sat on the top bar of a corral and rolled a cigarette; and when Sally Major came toward him from the house he had the feeling that the course of his thoughts had turned to substance before his eyes. He hardly ever saw her without first having had her in his mind; it showed him how much of the time she found her way into his thoughts.

He dropped to the ground as she came up with her quick, nervous stride. He saw that she looked worried, and her eyes were shadowed as if she had not slept very much.

"It sure is a lovely morning," he suggested.

"You're going up to the Crazy Mule with Grasshopper Tanner?" she asked at once.

"I'm one of 'em," he admitted.

"Who are the others?"

"Bob Macumber, and Art French, and Walk Ross."

He thought for a moment that there was a flash of panic in her eyes. "For heaven's sake be careful what you do. You look as if you're going on a picnic or something."

"Well, I guess it's nothing more nor less than a look-see," he said.

"How do you know it is? How do you know who you're with or what you're trying to do?"

"What do you mean?"

"Right over there is the window of the room we were in when somebody shot at you. That was hardly forty-eight hours ago, yet you seem to have forgotten all about it. The man who tried to kill you then has just as much reason to try to kill you now. Dad must be crazy to send you up there at all."

"Why, there's no reason I should stay one place more than another, child."

"Well, watch what you're doing in the Crazy Mule. I never in my life had as black a hunch about anything as I have about that canyon right now. That's all I wanted to say." Abruptly she turned on her heel and started back toward the house; she caught herself in her first stride, however, and turned back to regard him curiously. "You still don't mean to take my advice about going over the hill?"

"I just don't seem to be able to see my way clear," he told her.

She regarded him with a quirky smile; for a moment it seemed to him that something in her eyes made her seem very intimate and near. Then abruptly her face changed, and turning away sharply she went toward the house. He was not certain that he had seen in her eyes a glint of sudden tears. A sudden angry eagerness for battle filled him, so that he hoped that the seemingly inevitable outbreak of war would come soon.

One of Sally Major's sentences was ringing through his head as he lit his cigarette: 'You don't know who you are with.' Grasshopper Tanner . . . Walk Ross . . . Art French . . . Hardly knowing why, he found himself wondering which of those three, if any of them, could beat him to the gun, if ever he faced them with powder smoke between, and in his ears the roar of the forty-fives. . . .

It still lacked an hour of eight o'clock—the hour at which Grasshopper Tanner had agreed to rouse himself and take the trail to Crazy Mule Canyon again—when Jim Crawford's car, red hot and steaming badly from the pace of its approach, came careening up the road from Adobe Wells, and slithered to a stop before the ranch house of the Lazy M. With him were Bart Holt and Dick Major—the three of the Lazy M posse who had been left to hold the fort at Adobe Wells.

Clay Hughes had been sitting with Bob Macumber on the top rail of a corral; as the car pulled up Bob

Macumber dropped to the ground and headed for the house on the run, Hughes at his heels.

"What's bust?" demanded Macumber as they joined the arrivals.

"Everything," said Bart Holt curtly. The big door slammed back upon its hinges heavily as Holt thrust his way into the house.

Old Oliver Major met them in the hall. The questioning look of his stern old face might have been either anger or alarm, but he faced them silently, waiting for the others to speak.

"Mr. Major," Jim Crawford began; then he hesitated. It was as if he had been dreading this moment all the way from Adobe Wells, and now that he faced it, could hardly bring himself to convey the news he brought. "Mr. Major, they've took the jump!"

"What do you mean?"

"Mr. Major, I ain't sheriff any more."

There was a short silence while Oliver Major glared his incomprehension. "If you mean you resigned—" his voice rose angrily at last.

"No. I'd never quit under you, Mr. Major; I'm removed from office, that's all."

Once more the short silence of incomprehension, of disbelief. The loss of the sheriff's office meant abrupt disaster. Sooner or later, they had known, this blow was bound to come. But Oliver Major had thrown his every resource into postponing it long enough so that he might strengthen his hand. That it should have come so swiftly was incredible. He did not see how it could have been accomplished.

"It can't be so," Major said flatly. "Why, those county supervisors—when I left them yesterday, they were whipped to a frazzle! With Earl Shaw in the jug they're scared their whole machine will go to pieces, and leave 'em stranded. Until Shaw is free they're out of guts—and there hasn't even been time for Shaw's people to get a writ of habeas corpus!"

"It ain't the supervisors," said Crawford.

"Then you're still sheriff," declared old Major. "The supervisors are the only ones with authority to put you out."

"They done it by telegram from the Capitol," Crawford told him. "The order is signed by the governor himself!"

"The governor? Old Theron Replogle?"

"Governor Replogle," repeated Crawford.

The wind seemed to be knocked out of Oliver Major.

"Yes, he could do it," he said at last, "but I thought—I thought—" His voice trailed off. He turned away, and his hands seemed to fumble at the latch of the door as he led them into his office. An old wolf might have moved so, slowly drawing off into a recess in the rock, to recover from a shot that had stunned him.

At his ancient desk he turned and faced them. "I can't believe it," he said again. "How did this thing come through?"

"A whole batch of telegrams come in, relayed by

165

long distance phone from Walkerton. Billy Walters took them down like he always does. The first one was to me, ordering me to turn over the sheriff's office immediately to Alex Shaw."

"To Alex Shaw," old Major repeated.

"Yes; you said all along that if I was out, it would be him that they would put in. It come in the form of an emergency order. I got it with me." He handed Major a telegraph blank heavily scribbled in pencil.

Oliver Major studied it for what seemed the space of many minutes. "Yes," he said slowly, at last, as if still hardly able to believe, "I guess it's so."

"There was another one to Alex Shaw," said Crawford, "telling him to assume office at once; another to Earl Shaw."

"You saw that last one?" said Major sharply.

"Yeah, but it was in code. Billy Walters wouldn't give me any copy. I only got a quick look at it, and I couldn't make head nor tail of it; but it was a long one. Billy had a big time getting it took down right."

"I don't understand it; I don't understand it," Oliver Major kept saying. "Old Theron Replogle. . . ."

A silence fell upon them, the dazed, uncertain silence of men who find themselves suddenly frustrated by powers far beyond their control. The shadow of destiny, malignant and implacable, seemed suddenly to have become a monstrous thing.

Hughes had already felt before that old Oliver Major was leading them into the face of tremendous odds. Yet the old range wolf had slashed out at his energies savagely. It had been a bold move to seize Earl Shaw himself; but it had apparently been a successful one in that it had given the Lazy M a temporary grip upon the local law. However certain old Major might be in his own mind that Earl Shaw was behind the murder of Hugo Donnan, the Lazy M would be helpless as soon as Shaw resumed the reins of law enforcement. Major did not dare yield into the hands of Earl Shaw's gang either Clay Hughes, who was supposed to know more about the killing than he had told, nor Dick Major, whom Shaw would certainly try to make suspect of the killing of Donnan. Until he should be able to gather evidence against the true killers, Major's hold upon the sheriff's office was the only defense of the Lazy M.

It had been a precarious position at best, and obviously a temporary one; but while they held Grasshopper Tanner, whom Major now believed to hold the key to the mystery of Donnan's death, it had seemed that the boss of the Buckhorn water, by his very daring, might emerge victorious.

The striking away of that slender strategy had come with the force and unexpectedness of a thunderbolt. The abrupt power of the stroke was almost contemptuous in its arrogance, its irresistibility, and its finality. There was a long silence.

"You all see what this means?" said Major at last.

No one spoke; until Bart Holt muttered, "I guess it's pretty plain."

"There's two of us here," said Major, "who have to

167

see this thing through to a finish. The rest of you have no call to stay here and take your chance. If Earl Shaw has his way, and it sure looks like he's got a good chance, it's going to come awful dry weather for us all. The time to pull out of it is now, before it's too late. Will you go, Bart?"

"No," said Holt. "We're laughing at you. Unless Hughes—"

"I like it here too," said Hughes. "You give me a pain, Holt."

Major made a gesture of futility, the first of its kind that Hughes had ever seen him use. "There's just one chance," he said. "The governor don't know what he's done—of that I'm sure. I've always said that Theron Replogle was a small man, and a crooked one, but he wouldn't dare go as far as this if he wasn't riding blind. I don't doubt he's got a finger in the Silverado project and he's backing Earl Shaw because of that. What he don't know—and probably can't know from where he sits, is that Earl Shaw will never dare let Dick be brought to trial."

"He'll charge him, and he'll have Alex Shaw here after him, just the same," said Crawford. "Yes, he'll do that. It's his chance to bust the Lazy M, after all these years. But do you think he'd ever dare let Clay Hughes go on the stand—supposedly the only man that knows what Donnan said before he died? And do you suppose he'd dare let Grasshopper Tanner come up and testify, with nobody knowing what Grasshopper found out, nor what he'll say on the stand? What Theron Replogle can't know is that Earl Shaw will take the shorter way. Only a man that knows Shaw like I do can be dead certain of that, like I am certain now!"

"What do you think he's going to do?"

"I ain't telling you what I think. I'm telling you what I know. You youngsters keep forgetting what me and Bart Holt—and Earl Shaw too—will always remember: that there's many a cowboy deep under this prairie because of Shaw's trying to grab the Buckhorn water. Do you think he cares any more about the lives of two or three men, or sees any difference between the law and a gun in the dark when it comes to finishing a man off? I tell you, if Shaw makes a clean sweep of this range, neither Dick, nor Hughes, nor old Tanner neither, will ever live to see a court room."

"What's your play?" Bart Holt asked.

"We got to carry the fight higher. We got to tie into them on their own ground. I say Theron Replogle don't see what's going to happen. We got to show him. There's one man on our string that can talk to the governor and make him see it, and only one. That man's Stephen Sessions. I've sent for him. I had his wire in Walkerton that he was on his way. He should be here now—if he's coming at all. Why he isn't here I don't know. He's the only card we've got left."

"If he's going to be a day behind Alex Shaw he might as well stay home," said Bart Holt.

"And what if he doesn't come?" said Hughes.

"Then we've got to stand 'em off any way we can."

"Meantime," Macumber put in, "we can damn well go up to Crazy Mule Canyon with Tanner and see what we can find out there. We can do that much anyway."

"You're sure you want to do that?" said Hughes.

"Why not?"

"If Tanner's your blue chip, like you think he is, then it looks to me like you're throwing him into an awful risk by sending him up to Crazy Mule now. If I was Earl Shaw, the first thing I'd want to do would be to get Grasshopper Tanner cut out of the herd. The Crazy Mule looks to me like a fine place for him to work it. Tanner can't even hide out like an ordinary man, the way his dogs hang around and yell."

"Grasshopper find something, did he?" asked Dick.

In a few words old man Major told the three from Adobe Wells what was known about Grasshopper Tanner.

"Suppose he is cut off in the Crazy Mule," said Macumber. "He won't be alone by no means. I say leave us take him on up there, and if Alex Shaw comes up, don't make it any matter of just shooting our way clear! Let Alex Shaw worry about how he's going to shoot his way clear."

Old man Major appeared to consider. "No," he decided. "No, we're not ready for that. We're in awful deep. 'We don't dast get in any deeper—until Stephen Sessions comes."

"If he comes," said Holt.

CHAPTER TWELVE

That was a hard day to wait out. It is hard enough to wait for the turn of an event which is to happen at a known time. To wait for a thing which may be indefinitely postponed, or may never happen at all, can, if the turn is of supreme importance in many lives, strain human endurance to the cracking point.

After the held stock had been taken care of, nobody tried to work. The few horses that had been saddled drowsed unridden after the early chores. The cowboys were mostly silent behind the eternal restless smoke of their cigarettes. Even the cottonwoods seemed waiting, unwhispering in the hot air. Stephen Sessions and the possibility of his intercession with the governor, now seemed the only hope of the Lazy M. There was almost a prayer in the air that the next drift of dust on the southern horizon would mean that he had come.

For the moment they were helpless, unable to do anything but wait. They no longer even had access to a telegraph wire. The unsatisfactory Lazy M telephone was still out of commission, and would undoubtedly remain so; and no Lazy M man dared show himself in either Adobe Wells or Walkerton, now that Shaw was in the saddle once more. To do so would have been to risk a prompt choice between fight and imprisonment. None of them were ready for either one.

171

When in mid-afternoon a column of dust appeared to southward, marking the approach of a car upon the Adobe Wells road, watchful eyes picked it up a long way off. Most of the Lazy M had gathered with a vague, strained attempt at casualness before the ranch house by the time the dusty touring car wheeled to a stop before the house. And there was grimness and silence in the waiting group; for while the car was still a long way off, the shrewd-guessing eyes of the cattlemen had made out that it was not Stephen Sessions who had come.

Of the two men in the dusty touring car, one was the blond giant called Dutch Pete, who had stood behind Earl Shaw when the Lazy M posse had invaded the Bar S. The other Hughes had never seen before; yet he immediately knew that it could be no one but Alex Shaw.

Alex Shaw was younger than his brother by a good ten or fifteen years. He had more height and, less beef; more sinew and less bone. His hard-carved face, with its twisty grin, lacked the intelligence and the force of character apparent in that of Earl Shaw, so that at first sight Alex looked like a raffish caricature of his older brother. Where Earl Shaw would be ruthless, Alex would be merely reckless; Alex would be explosive in situations where Earl Shaw would hold back his hand and wait. Yet, Alex had a certain hard strength of his own. In some situations he would be more dangerous than his brother, because quicker in violence, and more careless of cost.

Alex Shaw swung down from the wheel, leaving his engine running, and approached Oliver Major with a quick business-like stride. His eye was sardonic as it ran over those ostentatiously casual, waiting cowboys in the background. All those men were wearing their guns; their faces were alert, interested, and expectant, but not nervous. This time it was Oliver Major who, physically, held the upper hand, able to make fight and win his fight—if only to do so was not to lose all else.

"You got the word?" Alex Shaw asked Major. His voice was impersonal, neither friendly nor belligerent. Of them all, this man, walking into the circle of his enemies, seemed surest of his ground.

"What word?" said Major.

Alex Shaw pulled his telegram from his pocket, straightened it with a snap like the crack of a whip, and thrust it under old man Major's nose. Dutch Pete, following more slowly, took up a position a little behind Alex Shaw and to one side, and hooked his thumbs in his belt. The big man's face was sleepy and expressionless; yet Hughes thought he had never seen harder eyes in the face of any man. They were hard as the eyes of a carnivore are hard, without effort of will or any particular malice of intent, but merely with the complete lack of any humane scruple known to men.

Oliver Major glanced at the paper only briefly. "I suppose that's the governor's order giving you the sheriff's office," he said.

Alex Shaw nodded. "Naturally, I have to jump onto the matter of this Donnan killing," he explained, evidently making an effort to keep his voice reasonable and detached. "I'm right sorry to trouble your outfit here; but it looks like I'm going to have to take up three of your boys, for questioning."

"Who do you want?" Major demanded bluntly.

"I'm afraid," Alex Shaw said, with the reasonable air of a man who knows he is asking much, but is pressed to it by duty, "I'm going to have to ask for Dick Major first of all." He watched Oliver Major.

The boss of the Lazy M gave no sign. "Who else?"

"Clay Hughes and Grasshopper Tanner."

"Well, they're right here; you see 'em. Go ahead and question 'em if you want."

"I'm going to have to take them back to Adobe Wells for that, Mr. Major."

"You question them here," said Major evenly, without heat.

Alex Shaw held Oliver Major's eyes steadily as he slowly shook his head. A shadow of his twisty grin crossed his face, somehow darkening it. "No; that won't do it, Major."

"Then," said Major, "you're out of luck."

"You mean you don't aim to give these men up?"

Major said contemptuously, "You knew that much before you come."

There was a long moment's silence. "I want to be reasonable here," said Alex Shaw at last. "All I'm trying to do is to carry out the regular process of the law, same as it's been put on me to do. I've got no charge to lay against any one of these three. All I ask is a chance to question them. You know I can't do that here."

"You'll do it here or not at all."

Alex Shaw folded up the copy of the telegram that had made him sheriff and stuck it back in his pocket before he spoke again. "I don't want trouble here. I can understand how you feel, Major, about letting your own boy go into the hands of the law. And I am willing to stretch a point so as not to stir no trouble up. I'm willing to leave Dick here, and only take the other two, Hughes and Tanner, and no more said."

"Not a man," said Major.

The twisty grin of Alex Shaw came and went again; the man seemed easy and relaxed. Certainly he was giving a good imitation of a man who is only trying to do his duty as he sees it, reasonably, without malice. Hughes for a moment wondered how any man could act the part so well, if indeed, the circumstance in the Buckhorn was exactly as Oliver Major supposed. He was turning this over in his mind when Alex Shaw spoke again.

"Major, you know what you're doing I expect; but I got to warn you just the same, if only for the sake of warning these hands of yours, that's standing here to back your play. They got a right to know what they're up against, I guess. You realize that if you refuse to hand up these men that you're making an open act against the due process of the law, and that if a charge of murder is brought against any one of your people here, you'll be liable as accessory after the fact?"

175

"I don't admit to that," said Major.

"I didn't ask you did you admit to it. I just wanted it clear to everybody what I said." His voice became more distinct, dropping all trace of apology. "You realize you're making an open stand against the law; and unless this killing clears up mighty quick in some way that ain't expected, the law will have to move against you according."

Once more there was silence; and abruptly Hughes thought he saw the explanation of Alex Shaw's casualness, his failure to resent the resistance he had encountered. This was not a man who took frustration lying down. Alex Shaw was relaxed and confident because he was obtaining exactly what he had come for. Probably he had had no hope that the three men he had asked for, or any one of them, would be given into his hands.

But the flat refusal of the Lazy M boss in itself gave the Shaw faction exactly what it wanted. Right here, now, in this quiet exchange of words, Alex Shaw was establishing the circumstance that would enable Earl Shaw to make immediate war upon the Buckhorn cattleman with all the ramified power of the law on the side of the Bar S. The decision which Alex Shaw had drawn from Major, inevitable to the character of the old range wolf, reduced Major and all his supporters to the technical status of so many outlaws.

And those waiting cowboys, ready as they were to back Oliver Major—they were not all of them so astute nor so experienced that some of them would not be trapped in the end into bearing witness to this act which gave a legal foundation to any raid against the Lazy M which Earl Shaw might now conceive.

"Mr. Major," said Clay Hughes, "for my part I think that Grasshopper Tanner and I had better go along with them."

Oliver Major turned a wondering eye upon Hughes. "Are you crazy, man?"

Hughes saw no reason for not saying plainly what was in his mind. "If we turn down his proposition of taking me and Tanner the Bar S will be holding every card in the deck. But if Tanner and I give up, their hands are tied, so far as the Lazy M is concerned, until they cook up their next move. There's nothing else to do."

Oliver Major was looking at him as if Hughes were out of his head. "It isn't questioning they want of you," he said slowly. "You act like I never explained all that to you at all!"

"As for me," Hughes said, "I'm ready to go along and take my chance."

The old man was iron in his convictions, and invincible in the stubbornness of his will. Yet now for a moment he seemed to hesitate, like a horse holding back for one last instant at the brink of a precipitous descent. It gave Hughes a queer sensation to see him waver, even for a moment. It was as if the rim rock itself had swayed, bending to the wind.

And now Clay Hughes saw that Sally Major had come through the scatter of waiting cowboys to her father's side. She had come silently, and how long she had been there he did not know. Her features were untroubled, and very still, except that deep behind her eyes was a suggestion of that slow hidden fire that Hughes had seen more than once in the eyes of her father.

The still face of the girl was an incredible contrast to the harsh uncompromising faces of the men, showing them for what they were. Behind the dark weather-scarred faces of the men lived the cross purposes, the ugly memories, and the hatreds which were once more sweeping the Buckhorn into war. As when he had first seen her, Hughes found himself unable to reconcile the fresh loveliness of Sally Major with her surroundings. It seemed to him that she made the best of the cowmen look like so many turbulent animals; while she herself was made to seem something infinitely delicate, infinitely precious, and unreal.

Sally Major's voice was very low as she spoke to her father. "If you let this man go, you'll never be able to lift up your head again; and you know that." Her phrases were incongruous to her voice, so quietly she spoke, without passion nor intensity; but somehow their very quiet gave them the sound of immutable truths, detached, unassailable by the turbulent wills of men.

Oliver gave no sign of having heard. "Hughes," he said, "nobody knows better than me that I can force no man to take my part; but I say—"

"It isn't a question of taking your part," said Hughes.

"But I say," old man Major bore him down, "you got no right to go. You've looked like a strong card in our hand, Hughes, and Earl Shaw knows it well."

"As to that," said Hughes, "I'll be the same card whether I go or stay."

Oliver Major shook his head. "They can't hold you, and they daren't leave you go. There's only one answer to that: and I think everybody here knows what I mean."

"Sure we can hold him," said Alex Shaw. "We can hold him on more counts than one. There's a charge lodged against him of impersonating a United States Marshal, for one thing."

"You'll never make it stick," said Hughes.

"We'll come almighty close to it!"

"That's beside the point," said Major. "Hughes, in the position we're in here, the Lazy M's got some right in this matter. I say you've got no right to go, no right to give yourself up to this gang. It's suicide to begin with; but even if you don't see that—"

"If we stand against this," insisted Hughes, "we'll be playing right into their hand. It's exactly what they want."

"What they want is fight," said Oliver Major. "If they don't get it one way, don't you ever fool yourself, they'll get it in another. Fight is what they want, and fight is what they'll get, and all hell can't stop that. If they can prune down our chances first by cutting you out of the herd, or Tanner either, don't you ever think that they won't be tickled to death. And the upshot will be the same, one way or the other."

Watching Alex Shaw, Hughes thought that the flicker of an unexpected hope had appeared in the eyes of the Adobe Wells sheriff.

"You heard what your boss said," Alex Shaw told Hughes; "and you Tanner—" Shaw's eyes searched out the figure of Tanner in the background against the wall of the house, and he raised his voice to carry to the old lion hunter also—"Major has as good as put you two men on your own responsibility, whether you stand against the law, or not. Hold out now, and you're outlawed where you stand; and don't you forget that sooner or later you'll be hunted down and called to pay up! Don't fool yourself that the law ever forgets, or falls down on the job in the end. The law says that you come to Adobe Wells and answer the questions that are asked you like reasonable men. Play an above-board hand and you've got a good chance of being free before night. But once you get yourself on the upwind side, there ain't going to be anybody you can look to to side you—least of all the Lazy M."

As Alex Shaw finished, Hughes realized that his own view of his position had changed. A minute before it had seemed to him that to surrender himself was to confuse the Shaw faction's strategy against Oliver Major, and that to refuse to submit to the technical authority vested in Alex Shaw was to play into the hand of Major's enemy. He now saw that this was not Alex Shaw's view; that although Shaw was willing to leave with no more accomplished than the technical outlawry of the Lazy M, he would be only too well pleased to take with him Tanner and Hughes himself. As for turning the force of the law upon the Lazy M, Shaw would only need later to force the matter of Dick Major's surrender—a thing which Oliver Major would never in the world concede.

"Go to hell," said Hughes to Shaw. "I'm staying here!"

For a moment Alex Shaw studied him as if testing the stability of Hughes' decision. Then his twisty grin flickered as he appeared to accept the insubmission as definite. His eyes turned to Tanner, waiting.

"If you're after me, I'll come," said Grasshopper Tanner, unexpectedly. He was answering Alex Shaw, but his defiant eyes were upon Oliver Major.

There was a moment's silence, while the old lion hunter's angular figure moved forward slowly, almost warily, as if he expected somebody to stop him. Then, "Why, you old fool—" Oliver Major exploded.

"Where do I get off, bucking the law?" Tanner demanded angrily. He had taken on the fiery look of a man who defends his own interests recklessly in the face of massed opinion. "This is your scrap, not mine!"

There was a general stir. Perhaps no one there had ever recognized before that the habitual bad temper of the old mountain man had concealed an impetuous instability. There was a queer intuitive genius in Tanner, but it was the type of genius commonly found in association with an unaccountable volatility.

Beneath his weird genius was to be found nothing upon which men could depend. Perhaps some unforgotten past experience had given Tanner an obsessive fear of the law; perhaps it was only that he was incapable of thinking of himself divided from his hound pack. A man surrounded by hounds cannot be hid; he is as easy to lay hands on any time as a man dogged by an active steam whistle.

"They've got nothing on me," Tanner's strident voice was saying. "And they won't learn nothing from me neither, as they'll damn soon find out! But I ain't gone crazy enough to fight the law without no reason at all!"

"Get in the car, Tanner," said Alex Shaw. Now that his work was done here, he seemed anxious to get away.

Once more for an instant Oliver Major seemed to hesitate. He opened his mouth, but closed it again, his face very grim. There was a movement behind him as some of the cowboys stirred, and Tom Ireland started to step forward. Major, without looking around, half raised one arm, palm backward, in a warning gesture; and they became still again, though their faces remained angry and uncertain.

The Adobe Wells car turned, and Hughes saw Alex Shaw grin as he said something out of the side of his mouth to Dutch Pete. Grasshopper Tanner's dogs were running forward now. Tanner stood up in the back seat, jerking his blacksnake from his belt. "Git back thar! You want to kill yourselves chasing a gas engine?" The whip snapped over the dogs; the nearest yelped, unhit, and they fell back, blooping their protest.

Oliver Major stood gnawing his mustache as he stared after the receding car, and his eyes were very bleak. Beyond any doubt, the old boss of the Buckhorn believed himself to be watching the departure of a man whom he would not see again. Sally Major suddenly covered her face with her hands and ran into the house.

Major turned upon the waiting cowboys, and his voice rose tremendously. He made a sweeping gesture of finality with one arm.

"You saw what's happened! This is the time for you to quit. This is the time for you to get out, before you're drawn in deep as me. Who wants his pay? Which of you has sense enough to take his pay and get out?"

No one moved, and there was silence except for the wowling of Tanner's forsaken dogs. The riders looked vaguely embarrassed; they studied the smoke of their cigarettes to avoid meeting his eye. Some of them exchanged expressionless glances, but none gave any sign of taking up Major's suggestion.

Major suddenly shouted at them, *"You damned fools, will you quit?"*

Still no one answered; and, after a strained moment, the old man strode through them, and into the house.

CHAPTER THIRTEEN

The Lazy M boiled up when the Adobe Wells car was gone. The cowboys, usually so frugal of speech, buzzed like a hive of bees. Not every one agreed that Grasshopper Tanner should have been allowed to give himself up to Alex Shaw; and not all of them understood exactly what had taken place. Nowhere among them, however, was perceivable any desire to avoid the approaching clash with the Bar S, whether the Bar S came with a pretense of law or without. Hardly a one of them would question his future if called upon to fight for the Lazy M. They made up a formidable fighting unit, not readily to be taken or put down. Yet they knew that while Shaw's control made the law itself a weapon and a mockery, not even an army could hold out against his resources long. More than ever they needed the ultimate intervention which Stephen Sessions could perhaps obtain.

Oliver Major had withdrawn to his office again. This form of retirement was one of the few indications that the boss of the Buckhorn water was growing old, for all his life he had been accustomed to think in the saddle, developing his ideas and his methods by putting them into effect. When he had withdrawn, the gang of cowboys in front of the house disintegrated slowly. Clay Hughes, after a short interview with the old man, rounded up the restlessly voicing dogs of Grasshopper Tanner and shut them in a stable. Then he set out to look for Sally Major.

This time he had no trouble in finding her. She was sitting in the patio, on the bench where they had last talked; her head was leaned against the wall, so that for a moment she seemed asleep, but as he approached she came to life, and indicated with a peremptory gesture that he was to sit down beside her. He obeyed, rolled a cigarette, and waited.

"Do you understand what has happened?" she asked in a low voice.

"More or less, I guess."

"Well, I certainly don't," she said. "In all my life I never saw Dad do anything like that before. What in the world has come over him? Do you suppose, after all, he is going to knuckle under to Earl Shaw?"

"No," said Hughes. "No, he'll never do that, not in a thousand years!"

"Then why in the world did he let Alex Shaw take Grasshopper Tanner?"

"Seemed like Grasshopper wanted to go."

"What's that got to do with it? Do you suppose Grasshopper knows what's good for him? Not any more than his own dogs!"

"You think Tanner's in danger?"

"Why, of course he's in danger! I know what happened this morning. I suppose there isn't anybody on the place who doesn't know that Grasshopper Tanner is hiding something. He's found out something that shows him who killed Donnan!"

"I'm only hoping," said Hughes, "that nobody outside the Lazy M knows that he has."

Her voice dropped to a whisper. "And what hope is there of that?"

"You think—"

"I think there's somebody here we can't trust. Someone right here among us is getting word to Earl Shaw of everything that happens here."

"What makes you think so?"

"It's perfectly obvious. Earl Shaw knew that the posse from here was on the way before ever it reached Adobe Wells. And I don't suppose you've forgotten that you were fired on the very first night you were here. Why it hasn't happened again is a mystery to inc. So far as I can see everybody here has acted just as if it had never happened at all!"

"Not quite that bad," he told her. "For my part, I'll admit to a very pointed interest in staying alive. I sure haven't stood in any more lighted windows. I don't believe there's been a minute since then when I could have been thrown down on, without a chance to fire back."

"Well, for heaven's sake, don't get careless. You have to remember that the man who fired upon you is still here, some place."

"What makes you think that?"

"Everybody is here now that was here then; nobody has quit his job nor disappeared."

"You don't think somebody could have ridden in from outside and—"

"Rubbish!"

"Maybe it was a mistake for your father to let Alex Shaw take old Tanner," Hughes said. "I didn't exactly understand it myself right then. But I've talked to the old man since, and—I believe he was right."

"For heaven's sake what was in his mind?"

"Well, it was this: he mentioned that somebody might be passing word to the Bar S of whatever happened here; but he didn't see how a spy could have got word to Earl Shaw since this morning, even if he wanted to. So he figured that Shaw couldn't possibly know that Tanner knew anything. After all, you know, maybe Tanner doesn't. He sure thinks he does, but maybe he's fooling himself."

Sally shook her head. "He knows enough to scare him plenty; and did you ever see a lion hunter that was easily scared?"

"Well, anyway," Hughes finished, "after Tanner made the choice of giving himself up, your father figured that to hold him by force would tell the Shaws that Tanner certainly did know something; but if he let him go, and Tanner kept his mouth shut, Earl Shaw would probably take him for just another meddling old fool, and let him go. Then Tanner will be back here."

"What makes you think he'll be back?"

"Because I shut up his dogs. They would have followed him in an hour or two if they'd been loose. But they won't follow him now. If it works out so that Tanner is turned loose and comes back here, that will sure be a big advantage over holding him by main strength."

"If," said Sally.

"Now," said he, "I want to know why you changed your mind about me."

"Changed my mind?"

"Yesterday when I talked to you, the last thing you said was that you wanted me to go over the hill; to get out and stay out."

She was silent for a moment. "Why should I tell you what I meant?" she said. "Why should I answer your questions, or tell you anything? You're not being open with me."

"I'm not?" he said, puzzled.

"Of course you're not. For one thing, I asked you how you made Earl Shaw give in; and you wouldn't tell me."

"Why, Sally—I even gave you the pieces of paper, with what I wrote on them."

"But you told me you didn't want me to see it, and that was the same thing as not giving it to me at all. Of course," she went on, "we all know now how you made him back down: you made him wonder if you weren't a federal man; and his fear of too big an entanglement tied his hands."

"Of course I know what you think about that."

"You can't possibly know anything of the kind. What I can't understand is why you wanted to make a secret of it—square in the face of the suspicion it naturally caused."

"I did have a reason," he said. "It was kind of a fool reason I expect, but it seemed real important to me."

"I'm not asking you what your reason was. I'm not asking you anything more at all."

"But I'm going to tell you anyway." He hesitated, for this was hard for him to say. "I promised you I'd stop a fight if I could. I'm never going to promise such a thing as that again. It forced me to lie our way out of a fight. At least, it amounted to a lie, in effect. I haven't the least doubt that everybody thinks I did it to save my hide. I'd rather have it thought that I was in cahoots with Earl Shaw."

"That's the most foolish thing I ever heard," she told him.

"I suppose."

"But why?" she insisted. "What do you care about people thinking a thing when you yourself know it isn't so?"

"I never did before," he admitted. "I don't suppose in all my life it ever made any difference to me what anybody thought; but when it came to showing my hand—I found out that this time it made a heap of difference."

"You thought Dad would—"

"I didn't care a hoot what your father thought."

"Then why did you run the risk of—"

"Because I knew you'd think I'd folded up in the face of a fight."

"You'd rather they'd think you were in with the Bar S than have them think you were afraid to fight?"

"Not them; you."

A silence fell between them, but presently a slow

189

smile came into her eyes. "Wasn't that kind of silly?" she said gently.

Through the quiet they could hear the voicing of Grasshopper Tanner's shut-up dogs, dulled behind walls, but mournfully persistent. "I was wrong," Sally murmured at last. "I take back what I said, about your not being open. I guess I understand a little bit better now." For a moment then it seemed to Hughes that the gulf had about closed.

"You still want me to get out of here?"

She answered slowly, her eyes on the pale blossoms of a vine which climbed a post before them. "I don't know."

"You were real set on it," he said, "at one time."

"The night I waited for you in the dark? That was something else. Because then I was thinking a different thing that wasn't so. I can't tell you what that was; but— something that I shouldn't have thought, I suppose."

"It was a natural thing to think," he said.

She glanced at him, startled. "What do you mean?"

"That first night," he told her, "you thought your brother killed Hugo Donnan."

Her face did not change; but watching her profile, he saw the slow color come into it. Suddenly she turned upon him, her grey eyes staring. "And what if he had?" she cried. "He went out to get Donnan because he thought it was the only thing in the world to do. If he had succeeded instead of failed, I wouldn't hold it against him for a single moment!"

"Of course not," said Clay.

"I blame myself for not believing him to begin with," said Sally. "Only—perhaps I shouldn't say this; but Dick hasn't quite always been willing to stand up and take the consequences of everything he's done. It was when I found out that Donnan had been shot from behind that I knew Dick could not possibly have done it. Dick doesn't know what fear is, physically, and never has, I suppose not for a single moment in his life."

"Sure," said Clay, "I understand."

"It was I who made Dick lie low at first when he rode in, the night after Donnan was killed. I'm about the only one that's ever had any influence with Dick. I shouldn't have done it; it was just a mistake of mine. But at first, when I thought Dick was the one who got Hugo Donnan, I was afraid that Donnan had really said something to you before he died that would convict Dick. Right or wrong, guilty or innocent, I would have stuck by Dick all the way through. Now you know why I wanted you to leave that first night."

"Sure," said Clay.

"Of course, after I knew that Dick did not do it, I hoped that you would stay, to help us with what you knew. And I was wrong again. Why should you come in here, and run every risk that a man can run, when all the time—" She hesitated, and stopped.

"When all the time what?"

She lowered her voice. "It's a good bluff you've made, Clay," she said softly. "A game bluff, and a nervy one, and I appreciate it, because you did it to help us here. But it puts you in the worst possible danger; and I don't see how it is going to help in the end. I don't know what the others may think, but it looks pretty clear to me, Clay, that Hugo Donnan told you nothing at all!"

He had seen that coming. After all, he could not remain silent forever without having it suspected that his silence hid nothing at all. Yet it was in his mind that his slender, tenuous bluff might yet, in the end, prove the key to a door. What he recognized at once was that if he was to maintain that tenuous hope he must never for an instant seem to admit that he was bluffing, not even to Sally Major. A great sense of loneliness overwhelmed him as it was once more forcibly borne in upon him that he was playing his cards alone; not even Major, whatever he might suspect, could be perfectly certain that Hughes had nothing to withhold. But he had never felt quite so much like one man alone as now, knowing that he must guard the truth from Sally.

He trusted her implicitly; but he could not expect her to know the truth without confiding it to someone nearer to her than he was—perhaps to her brother, or to Mona. After that the grape vine telegraph, wholly innocent, but ruthlessly efficient, would carry the word all through the ranch, and so at last to Adobe Wells itself: "Hughes knows nothing."

"Are you sure?" he said slowly.

"That Donnan didn't tell you anything? It looks pretty plain, Clay."

"Are you sure?" he said again. She would never

know the effort it cost him to bring that faintly mocking smile into his eyes. There was something in her own warm eyes that dissolved his will, broke down all barriers, so that before them nothing seemed thinkable except open honesty to the depths. Yet, now he knew that he must look squarely into those eyes and make his own impenetrable and expressionless—except for the smile which was in itself a lie. That smile had made Earl Shaw back down and give himself up; it now defended the little slender bluff which was perhaps a key.

"Are you sure?" he said again.

He saw puzzlement, then doubt come into her face, and he winced. How could she ever forgive him for this, or trust him again, when at last the truth was known? But he knew that Sally's future was inextricably bound up in that of the Lazy M and the Buckhorn water. To deceive her now was his only means of retaining the single fragile weapon which he could bring to its defense.

"I don't understand you," she said dimly. "I think I don't understand you at all."

"My first promise stands," said he. "I won't tell any one what I learned that night in the Crazy Mule until I've told you."

She regarded him thoughtfully, her grey eyes almost dreamy in her quiet face. He wondered why it suddenly seemed that once more she was looking at him from across an all but impassable canyon. "I'm beginning to think," she said, "that you know what you're doing better than anyone else; a whole lot better than I do, certainly. You must do what you think best."

"I think it would be the best thing to sing you a song on the banjo," he suggested.

She shook her head, and a twinkle appeared in her eye. "You can't; you broke a string."

So she had been watching him then, he thought, as he had stood in the patio alone. "I'll fix the string."

"I have to go and find Mona. Sometimes I think she's never going to snap out of it again. She eats if you tell her to, and walks if you tell her to, but never makes a single move, hardly, of her own accord. It's the saddest thing I ever saw—almost as if she were dead. If Donnan had lived she would have got over him presently, and seen that he wasn't so much, but now that he isn't in the world any more—"

"I know," said Hughes.

CHAPTER FOURTEEN

Clay Hughes went out of the house, instinctively hitching his gun into position as he stepped through the door. It seemed a long time since there had not been a keen edge of necessity upon the watchfulness of his eyes. But there was still a relaxed laziness in his stroll, and a jaunty angle to his disreputable hat as he jerked it over one eye. He was glad to be alive, and in the same county with Sally Major. Nor could he help a sort of joyous anticipation of the fight that was ahead. What his part would be in it he did not know;

but whatever it might be, he could expect it to put him into action in Sally's behalf.

There was a gloomy anxiety, however, in the face of Bob Macumber, who came toward him now.

"Clay," said the chunky foreman, "this is sure getting to be too much for me. It begins to look like I pulled another bull."

"What's the matter now?"

"Well, right after Alex Shaw went back to town with Grasshopper Tanner, I sent Art French and Walk Ross down to Twelve Mile Corral in the flivver to turn the stock out. Seemed like we wasn't going to be having time to feed and water no stock twelve miles away; I wanted 'em thrown on the range. That was two hours ago. Clay, they ain't got back."

"Give 'em time, Bob."

"Heck, Clay, all they had to do was to throw down a couple of sets of bars!"

"Maybe their car busted down," Clay suggested.

"I'm hoping so," said Macumber gloomily. "It's about the least thing that could happen. Even so, it's bad enough. This is an almighty poor time to have hands lying around loose all over the valley, Clay."

"Why don't you send somebody after them, then?"

"How do I know that Alex Shaw isn't holding Twelve Mile Corral, and fixing to pick up anybody that comes down there? He can hold any man of us now, as an accessory to not letting him have Dick Major. Damn this accessory business anyway. I thought accessories was something that went on automobiles."

Hughes thoughtfully whistled a few bars of "Stony River." "Poor old Tanner," he said at last. "There's nothing we can do about it now."

"What you mean, Clay?"

"Art French and Walk Ross—I haven't known the people around here as long as you have, Bob; and I don't take 'em at their face value quite so much," he answered.

"They've both worked here a long time," said Macumber, impatiently. "But another thing's happened that may turn out even worse. That damn cook should have had chow started long ago, and where is he? He ain't any place! I've hunted high and low, and it sure looks to me like he's disappeared hisself. I got them old Mexican women that takes care of the house to go to work on it; but supper will be an hour late, and will probably beat hell when we get it. The old man will sure make the air blue."

Macumber wandered off again in the kind of wavering hustle of a man who feels he must take care of everything, but doesn't know just how to go about it. Macumber had changed, becoming nervous and jumpy; he certainly would have to get over that if he was ever going to be a good cow foreman again.

There was going to be a lot of trouble around there about the disappearance of Ross and French; Hughes had known that as soon as he had heard of it. By nightfall everyone in the outfit knew that the two cowboys who had started for Twelve Mile Corral in a flivver had not returned. The cowboys, as one man, were in favor of going after French and Ross to make a rescue—or a capture, whichever seemed required under the circumstances. This Oliver Major did not want. He ordered that no one should leave the immediate vicinity of the ranch buildings; and he backed up his order by gathering up the keys of the three cars remaining on the place, and shoving them into his own pants pocket, where they stayed.

Even so, four of the cowboys had saddled up for a raid of their own, and probably could not have been restrained in time, had not a new turn changed their plans. Shortly after dusk a rider came jogging into the Lazy M; and this proved to be Art French himself, riding a spare saddle and a cayuse he had picked up at Twelve Mile Corral. The whole Lazy M swarmed from all quarters to hear his story.

This, told in the unexcited drawl of Art French, proved to be disappointing enough.

"Nobody jumped us; the car didn't bust down; there wasn't no fight," Art French leisurely answered the questions shot at him by the old man. "All it was, Walk Ross seems to have gone nuts, on account of he figures old Tanner is liable to get it in the neck. Seems like Walk used to hunt with old Tanner, over in the Mogollon Country. Didn't realize old Tanner had a friend; but seems he has, and Walk is it. Walk is good and sore at us all for leaving old Tanner go with Alex Shaw. He tried to get me to go with him on to Adobe Wells, so as to be on hand if it works out that Tanner needs help. Me, I'm going to stay with the old man's orders, and I won't go. Walk, he says he'll be damned if he'll come back to the Lazy M and sit around twiddling his thumbs, with old Grasshopper in trouble. He can't get it out of his head that Tanner is in right immediate danger. After we argued a long time we split up, and Walk took the car on to Adobe Wells, and I caught up a cayuse and come back."

"So it was Ross," said old man Major to Hughes and Macumber when they were alone again.

"So what was Ross?" said Macumber.

"The man that's been giving away our hand to the Bar S," said Major, his face very grim. "I wouldn't have thought it of Ross in a thousand years. Why, Walk has worked for me for four years; and how Earl Shaw ever got to him is past me."

"I never did like his looks much," said Macumber.

Old man Major roared at him, "What's looks to do with a man?"

"Looks like they told the truth this time, the way it worked out," said Macumber.

"It's getting so a man doesn't know where to set his foot to find solid ground," said Major, bitterly. "Well, thank God he's gone!"

"It looks to me," said Hughes thoughtfully, "that if you know Walk Ross so well, you might still take him at his word. His going to Adobe Wells because he wanted to be on hand to help Tanner, if he needed it, is a pretty tall story, that's true; but," he added sarcastically, "this thing of one man siding another through a siege of trouble is still known in some places, strange as it may seem."

"Ten million fiddlesticks," snapped Major. "Grasshopper Tanner didn't have a good friend in the world!"

"As for me," suggested Clay, "I'd like to know a little more about Art French."

"He come back, didn't he?" snorted Major. "He come back, while Walk Ross jumped the outfit and headed for Adobe Wells. Can you see a thing when it's written plain on the face of the facts, or do you want me to draw you a picture of it?"

"Let it go," said Hughes.

The people of the Lazy M slept in shifts that night. At all times one or another of the cowboys was on watch from a roof, waiting for headlights to show on the Adobe Wells road. If one thing was certain to the people of the Lazy M, it was that Alex Shaw, who had come and gone that day, would come again; this time very strong. And if Alex Shaw went back empty handed when next he came, it would be because he was sent back, and behind him there would be gun smoke mingled with the dust.

It was an hour after daylight, however, when a general alarm brought the Lazy M people once more into the space in front of the house to watch a lone car wheeling slowly up the road from Adobe Wells. This time there were rifles in the hands of some of the cowboys, in addition to the guns that swung at every thigh.

As the car drew near, however, they saw that it was

of a type unfamiliar to the Buckhorn; and the man who drove it was alone. When at last the big roadster wheeled to a stop in front of the ranch house, it was a ruddy faced old man with hair as white as his immaculate shirt and collar who got stiffly down from the wheel.

It seemed to them a long time that they had awaited the half known quantity called Stephen Sessions. So long had seemed those few days that the man had become almost a myth, a legend. After it had become uncertain whether or not he was coming at all, the Lazy M people had come to feel that only his presence would be needed to turn disadvantage to advantage, and make one roaring sweep of victory out of an otherwise hopeless contest with irresistible forces. It is only the footloose and irresponsible criminal who can slip the grip of the law for long. They were learning that the same law which finds itself puzzled and ineffectual before gangster and racketeer can close with a remorseless grip upon well-rooted and responsible men.

And the roots of Oliver Major's very life were deep in the Buckhorn water. He could no more take to flight than he could surrender; and it seemed that his enemy was able to bring all the power of the commonwealth against him in open battle. In this situation only Stephen Sessions offered hope of intervention in the high political circles which had, by a single quick stroke, given the law into the hands of Earl Shaw.

And now, the long delayed Sessions was here at last!

Hughes, watching Stephen Sessions shake hands with Major, wondered if after all they had placed their hope in the right place. Certainly Stephen Sessions looked as if he could intercede successfully if he wished. There were already two men in the Buckhorn—Oliver Major and Earl Shaw—who had the unshakable look of granite. To these Stephen Sessions now added a third. The solid hulking weight of his slightly bent shoulders, the square solidity of his face, and above all, the complete unconscious assurance of the man, visible in his every move, gave him a look of great static power. Yet, there was a blandness in the heavy ruddy face, which, no less than the half-humorous shrewdness in the old blue eyes, suggested that this was a man who made his own decisions; and having made them, was persuaded by none.

"I laid overnight in Adobe Wells," Sessions was saying to Oliver Major. "What's got into this valley of yours, Oliver? You people trying to get back to the old days?"

"I only wish we could, Steve!" said Major.

"It's time I got here," said Sessions, half jocularly. "From what I hear, things are sure shaping up into one sweet mess. Was that one of your men who was killed in Adobe Wells last night?"

"A man killed, Steve?" said old Major slowly.

"Didn't you hear? Don't you folks even keep a telephone any more?"

"The telephone's been out of whack for four days," Major told him. "Do you remember the name of the man that was killed?"

"I've never forgotten a name yet," said Sessions. "It was a man being held as an essential witness, and he was killed making a jail break. His name was Grasshopper Tanner."

"*Grasshopper Tanner,*" Major repeated: He swung upon Hughes. "Do you doubt now what would have happened to you, if you'd gone with Alex Shaw?"

"No," said Hughes.

For the first time he saw the incredible assumptions of Oliver Major as parts of a grim prophesy already coming true.

"He wants you next," said Macumber. "You can go in there now."

For three hours Stephen Sessions had been closeted in the old man's office with the boss of the Lazy M. From within the office came a steady growl of conversation; sometimes old Major's voice seemed to rise in harsh emphasis; but what all the parley was about, nobody exactly knew. They had become accustomed to thinking of Sessions as the man who was going to intercede in their behalf with the governor; the man who was going to make the wires hum, revert the advantage that the Bar S had been given, and put the law once more in the hands of Jim Crawford and the Lazy M. It was beginning to look as if there was a hitch some place in this program. Knowing little, they worried. The word of Tanner's death, with its impact of harsh, immediate certainty, had set them on edge.

"Does it look as bad to you as it did to Tom?" Hughes asked Macumber.

Bob Macumber's face was both dazed and puzzled. "I don't know what to make of it, Clay. This here Sessions just sits there with his big square pan hung out in front of him, without any expression on it. I can't make head or tail of him. But the old man's looking mighty black. Clay, it looks to me like something's gone haywire."

Sometimes during those three hours since the arrival of Sessions some of the Lazy M men had been called in to answer certain questions before Stephen Sessions. Bart Holt had given, for Sessions' benefit, his version of the appearances at Crazy Mule canyon. Harry Canfield had been asked some questions about the shot that had been fired at Hughes. Jim Crawford had been on the carpet for almost the whole of a bad half hour, and had come out angry and puzzled; refusing to discuss what had evidently been an ordeal. Tom Ireland had been called in and asked some puzzling and apparently irrelevant questions about the character of Grasshopper Tanner; and Art French, and Bob Macumber had each had their say as to obscure points of recent happenings.

"He asked me quite a few questions about you, Clay," said Bob Macumber. "Well, I gave you a clean bill of health. You better be getting on in there, boy."

What struck Hughes as he entered old Major's office was the change that had come over the old boss of the Buckhorn water himself. He saw instantly what those others who had been questioned here must also have seen, but had been reluctant to say. The old man's face had been grim before; it was now grey and haggard, and so bitter hard that he looked more than ever like a cross between a range wolf and a hunk of granite from the rim. A lank lock of grey hair dangled before his eyes, and through it he stared redly, unaware that it was there.

"This is Hughes," Major growled shortly.

"You were the only man in Crazy Mule canyon the night Donnan died," said Stephen Sessions. "Is that right?"

"I was the only one with him when he died," said Hughes. "But I allow there were others in the Crazy Mule that night—or Donnan would never have come by his finish."

"I understand you left this forty-five caliber shell in the ashes of your fire," said Sessions. The old politician's voice was quiet; he was watching Hughes gravely, just as he must have watched many a man from the bench in the days before he had retired from public office forever. He sat leaning forward, with his shoulders hunched up by the arms of his chair, so that his unweathered face was thrust out before him, a suave mask.

"You understand wrongly, then," said Hughes. "I left no shell."

"How do you explain the presence of the shell that Bart Holt found?" Sessions asked.

"Grasshopper Tanner's explanation sounds as reasonable to me as any," said Hughes.

"Tanner is dead," Sessions reminded him, "and can give no explanation."

"I have no doubt," said Hughes, "that you know what he thought about it, just the same."

"And what," said Sessions, "did you say Donnan told you before he died?"

"I didn't say."

"Clay," said old man Major, "if there's ever going to be a time to speak out, that time has come now."

Yes, surely, thought Hughes, old Major had come very close to the end of his string. A litter of paper on the desk beside Major, and overflowing onto the floor at his feet, made the room look disheveled. Hughes saw now that those big curling papers were surveys and geologic charts. They had been arguing, then, about the Buckhorn water.

"Are you going to answer my question?" Sessions said dryly.

"I did answer it," said Hughes.

"You are evading me," said Sessions. "I put it to you: Donnan said something to you in Crazy Mule Canyon."

"Well?"

"Are you ready to state what that was?"

Hughes shook his head slowly, his eyes steady on those of Stephen Sessions. "Not yet," he said at last.

An unexpected smile jerked the corners of Sessions' mouth as Hughes and Sessions stared at each other; and Hughes saw that Sessions disbelieved. And he

205

realized now that he never in his life had been before a man so difficult to bluff, so nearly impossible to deceive.

Once more—and he was fervently hoping that it was for the last time—he brought that faint ironic smile to the surface, this time a smile of the eyes alone. With it he had bluffed Earl Shaw so that Shaw had surrendered himself into the hands of the man he hated; with it, God forgive him, he had brought Sally's accurate guessing to nothing. Even old Oliver Major was in doubt, to this very moment, as to whether Hughes withheld something he knew, or had nothing to withhold. But now, for a moment, it seemed to Hughes that the world-weary blue eyes of the old man could look through that bluff as if it were glass, and see the emptiness beyond. Yet Hughes stood silent, playing out his bluff to the very end; and as Sessions' smile slowly faded, he hardly knew whether to think that he had won, or lost.

"If you know something," said Sessions, "what do you expect to gain by holding it back?"

"There's one link still missing," Hughes heard himself say. "I'm thinking now that it won't be missing very long."

He thought he had never heard such blatant nonsense as his own words then. In spite of the slow assurance of his voice, it seemed to him that the utter lack of meaning in his words must be impossible to conceal.

Yet, when Stephen Sessions spoke, Hughes recognized that a note of uncertainty came into his voice. "I'll admit that I don't understand this boy, Oliver. Personally, I doubt that he knows anything at all."

"Maybe he doesn't," said Major stubbornly. "But it's pretty plain that Earl Shaw thinks he does!"

Sessions slapped the arm of his chair impatiently. "Oliver, I tell you, you don't know that."

"He was fired on, wasn't he? As he stood in this very house?"

"But you don't know by whom," said Sessions, flourishing an eloquently judicial finger. "It's time a little cool reason came in here, Oliver. To begin with, you don't know this boy. Except for the word of Bob Macumber, who hasn't seen him for years, you don't know a thing about him—where he's from, or what's his record, or who are his enemies. For all you know, there may be fifty men in the southwest who are anxious to even up old scores against him that you know nothing about."

"But I know the rest of my boys here," said Major, "and I tell you there isn't a one of them that—"

"And do you know that? You don't even know your own men, Oliver. You thought you knew Walk Ross; he's worked for you four years, yet you yourself are willing to have me believe that he's carried some wild yarn to Adobe Wells, and got Grasshopper Tanner killed thereby! Maybe you don't know this—but personally I never forget a name—there was a Walker Ross in a bad shooting scrape up in Idaho about five years ago."

"Yes, I knew that," grunted Major.

"And who is this Art French? Do you know? Maybe you'd like me to dredge down in my memory and bring up a fact or two about this man who calls himself Art French. Just as I never forget a name, neither do I ever forget a face, Oliver. I can call half the people in the southwest by name, history, and reputation; and when it comes to Art French—"

"That isn't the point," said Major. The old man seemed badgered, beset. He could wrest a fortune out of the stubborn hills, and throughout his life he had worked his will with a vast valley; but when it came to demonstrating something that seemed to him obvious, he found himself at a loss. "The past or future of Walk Ross is not the question in hand." His fist drummed the desk top, heavy and slow. "I offer you Grasshopper Tanner. He's a sample of what happens to Shaw's enemies—when they put themselves into the hands of the law officers Replogle has foisted on us! I let Tanner go because I hoped Earl Shaw didn't know Grasshopper had discovered anything. The minute word got to Adobe Wells—evidently by Walk Ross—that Grasshopper Tanner was a dangerous man to the killers of Hugo Donnan, that was the end of Grasshopper Tanner! It'll be the same story over again if they take Hughes. It'd be the same story again if they took Dick—but, by God, they'll never do that while I live."

"Grasshopper Tanner was killed trying to make a jail break," droned Sessions wearily.

"If he made a break at all—which I doubt—it was because it was the only hope left to him. Grasshopper gave himself up to Alex Shaw of his own free will."

"Yes, yes," said Stephen Sessions. "We've been good friends for a long time, Oliver; and I certainly hope nothing is going to come up to spoil that now. God knows, Oliver, I'm only too willing to do all I can to—"

"There's only one thing in the world that's reasonable to do," said Oliver Major. "Theron Replogle has rammed into this business and put the sheriff's office in the hands of Alex Shaw. Now Theron Replogle has got to yank Alex Shaw out again; as matters stand, he looks like the only one who can. Otherwise, I tell you, there's going to be the damnedest scrap in the Buckhorn that the southwest has seen in many a long year!"

"Of course," said Stephen Sessions, with only the faintest trace of unctuousness, "I don't decide these things, Oliver. I am here as an observer for the governor, as I told you before. All I can do, at best,—"

"The whole state knows that you are the man closest to Governor Replogle. I'll say more. There's a good many of us has a pretty plain idee, Steve, that Theron Replogle is only a dummy—with you and a couple of others working the strings!"

"Now, now," said Sessions, "that isn't the sort of impression we want to create at all!"

"I expect not," said Major dryly.

"I ask you to look at what you're asking me to do,

Oliver," said Sessions. "By the way, do we need this man any more?"

"Yes," said Major unexpectedly. "I want him to hear this."

Sessions shrugged. "Let me speak plainly for a couple of minutes. In the first place we have the murder of Sheriff Donnan. By the greatest misfortune it appears that Donnan has previously been threatened by your son." He raised a hand quickly. "Of course, we know he didn't do it, but there is the situation. The first deputy under Donnan happened to be a man very much under your influence, Oliver; you certainly won't deny that. Under your influence, acting-sheriff Crawford stepped forth and imprisoned, absolutely without evidence, one of the most influential citizens in this part of the state, together with several of his employees. Naturally, a sharp protest arises, literally forcing Governor Replogle to replace acting-sheriff Crawford with somebody better prepared to act impartially."

"Impartially!" exploded old Major.

"I realize, of course, it doesn't seem exactly impartial to you," Sessions conceded. "But certainly Alex Shaw has acted entirely within the limits of his duty. What has he done? He has attempted to gather together for questioning the persons nearest the case: that is, Tanner, the old tracker; Hughes, the last man to see Donnan alive; and, of course, though we are sorry for it, your son, who in his own interests, certainly should wish to have his name cleared as promptly as possible by due process of investigation. A very reasonable procedure, certainly. Yet, see what you now ask me to do! I am to persuade Replogle immediately to remove Alex Shaw from office—on no charge at all, unless it is that a man unfortunately lost his life while attempting to break jail."

Oliver Major opened his mouth, but shut it again, and turned away his face, as if sickened. *"Dear God, Steve!"*

"I was glad to come down here when you wired me," Sessions went on; "though, coincidentally, as I have said, I am also acting as an observer—an impartial one, I hope—on behalf of the governor. It's nothing new to you, of course, when I say that the Buckhorn has always been an uncertain element in the state. The peculiar position of the water—"

"The only thing peculiar about the water," said Major, "is that Shaw has forever wanted to get it for his own!"

"That's naturally your view of it, Oliver. I must say that I think your stand against the Silverado project is not wholly tenable. The laws of conservation naturally provide that wherever water is running to waste, that surplus which is lost may be diverted to other points were it can be put to use; and as for the Silverado—"

"Steve," Major began. "Steve—" One hand reached uncertainly for a map, but dropped again, relaxed and futile, in his lap. There was a silence in the room while Major stared at the strewn litter of the maps. He looked weary and very old—an old wolf still, but infinitely beset.

Yet, Hughes could see the visions that were in the old man's mind. All his life he had worked to build up the capital that was to bring the Buckhorn water to fruition. He knew where his dams should stand, and where his reservoirs should spread their sheets of stored water. In his dreams he had looked forever forward to the day when the Buckhorn should come into full flower, supporting not an outfit, but a people. And that development was to be a sound development, steady and sure. Never was there to be the rush and clutch of the land sharks, nor scores of little homesteads springing up in the light of false hopes and misworded claims—each presently to leave a skeleton shanty and a broken windmill to commemorate the heartbreak of a poverty stricken family, and the wastage of a dirt farmer's toil. But how could Major hope to convey to that suave, many-argumented man the visions he was seeing behind those maps—old Oliver Major, who all his life had expressed himself only through the actualities under his hands?

"Oliver," said Stephen Sessions, "I'm sorry to say this, but it seems to me that there's only one way for you to handle this thing. Stop bucking the regularly constituted legal authorities. If you can't cooperate with the due processes of the law, at least submit to the law's reasonable demands. Once you've made your mind up to that, no problem exists, whatsoever. I realize you can never reconcile yourself to the Silverado project, but you are entirely wrong in confusing it with the case in hand. The case in hand is the simple murder of a sheriff by parties unknown, and everyone associated with the unfortunate occurrence must naturally expect to assist the investigation. Of course, it comes hard to you to—"

On and on droned the smooth, plausible voice from the square implacable face. Almost, listening to that voice, a man could believe that there existed no problem at all, and no trouble at all, and that all men must do in order to have all things come smooth and clear, with justice to all, was to walk in peaceful ways.

Then, as Stephen Sessions paused, and the silence again returned for a moment to that room, there came across the sun-drenched heat the mournful keening of Grasshopper Tanner's dogs.

Major smashed a fist upon the desk, and his voice came in a rising thunder. "Steve, I tell you, as God is my judge—"

A quick rap on the door interrupted him, and without waiting for summons, Bob Macumber thrust into the room. "Mr. Major, there's a car coming up the Adobe Wells road like all hell was on its tail!"

"Just one car?"

"That's all we can see yet."

"The boys know?"

"They're ready, Mr. Major!"

Major came to his feet and strode toward the door.

"For heaven's sake, Oliver," Stephen Sessions began, "be careful what you—"

Major whirled on him savagely. "Shut up!" he snarled, his voice vicious with angry contempt. He went lurching toward the front of the house like a man saddle drunk from too long a season in the leather.

CHAPTER FIFTEEN

Once more the people of the Lazy M waited silently before the sprawling adobe, as the approaching car, careening crazily, tore up great geysers of dust from the Adobe Wells road. There was a stir among the cowboys as it was seen that the car was again that of Alex Shaw.

As it wheeled into the space before the house, however, they saw that the driver, who was also the sole occupant, was not Alex Shaw. The man who eased stiffly and unsteadily to the ground was Walk Ross.

There was a moment's silence while Walk Ross faced those many pairs of watching eyes. Then Tom Ireland raised his voice in a sort of a smothered bellow, and thrust himself hulking forward. "You got guts to come back here!" he roared.

The face of Walk Ross was bloodless, and he seemed dazed. "I got guts to—what?" he said vaguely.

Tom Ireland roared, "This is the coyote that crossed up Grasshopper Tanner! I—"

He stopped abruptly as they saw the legs of Walk Ross slowly buckle under him, so that he sank to his knees, and then to all fours.

"Get back, Tom!" Oliver Major ordered.

Walk Ross was already getting up under his own power as Clay Hughes and Oliver Major reached him. "You hurt, Walk?

"Ain't anything that amounts to hell," Walk Ross mumbled apologetically. "It's just a little nick, but I guess it got to bleeding some, as I come over the bumps."

"Here," ordered Oliver Major, "help me get him in the house."

"Listen," said Walk Ross. "Listen: you only got a few hours! They've got together a posse of anyway forty men—most likely it'll be fifty before night. Their aim is to swarm down on us the first thing tomorrow. They got men enough to clean us out quicker than a whistle, if we don't get set to stand 'em off! Somebody gimme drink of water. Ain't you got any water?"

Everybody trailed after them as they helped Walk Ross into a room and propped him on a bed. Sally Major brought water and rolls of gauze, and Oliver Major himself set about rebandaging the man's wounds. Walk Ross had been but lightly hit. A grazing bullet had struck a furrow across the inside of his upper left arm, disabling it for the time; and though he had improvised bandages, the loss of blood had weakened him tremendously. Hughes saw that Walk's haggard weariness had brought a human quality, which he had not observed before into the man's sharp, hawk-nosed face; and though the eyes were still as curiously light as bits of shell, the odd, expressionless quality, as

215

of a noncommittal lynx, was no longer evident.

"Earl Shaw himself is coming with the posse," Walk told them. "Of course, Alex Shaw stands as sheriff, but Dutch Pete will be the leader of the main mob, and Smoky Walters and Frank Muldoon are the real gun throwers, that we have to look out for every minute. God knows what we're coming to here. It seems like—"

"How come you to go to Adobe Wells, Walk?" Major asked.

"We never should have let Tanner go to Adobe Wells. We should have held him here if we had to hog-tie him," Ross answered. "Letting Tanner go with Alex Shaw was just the same as if we'd shot Grasshopper where he stood. I—"

"How'd you get hit?"

"I had two brushes with 'em," said Ross. "Once last night when Tanner was killed, and once today when I swiped this car and broke clear. It was last night that they clipped me, though. Oh, lord, if I only could have winged one of 'em if only just to mark him! . . . You people never understood Grasshopper Tanner. He was hard-mouthed and crotchety, mostly because he was old. But I've worked with him, and ridden with him over in the Mogollon, and I tell you I know him, and a better man never stood up. I couldn't stand by and not do nothing when I knew what was ahead of him. I went to Adobe Wells to do anything I could if I was needed. I don't know how some of you fellers are going to explain it to yourselves that you wasn't with me. God knows, hard-mouthed as he was, Tanner never went back on a man in his life."

"Yes, sure; but what happened?"

"It was after dark when I got to Adobe Wells. I parked the flivver back of the town corral, and I walked through the town with my hat pulled down, and I come to the jail. I managed to get around to the side to talk to Tanner through the window a little bit. The old fool didn't see what he was up against, even then. I told him I'd come to crack him out of there, and he cussed me like always he did, and told me it wouldn't do. Then Dutch Pete come ramming around the corner of the jail, and I had to duck out.

"I went and bought me a couple of drinks, and I was recognized; but I knew what was ahead all the time, and I didn't care. In about an hour I went back. You know that little mud shack they use for a jail. Well, when I got back it was empty. I called out Grasshopper's name at them two little windows that opens into the two cells. But there wasn't even any deputies there, and Tanner was gone.

"There wasn't any moon but the stars was clear; and off in the dark, maybe a hundred yards away, I thought I seen somebody move. You know where that gully strikes along there, right back of the town, and there's a rift of brush? It was over there. What I seen could have been a horse or a cow, but something told me it wasn't that. I begun moving toward the place where I thought I seen something, quiet as I could. I got about half way to the place when I heard

Tanner's voice, from up ahead.

"Poor old Grasshopper—maybe I shouldn't tell it on him—but there at the end the poor old feller whimpered like a—like a cat. He hollers out 'I don't know anything, I don't know anything,' and then he's stopped off as if somebody slapped a hand over his mouth. And then somebody says 'No powder burns now' and—Wham—one shot, and two more.

"I comes up with my gun and lets go pretty near blind, and lets 'em have three blasts. I seen two fellers run, and they blazed away at me as I come running forward, and one of 'em give me this clip. I found Grasshopper Tanner. They'd finished him, all right.

"I high-tailed it out of there and tied up my arm, and laid low. Pretty soon when I went back to the flivver there was fellers sitting on it, and I guess there's fellers sitting on it yet. It wasn't until just now that I finally made a break of it, and swiped this car as it stood with the engine running in front of the store, and come on. They peppered the old bus plenty as I went, and there was a couple of cars following me almost all the way to Twelve Mile Corral. But the old baby stepped out pretty, all right. They never was close after the first few miles."

"Who was it done in Tanner, Ross? Did you get a look at 'em? Could you make a guess who they was?"

"I'm afraid I couldn't say for sure, Mr. Major."

"Can't you make a guess at all?"

"Mr. Major, I'm afraid I can't even do that. You people got any more water here?"

Major drew a deep breath. He squared his shoulders with an effort as he turned to the others. "Get out of here, and quit using up the air," he ordered. "The poor feller's all in. Bart, you stay with him, so if he thinks of anything else, or wants anything."

He led the way himself as they all trooped out. Sally Major was weeping silently. Hughes heard her murmur, "That poor old man, that poor old man . . ." Outside the door, in the cool of the hall, Major stood waiting, wiping his hands; and presently when everyone but Stephen Sessions and Clay Hughes were gone, he spoke again, his voice harsh and low.

"There you have it," he told Sessions. "There you have the story, plain and square in front of your eyes! Now you know what would have happened to Hughes here, yesterday, if I'd left him go. And you know what would have happened to Dick, and will yet, if ever he gets into Earl Shaw's hands!"

Stephen Sessions shook his head slowly, and that weary, infinitely exasperating smile of his crossed his face. "You're illogical, Oliver. An hour ago you were asking me to think that Walk Ross was the one who influenced Earl Shaw to get rid of Tanner. Now Ross comes back with a different story, and you want me to believe that! Why, Oliver, that man would be discredited as a witness in any court in the world. An hour ago you had it that Grasshopper Tanner didn't have a friend, and Ross was his worst enemy. Now you want me to believe that Ross held Tanner so dearly that he risked his life in order to—to do what? To defend

Tanner from unidentified enemies in Adobe Wells. If you'll just stand off and look at that proposition, Oliver, you'll have to agree with me that—"

"What can I say to you," said Major with repressed savagery, "if you can't look at a man and tell when he's telling the truth? Why do you suppose Walk came back here if he isn't on the level?"

Sessions shrugged. "We don't even know why he went to Adobe Wells in the first place. If you're going to try to hang weight on the wild stories of every shifty, gun-throwing cowboy in the southwest, you're going to lose yourself entirely. I suppose he came back here because he was run out of Adobe Wells—for gun throwing of some kind. Speaking of questions, you haven't explained yet how the idea was conveyed from here to Earl Shaw that Grasshopper Tanner knew anything to begin with."

"There's that missing Mexican cook," Major offered.

"You think Shaw is fool enough to take the story of some irresponsible mess shack hand? Oliver, you've believed exactly what you want to believe for so long that you expect everybody else to do the same. You didn't even bother to ask Walk Ross what he thought about that side of it."

"We'll ask him now," said Major. He thrust his way back into the room in which Walk Ross had been put. "Walk," he asked the wounded man, "did you talk to anybody in Adobe Wells about Grasshopper Tanner?"

"Mr. Major, I didn't talk to anybody about anything."

"Then what is your theory about how word got to the Shaw outfit that Tanner had found out something—maybe could name the killer of Hugo Donnan?"

"Mr. Major, that's the question I been asking myself. "Walk, are you dead positive you didn't let drop anything?"

"Dead certain! I didn't speak a soul."

"All right, Walk, that's all I wanted to know."

"You see?" said Sessions.

"I suppose," said Major slowly, "that you think his story about the posse coming out here is pipe smoke too."

"No; I'm afraid that part of it has the look of truth. What would you expect, Oliver? You've refused to cooperate with Alex Shaw in his position as sheriff. You've held back from him by force—or what amounts to it—the very men he has to question in running down the Donnan case. Ask yourself what would become of the law in this state if that sort of thing was tolerated. Alex Shaw hasn't any choice. He has to come here and get his men if it takes twenty men to do it, or fifty. You ought to be able to see that."

"He isn't going to get 'em, Steve!"

"The trouble with you," said Sessions, "is that you're living in the past. This is the day of law and order. The old shoot-out days are gone."

Oliver Major stared at him for a long time. Sessions had as good as admitted that, as an observer for the governor, he was in a position to advise Governor

Replogle what to do; and his effort to suggest that his advice would not be acted upon was feeble at best. Yet, his monstrous incredulity, his supremely placid assurance that only he saw to the bottom of all things, composed an impenetrable shell, apparently more invincible than a wall of stone or a cordon of guns.

Here, within this man, lay the influence which alone could extricate the Lazy M from the ruination of open battle against the travestied authority of the law. Yet Sessions remained blind, either unable to comprehend or unwilling to acknowledge the danger which overhung them. His suave plausibilities turned aside every argument converting the obvious and inescapable to paltry imaginings with a word.

The tantalizing nearness of the unattainable must have been unbearable to Oliver Major; yet his voice was quiet as he spoke again. "Steve, look back," he urged. "Look back to when you and me and the rest opened this country up." He was trying to bridge the years, carrying their relationship back to the days when Sessions and Major had looked alike and thought alike, cattlemen in a raw cattle country. "I'm not asking you if there were ever notches on your own gun, Steve. I'm only saying those were hard days, those old days behind."

"Thank God they're behind," said Sessions.

"Are you sure they're behind? Can they ever be behind, while the men that made them are still alive? How many men do you think are down underneath the bunch grass, because Earl Shaw could never give up

222

the idee of jumping my range? Two? Five? Steve, many more than that. Do you think Earl Shaw's the man to flinch at downing one or two men more? There was Tanner last night; you can try to tell yourself different all you want, but you know now exactly how he died, and you know why. You know that if we give in now the same thing will happen to Hughes; and to my son! You'll learn some day why Shaw *wouldn't dare anything else!*"

Stephen Sessions made a vague, uncomfortable gesture. Then suddenly he turned to grip Major's shoulders with his big pale hands. "Drop it, Oliver!" he urged. "Forget this damn fool fight. In heaven's name, if you can't bring yourself to cooperate with the law, take Dick and hide out until this thing blows over! Man, man—with the whole commonwealth against you, don't you know when you're licked? Pull out and go over the line, and I'll—"

"There's no hope in that," said Major in a dead voice. "We got to stand and fight it here. Do you think I've put my life into the Buckhorn, just to turn tail now? What's left? A riding job, some place, under a different name? I'm too old for that, Steve."

"Then for lord's sake let Shaw take and question Dick and Hughes. If your son comes to trial, I'll defend him myself, and clear him, too! But for the time being, you've got to hand him over."

There was an unsteadiness in old Major's voice as he answered, "I'd as leave kill him with my own gun."

"But you damned old fool," cried Sessions, his

voice rising nervously for the first time, "what can you gain?"

"Listen," Major commanded. "Theron Replogle is a crook, and he's got rich off the state—but he's not equal to murder for common profit, and that's what this is. Theron Replogle is blind to what's happening here—he must be blind. I'll stand and fight until he opens his eyes! And when he does, by God, you'll see me sweep the Buckhorn, as I cleared it twice before!"

Stephen Sessions threw up his hands. "I've done all I can," he said shortly. "What happens is on your own head now."

"What are you going to report to Governor Replogle?"

"The only thing I can report: that the law here is functioning in a regular and legal way—and that an old fool who's trying to live in the past will probably have to have the obstinacy knocked out of him."

"For God's sake, Steve," cried Oliver Major, *"can't you see what you're doing?"*

"There's no earthly use arguing with you," Sessions turned away. "I may just as well be starting back."

Major's voice was low again, but very bitter. "You guess you'll leave, do you? You guess you'll leave! For my part, I guess you won't do anything of the kind. Not yet, you won't!"

"What do you mean?"

"You're staying here, Sessions."

"Why, you can't hold me here!"

"I can't? I'm doing it though! Governor's observer,

is it? By God, I'll give you your belly full of observing. Hughes! See that this man doesn't leave the house!"

"Right," said Hughes.

CHAPTER SIXTEEN

If Stephen Sessions was to remain at the Lazy M, there were others for whom Oliver Major had other plans. They had supposed that he would confront Alex Shaw's posse with the entire personnel of the Lazy M; but it appeared now that this was not to be the case. José and the three or four other Mexicans were first to go, fired outright with a paternal warning to get out of the troubled range while the getting was good. They trailed off into the heat waves of the afternoon without complaint, the scanty belongings of each behind his saddle. This proved to be only the beginning, however.

Major called his hands about him. "Maybe some of you boys aren't going to like this," he drawled. "Maybe some of you aren't going to like it at all. No cowboy ever yet knew what was good for him, I suppose. You all heard the word that Walk Ross brought. Some time between now and tomorrow noon hell is going to bust wide open, right here where we stand. Naturally, I don't want Sally and Mona on hand for that. I'm going to send them across the Gunsight, then westwards and up-country across the state line. There's a brand over there called the Pot Hook just a little broke-down, two-man spread, but they'll be with friends. Now, for all I know, the Shaw men have closed the Gunsight by now."

He hesitated. Hughes wondered if he was going to say what must be in his mind—that Mona, whose affair with Hugo Donnan had led Dick to threaten Donnan's life, could certainly be made into a powerful witness against her brother, if ever her testimony could be drawn from her; and that the Bar S might be eager to hold her as such. Major made no mention of this, however, as he proceeded, talking slowly.

"I'm sending enough of you boys with Sally and Mona to force that Pass, even if it's closed. But when that's done, I don't want to see any of you come trailing back. You're to go on with the girls to the state line. It's a four day pack, more like five, but you have to go with them all the way."

There was a silence. "Who's going?" Canfield asked at last.

"I'm sending five men. Some of you I'm sending because they're the best I have. I'm sending Bob Macumber; and you, Tom; and Harry Canfield and Jim Crawford; and while I'm at it, I'm sending Rowdy Lee." The men whose names had been called off looked stunned, as if they could not believe that they had been read out of the fight they had waited for so long.

"Why, Mr. Major—" said Tom Ireland at last, "Why, Mr. Major—it'll be eight to ten days before we're back!"

"And what if it is?"

"Why, the fight will be all over, settled and done, before ever we make it to the state line!"

"I know," said Major. "It's the harder job, Tom, in a way. But it's got to be done. . . ."

The five men who were to escort Mona and Sally over the Gunsight went about the assemblage of their packs and horses slowly, behaving more like doomed men than men reprieved. But if Major had met reluctance on the part of the men, he met open rebellion when it came to Sally Major. Mona, who continued to walk through the world as if she were no longer a part of it, assented listlessly; but Sally Major exploded in her father's hands, flatly refusing to go.

"It isn't right, it isn't fair," she declared. "I belong here as much as anybody else does, and a whole lot more than some! I won't go—you can't make me go! How do I know that I'll see you or Dick, or anybody else here, again?"

"Sally, you're going just the same." In the end not even her tears moved the old range wolf's decision a hair's breadth. "If you won't go willingly, you'll go tied on your horse. Child, I'm asking you not to force me to that."

Thus, when shortly after dusk the trailing pack train pulled out of the Lazy M corral, Sally mounted with the rest. At the last moment Clay Hughes went forward to the stirrup of her pony. "Set easy," he said, taking one of her hands from where they lay folded lifelessly upon the horn; "and I'll be seeing you."

For a long moment she looked downward at him through the dusk. The nigh stirrup leather creaked as she swayed toward him, as if even yet she would swing down and refuse to go out with the pack train. But in the end she only gave his hand a quick pressure and turned away her face.

Oliver Major, motionless as a gaunt, tall post, stood a long time watching the last slow dust of the plodding pack train, listening to the yip of Rowdy Lee as he rounded a pack horse that was trying to turn back. Far off in the dusk Clay Hughes saw Tom Ireland, trailing behind the others, turn his horse broadside, and sit looking back at the Lazy M for a space of long minutes. Hughes could not make out Ireland's face; but he would not have been surprised to know that the man wept. To those cowboys the Buckhorn was their country, their range. It was a hard thing to drive them from it in the very hour in which they were most needed for its defense.

Oliver Major snapped into motion again. "We'll get fixed to hold the pump house," he told the others. "We can't hold the main house against a swarm like the Shaws will bring. They'd cut off our water, first thing. Gustafson, get back on top of the house and watch the road. Keep your ears open! The rest of us will move bed rolls, rations, and all the arms on the place to the pump house."

"How much grub you want?" Dick Major asked.

"Not much. A few days. This game is going to turn one way or the other very soon. We'll hold three—no, four ponies inside the pump house."

"There's seven of us here," Dick pointed out. "We'll have room for a full string by putting the stock in the lean-to."

"The lean-to has got to be tore down; it won't keep no bullets out, and it's only in the way. We'll pick up extra ponies easy enough, if we make a play. Put four good quiet cut horses in the pump house, and turn out all the rest of the stock. . . . Who's staying with Walk Ross?"

"Dusty Rivers."

"Go tell him to put out the lights in that window. A man could put a rifle shot in there from pretty near a quarter mile."

They went about their work almost silently, dividing their tasks tacitly with the accord of self-sufficient men who are used to working together. The building that was now the pump house was very old, the oldest at the Lazy M. It had been Oliver Major's own house when the Lazy M was new. Besides the shackling lean-to it had but two rooms, the larger of which was now occupied by the gasoline pump that lifted the Buckhorn water in dry season. In spite of its age, that first little house was very rugged and strong. Its three-foot walls of adobe had been washed over with cement in its later years, and thus protected the adobe stood against the weather like rock.

The great mass of junk that had been stored in this building was now made to melt away, giving place to arms and supplies. The dozen gasoline drums that were kept here were rolled far off, lest a ricocheting bullet create hazard of fire and explosion. The lean-to was reduced to debris, which was in turn removed. It was a work of hours, but when it was done the adobe was a stubborn blockhouse, well fitted to stand off a prolonged attack.

As they moved through the big ranch house, gathering up by lantern light the last stray odds and ends of arms, it seemed to Hughes that he had never seen any habitation become so swiftly desolate and forsaken. The lanterns cast the shadows of the long-legged, slow-striding cowboys as monstrous, swaying shapes that seemed to lurch through cloisters long abandoned. The click of their high heels upon the tiles induced mournful echoes that Hughes had never noticed there before; and there was upon the whole place an odd brittle silence, so that men spoke with unconsciously lowered voices.

Hughes wondered if Oliver Major, as he had added section after section to this commodious house that was to last through the years, had ever imagined that he would be driven to abandon it as he neared the end of his long trail, and return to that first little two-room adobe which he had set up beside the Buckhorn water first of all. It occurred to him that perhaps Oliver Major was going to end his Buckhorn career in the very spot where he had begun it—within the walls of the little adobe shanty which he and his brother had built so long ago, putting into it the labors of their own hands.

"They're liable to fire this house, Oliver," said Bart Holt.

It was very hard to imagine that by tomorrow night the place might be a smoke-blackened ruin. The suggestion made the enormity of their predicament suddenly harsh and real, though at the same time the harder to believe. This house, more than. any tangible thing, represented the comprehensive dream of Oliver Major, built slowly and soundly through the years.

Oliver Major's voice was so hard and unsentimental as he answered that they did not notice several moments had elapsed before his reply. "Let 'em. The house will grow up again because there's water under it. Nothing but the water counts. . . . This valley should have kept its old Indian name."

"What was that?"

"Washog Kickaninny Two Whoop," said Holt. "Or something like that."

"Huh?"

"It means 'The Valley of No-Peace.'"

Dick Major went into Sally's room and brought out his sister's own gun, a light thirty-thirty rifle, beautifully made. And now Hughes suddenly realized why the place had relapsed into such empty desolation. Those leather-faced men of the saddle with whom he walked—a hundred of them could tramp about upon the ringing tiles and the place would still harbor a sense of utter loneliness, a dismal void. The heart and the meaning had gone out of the Lazy M with Sally Major. Here were the halls through which she had walked so often with her quick, vitally energetic stride; here was the bench where she had sat and listened to the banjo thrum; under these cottonwoods she had stood with the night breath of the desert stirring the faintly gleaming mist of her hair about her throat.

If she returned, this house would come alive again, filled with a merry hope of the future, though the walls themselves were debris. If she did not come back, the place would be empty and lonely forever, and the Buckhorn water itself would have no meaning at all.

It was drawing on toward morning by the time their work seemed finished at last. Oliver Major turned to Clay Hughes. "From now on I'll keep my eye on Sessions," he said. "You don't need to worry about him no more. You go and get Walk Ross moved. He ought to be feeling all right by now."

Bart Holt and Dusty Rivers were in the room where Walk Ross was lying. An argument that was going on there checked as Clay Hughes pushed in, but picked up again.

"Walk," Bart Holt was insisting, "you re absolutely the only man from here that's been to Adobe Wells since Tanner spilled his story. You must have dropped some word. It's up to you to figure out who you dropped it to."

"I never so much as—" began Walk Ross. His voice was very dry and thin.

"I tell you you must have," declared Bart Holt. The room was very dark. Hughes could hardly make out

the figures of Holt and Dusty Rivers, and the dim outline of the man on the bed.

Dusty, at the foot of the bed, stirred restlessly. "Oh,
leave him alone, Bart," he said wearily.

"The old man wants you to move to the pump house
now," Hughes told them. "You need a hand, Walk?"

The figure on the bed raised itself slowly, and for a
moment sat head in hands. "I sure feel goofy," said
Walk's voice. "Just a minute. . . . Just a minute."

"Here, catch hold of him on that side, Dusty," said
Bart Holt, moving forward.

Walk Ross suddenly sat bolt upright, and his voice
snapped out sharply. "Wait a minute! I got it! By God,
I know what it was! I got to see the old man."

Walk Ross heaved to his feet, so that for a moment
Hughes saw him outlined, a black swaying figure,
against the dim starlight of the window beyond. Then
the silhouetted figure disappeared as if a trap door had
opened under it, as Walk Ross lost his balance and fell
forward to hands and knees. Springing forward to
assist him, Hughes found that Ross was stripped to the
waist; his skin was so hot that it almost burned Clay's
hands. They put him on the bed again, where he sat
braced unsteadily on his good arm.

"Good God, I've sure been a fool." His voice came
dimly through the dark. Then more sharply, as he tried
to rise again, "Quick, I got to see the old man! I tell
you, I see through it all!"

"Set easy," said Bart Holt, holding him down.

"Maybe he's gone delirious on us," suggested Rivers.

"Delirious, hell!" Ross declared. "Let me go! I got to—"

"I'll get the old man," decided Bart Holt abruptly. "Here, keep him where he is, Dusty."

"I got him."

Bart Holt swung out of the room. They could hear the pound of his feet as he ran stiffly down the tiled hall.

"What is it? What is it, Ross?" Dusty was demanding.

"It's all my fault. It's my own damn fault!" Walk's tormented voice sounded very loud in the dark. "If I had any sense, Grasshopper would be alive right now!"

"Walk, what is it?"

"I—"

At the window the black outline of the casement seemed to bulge and close slightly, as if by a trick of the eye.

From the shadow at the window's edge burst a red flash, and the smashing concussion of a shot, unexpected as a dynamite blast within the confines of that narrow room, almost jumped Hughes out of his boots. Walk Ross jerked convulsively, and fell sideways, face down upon the bed.

Dusty Rivers, jerking out his gun, fired twice through the window into the empty starlight. Hughes, however, checked the streak of his hand to his gun. He caught up a chair as he sprang to the window, and with it smashed out the wooden bars. Dusty Rivers, whimpering curses, launched past him toward the opening he had made.

Hughes caught at Dusty's sleeve. "Wait! Not yet!"

His fingers slipped their grip as Dusty sprang to the four-foot window ledge and drove through the shattered bars. Once more a gun spoke, this time beyond the massive walls. Dusty Rivers crumpled in the act of leaping to the ground, and, pitching forward heavily, was lost to view.

Clay Hughes set a foot on the window ledge and counted five. Then, and not before, he sprang outward to the ground, across the body of Dusty Rivers. Once more a gun cracked, the bullet droning over his head. A black hulk was turning the corner of the house, away from him, to the frantic hoof-drum of a viciously spurred animal. Hughes fired once at the vanishing shape; his bullet clipped the corner of the adobe, and he heard the brief explosive growl of the ricochet as it hurled itself off into space. Running to the corner of the house, he fired twice more, by sound, as the running animal disappeared into the night beyond the cottonwoods. He heard Gustafson's gun speak twice, slowly, from the roof as he holstered his gun, and he ran back to Dusty Rivers.

Dusty spoke in hoarse gasps as Hughes bent over him. "Clay—quick! Find out what Walk knows! If he cashes in—"

Hughes obeyed. He went in through the broken window bars again, and bent over the figure on the bed.

"Walk; can you hear me, Walk?"

Walk's chest labored under Clay's hands but he did not speak.

Now lantern lights showed outside the window, as Bart Holt and Oliver Major came up from the pump house on the run. Behind them, coming more slowly, Hughes could hear the voice of Dick Major, to whom Stephen Sessions appeared to have been turned over, urging Sessions to "shake a leg, before I take a crack at you!"

"It's Dusty!" came Major's voice. "Dusty, have they got you?" Rivers did not answer.

"Where's that damn Hughes?" snarled Bart Holt. "I've known all the time that he——"

"Here I am," Hughes sung out to them from within. "Somebody got Walk Ross; and he got Dusty as we started out through the window after him. Somebody get a light in here!"

There was a sound of ripping wood as Oliver Major tore a shutter down. "Get Dusty onto this, and carry him down to the pump house. Here you, Steve Sessions, play a hand here." Major climbed stiffly through the window and his lantern filled the room with light.

The first shot, they found, had apparently gone high, and the pull of the trigger had thrown it a little to the right, saving Walk's life. As it was, he had no worse than a smashed shoulder, but the wound was bleeding fast. Oliver Major snatched up a pillow and tore open a seam with his teeth. He pulled out of it a huge

236

handful of feathers, and with them packed the wound of the unconscious man.

"They got Dusty through the ribs," he said. "It looks like it might turn out awful bad. Take this pillow and run like hell to the pump house with it. There's nothing like feathers for a lung wound. Take 'em and run like hell!"

When Bart Holt had seized upon this extraordinary remedy for chest wounds, Clay Hughes went back to the house to lend a hand with Walk Ross. As he joined Major again, the broad shoulders and big shaggy head of Chris Gustafson were thrust in through the broken bars of the window.

"Somebody's got Walk Ross and Dusty Rivers," Major told him shortly. "Looks like we can patch 'em up—though Dusty's hit awfully bad. Now get back up on that roof and stay there!"

"I guess I seen the feller that shot 'em git out of here," said Gustafson slowly, in his deliberate heavy way. "At least, I seen a man on a horse go tearing out of here right after the shot, and somebody was shooting at him when he went."

"And you never threw down on him? Why, you big—"

"Yeah, I took a wham at him," Gustafson said. "I got his animal as he went past the far corral. The light was awful bad; but I managed to get a fair plain shot, and I killed his horse."

"Then," said Hughes, "we can mount up and catch him yet."

"I don't know about that," said Gustafson. "The feller got up and ducked around a shed. I seen him once more, running for the Adobe Wells road, or in that general direction, kind of; and I took two more shots, but didn't get him. And then I lost sight of him in the dark. I don't expect we'll ever pick him up again now, Mr. Major. It's awful easy for a man on foot to dodge and lose hisself in a gully or somethin', in the dark."

"We'll have a try at it anyway," said Major. "Now you better get up on the roof again, Chris."

"What I come down to say," said Gustafson, "was that I can see lights on the Adobe Wells road."

Major roared, "Why didn't you say so before? How close on us are they?"

"They're hardly more than in sight. I doubt if they're any closer than twenty-five miles, where the road makes that bend this way. There's an awful mess of 'em, too; though it's hard to say how many, the way the lights double in the ground mirage."

"Well," said Oliver Major slowly, "that gives us between half an hour and an hour, anyway. I reckon we won't take time to look for the gun-throwing hombre, though. One more or less isn't going to make much difference, I guess. I sure would have liked to know who he was, though."

"Then which of us is missing?" Hughes suggested.

Major considered a moment. "Ain't all the boys here?" he said.

"Where," said Hughes, "is Art French?"

CHAPTER SEVENTEEN

If there were any doubts as to the identity of the man who had fired upon Walk Ross and Dusty Rivers, it fell away when Chris Gustafson had walked out to examine the horse he had shot out from under the fugitive.

"You're right sure that's Art French's saddle?" Major questioned him.

"I've ridden alongside that saddle too many times, Mr. Major, in the four, five months he's been with us, to make any mistake about it now."

"I wouldn't have believed it," Oliver Major admitted. "I can hardly believe it now. He was a wild, crazy rider, Art was; and not everybody liked him, I know, but I never thought— It was his own horse, I suppose?"

"No, Mr. Major," said Gustafson, "that was a funny thing. It wasn't any horse he was startin' off on at all. It was a mule."

"A mule?" repeated Hughes.

"It was the mule we always called Henry Milligan."

"A mule named Henry Milligan," marveled Hughes. "What are you giving us here?"

"That's what we always called her," Major corroborated. "She was the smartest mule in the Buckhorn. We used to use her back in the mountains when the wild horses got pesky, and run some of our stock off. She could take short cuts like a man would be afraid to take on an ordinary horse, and fast, too. But lately I didn't realize she was around."

"She come wandering in yesterday morning," said Chris Gustafson. "I seen her standing by the hay gate, like she used to do, and I hayed her off. I supposed somebody had been using her for a pack; there was a saddle gall on her, just a couple days old."

"So it was the voice of Henry Milligan," said Hughes, "I heard the night Hugo Donnan was killed!"

"What makes you think so?"

"Maybe you remember it was something about a mule that was worrying Grasshopper Tanner. Ask yourself why French rode off on Henry Milligan instead of taking his own horse."

For a moment Bart Holt seemed to forget that he had never been wholly convinced of Hughes' innocence. "By gosh," he put in, "I think he's on the trail of something there. A man on the Milligan mule—especially this wild-riding Art French—could get up onto the rim and down again in a hundred places that no sober man on an ordinary pony would ever think of trying."

"Is this any time to be making a lot of crazy guesses," demanded Dick Major, "with the Shaw posse almost on us?"

Old Oliver Major looked him over sadly. "Seems like there isn't anything more we can do for the boys that's hurt," he said. "What else can we do but wait?"

"Wait, hell," stormed Dick. His voice sounded as if it would crack with nervous strain. Obviously he was trying to be cool and hard, like his father and Bart

Holt, but his stormy uncontrolled vitality was making a bad job of it. "We should go to meet 'em," he declared. "Throw a car across the road where she crosses the Buckhorn! We could lay back and pepper hell out of 'em as they come up. Let them once get in among the adobes here——"

"No, that won't do," said Oliver Major wearily. "Don't think it didn't come into my head, boy; we could give 'em an awful raking there, right where you say. It would sure be a diminished posse that come on from the bridge. But the 'Horace hold the bridge' stuff is out. It's a hard play we're making as it is. It would put Governor Replogle where he wouldn't dast turn and call off the dogs, if we was to ambush the posse and kill a bunch of 'em before they ever opened with a shot."

Stephen Sessions spoke for the first time in a long time. "You still think Theron Replogle will turn?" he said, an amused weary contempt in his tone.

"By God," said Oliver Major, a deep stubborn conviction in his voice, "I'm thinking it'll be the end of him if he don't! The old cattlemen of this state know plain facts when they see them yet. If Replogle keeps on with the stand he's made, you think this state can ever hold him, once the facts of this business are known? And known they will be, you can mark me that! The newspapers didn't amount to much, Steve, in the old days, the days of Black Plains and Tonto Basin; but they amount to something now. Within two days there'll be headlines all over the southwest—all

241

over the country, Steve!"

"'Two Killed As Posse Takes Gunman,' maybe," said Sessions contemptuously.

"You'll soon know," Major told him. "It'll be put to the test right soon."

It had been shortly before three o'clock when Gustafson had first reported headlights upon the Adobe Wells road. At 3:18 he brought word that a fresh observation had shown that at least eight or nine cars were on the way. Though the distance made them seem to crawl, their steady approach indicated that they were making good time upon the road. One car, he said, appeared to have drawn some distance ahead of the rest.

The earth curves and the faint indiscernible roll of the valley floor still concealed the headlights from the watchers on the ground at 3:35 when Gustafson reported that the main body of the approach had lost itself to sight at Twelve Mile Corral. Either they had gathered there to wait for daylight; or else they were at that very moment approaching without lights. Ears applied to the ground could detect no purr of engines as yet, however. The lead car, proceeding with full lights, had done a peculiar thing. It had turned off the road at the Twelve Mile bridge, and was swinging out in a wide circle, through the sagebrush.

"By running the old salt pans," said Bart Holt, "they can swing round us to the east about as far as they want. Maybe they figure to outflank us or something. Though I must say, I don't see no idee in that."

It was still dark as the intention of the far flanking car became plain. It had swung wide of the headquarters buildings of the Lazy M, and now its dimming tail light could be seen twisting its way northward along the horse trail to Gunsight Pass.

"He thought of that too late," said Major. "He's putting a bunch there to cut us off from the Gunsight, for fear we'll sneak out the back way and get across the state line, like we sent the boys with Sally and Mona."

"We could get out plenty other ways," said Bart Holt.

"Naturally; but I wouldn't doubt he'd rather take a chance of running us down after we was busted up and scattered in the rough country, than try to catch us from behind on an open trail."

Now the cars which had stopped at Twelve Mile Corral once more proceeded with lighted lights. The distant flash of their head lamps could be seen by them all now from the ground; though it still required elevation to count them correctly: there were no less than nine.

Then, as the people of the Lazy M watched the approach of the cars from Adobe Wells, their attention was diverted by the approach of a furiously running horse. They looked at each other.

"Watch what you're doing now," Major cautioned, as the hard-ridden animal drew near. "Lord knows who this is; but you fellers keep your guns in their leather. If it comes there's any shooting to be done, I guess I can take care of one horse-load of enemy, all right."

A froth-lathered pony burst into the far reaching white light of the gasoline lantern, and was jerked up, open-mouthed, upon its haunches. The rider was Bob Macumber.

"Is she here?" he yelled at them, without concealment of the panic in his voice.

"Who?"

"Sally! Ain't she here?"

"No, she isn't here! Where— Have you—"

"She must be here! She's got to be here!" insisted Macumber crazily.

Oliver Major cried out, *If you've lost that girl—*

Hughes, perceiving Macumber's instant intention, sprang forward just in time. Bob whirled his pony with a savage wrench and struck in the spurs as Hughes seized the reins at the bit, and, with all his weight in the ground grip of his high heels, dragged down the pony's head.

The frantic pony, caught between the strike of the spurs and the wrench of Clay Hughes' weight upon the bit; whirled in a crazy plunge, and for a moment Hughes was lifted clear of the ground as it reared. Then abruptly, with the odd, sudden acceptance common to cow horses, it quieted and stood motionless, quivering slightly, on braced legs.

"Let him go!" Macumber begged. "I've got to go back!"

"All right," said Hughes, "but I'm going with you, damn it! Now quick—what happened?"

"We got through the Gunsight all right—nobody

tried to stop us. Sally kept changing her place up and down the train, all night. She'd go up and ride with Tom for a while, then drop back and ride with me. Then for a while I thought she was up with Tom, and Tom thought she was with me. She must have turned out and held her horse quiet with a hand over his nose, in the shadow of the timber, until we'd all gone by, and then started back. Just beyond the peak of the Pass, Tom come riding back along the train saying he hadn't seen her for an hour. . . . I made all the rest go on with Mona. I knew if there was going to be any trouble it was ahead, since the Pass was clear. I couldn't believe but what Sally must be only a little way back. I follered back along the trail at the high lope. I don't believe any animal has ever come down that trail the way I put this horse down it tonight. But Sally ain't on the trail, I can swear to that!"

"You missed her! You *must* have missed her! Lead them horses out!" snapped Oliver Major. "Bring my saddle, Dick. Chris!—Chris, where are you? He'll have to stay with Walk and Dusty—the rest of us will go back up with Bob."

"What about Sessions?"

"To hell with Sessions! Bob, I promise you, I'll kill you if you've lost that girl!"

"I hope to God you will," said Macumber dimly.

"Here goes the Buckhorn water," said Bart Holt.

"Damn the Buckhorn water!"

Hughes, the first saddled, already had his foot in the stirrup, when a faint, far suggestion of sound brought him to a frozen stop. He listened. "Keep still a minute! Stop everything, will you? Make that cayuse stand!" Hughes could bring into play a voice that animals obeyed; and those over-keyed men obeyed him like animals now, freezing motionless to his command. Even Major checked his hands in the act of jerking tight his latigo, and listened with the rest.

The drone of the approaching cars, within the two miles now, gave the darkness a deep humming undertone that seemed to come from the ground itself. Under this handicap Hughes at first could hear nothing more. Then, very faintly, almost as if he imagined it, he thought he heard the sound of hoofs, coming in at a running walk.

"Stand where you are!" he ordered the others savagely. "If I'm wrong I'll sing out, and you can come on."

He had hardly believed that they would acknowledge his abrupt usurpation of authority; yet they obeyed, waiting, finishing their saddling as he eased his pony at a quiet singlefoot into the dark.

At three hundred yards he drew up and listened again, then booted his horse forward at a dead run. Bending low on the withers he made out a mounted figure against the stars of the high horizon. It shied as he drove down upon it, and broke into a lope to circle him.

"Sally," he shouted, "is it you?"

The other rider pulled up. "I guess so, Clay," Sally's voice came to him, small across the dark.

He turned his horse and brought it close, stirrup to stirrup with hers. He wanted to speak to her, but found he could not. The iron had gone out of him, leaving him limp in the saddle. For the moment it seemed to him that all struggle had found an end with the return of this girl. The roar of guns and the death of men, the destruction of a range, the throttling of the Buckhorn water itself—all that was only a little stir in the desert dust, of no significance compared with the overwhelming relief that swept him with the reappearance of Sally Major.

She swayed against his shoulder as he brought his pony close, as if very weary, and very glad to be back. The pressure of that slight leaning weight was electric. As if by reflex he flung an arm about her shoulders, very strong and steady, but gentle too; for the one thing he was utterly sure of in a world of uncertainty was that here beside him, stirrup to stirrup, knee to knee, was one reality infinitely precious, wholly irreplaceable. For a moment her high-strung vitality seemed to sag, and she leaned her head against his shoulder like a tired child. "I had to come back, Clay. Don't let them send me away again! I want to stay here."

"I don't know," he said, "if I'll ever be able to let you out of arm's reach again."

For a few moments they rode so, very close together. Then she straightened up and lifted her horse ahead to meet the others. They were coming out now on a run, no longer to be restrained. Clay dropped the reins on the horn, letting the pony go back as it might, and stretched his arms luxuriously over his head. A grey light was showing beyond the trail-off of the Sweetwaters, bringing a day that Earl Shaw and the Lazy M had awaited, not through one night alone, but through the restive years. Clay Hughes shot a glance at the coloring sky, and grinned, ready to meet whatever turn of the luck with a glad heart. Sally Major was here. . . .

"Fool kid," mumbled Oliver Major. "Fool kid. . . . Get them ponies back in the 'dobe! They're nearly on us now."

It was typical of that family that neither Dick nor old Major demanded of Sally why she had returned. Now that she was here it was as if they had half expected her to break away and ride back, all alone. While Dick explained to Sally what had happened meantime, Hughes sought out Bob Macumber.

The foreman stood well apart from the others. He was leaning against the wall, and rolling a cigarette with dull, fumbling hands.

"Don't take it so hard, Bob," said Clay.

Macumber raised his head, and Hughes was surprised to see in that first faint light that Macumber's face was the peculiar grey-green of seasoning grass. "There's no possible chance of getting her away from here now," said Macumber. "They're almost on top of us—they've cut off Gunsight Pass—"

"She'll be all right here, Bob."

Macumber looked at him sharply, incomprehension

in his eyes. "Are you daft?" he demanded. "Why Clay—why—one chance shot angling in through a window—one wild ricochet, sweeping end to end through the inside of that 'dobe—good God, Clay, don't you realize she'll be under fire, here with the rest of us?"

It was a strange thing to see Bob Macumber's face gone green and slack with fear; the astonishment of it knocked away Clay's own presumption of Sally's safety here. He could not conceive of a world going on with Sally Major struck out of existence; and perhaps this very incapacity had induced in him too great a faith in those solid old adobe walls and the abilities of their defense.

"That's something," he said, "that we can't possibly let happen, Bob."

"It's my fault," Macumber accused himself. His voce sounded tangled and unfamiliar. "She'd be safe beyond the ranges now if I hadn't of fell down. All my life," he added, almost inaudibly, "I've fell down on near everything I tried. But I never reckoned I'd come to a fall down like this. It's a sorry thing I ever lived to come to it."

Nothing anybody could say, Hughes knew, could be worse nonsense than that. If there was a man in the world who could be depended upon to carry a thing through with all he had, it was Bob Macumber. Anybody could see that, except Macumber himself.

Bob jerked upright, and the abortive cigarette fluttered from his fingers, a shapeless rag. "I tell you,

Clay," he said, lifting his hands in front of him in an awkward, rigid gesture, "I tell you I'd have gone to the end of hell for her, and two miles beyond! All the Buckhorn, and every soul in it isn't worth the little finger of her. I tell you—"

Suddenly Hughes saw what he might have guessed before: Macumber was another who judged everything only in its relationship to Sally Major. "It'll come all right, Bob," he said.

Macumber jerked away from him, withdrawing a couple of paces. He fumbled for his makings, and began another cigarette. "I'll do what I can to even it up," he mumbled. "God knows it'll be little enough."

The first car of the Adobe Wells string was rumbling across the wooden bridge below the farthest Lazy M corral. "Get inside!" Major was ordering them. "I aim to take no chances here."

Unhurriedly the waiting men obeyed. "Ain't you even going to stand out first to speak to them?" said Bart Holt. "I think we ought to—"

"Stand out, hell!" said Major. "You ought to know by this time that they'll gun either Hughes or Dick with the least excuse, or none!"

"Or you either, for that matter," said Bart Holt.

"I aim they'll gun nobody at all," declared Major. "Where's Sessions?"

"I got him in here."

"Come on, Hughes—Macumber! Damn it, will you come on?"

It seemed strange to take to cover without the

exchange of a single shot, without even waiting for the formal challenge of Alex Shaw. But the time for formality and pretense was a long time past. They were up against the reality of war. It was a game in which the least penalty of error was the life of a man, and instant and conclusive disaster was the price of misplay. They had little enough to work with: six men, fighting behind adobe walls, against the law; six men, with their wounded—and a girl. They might ask themselves, surely, just how they expected to emerge victorious from open combat with the law; but they had the fate of Grasshopper Tanner to warn them that submission was the one course entirely out of the question.

Up by the house the first of the Adobe Wells cars passed the main doorway without hesitating, and came on directly for the pump house. Art French, of course, had tipped them off about that. The following cars seemed to draw up as they disappeared behind the house, for none of them reappeared. The one car came on slowly, alone, already within the hundred yards. Twenty yards from the pump house it rolled to a stop, and Hughes saw by that first grey light that it was the roadster of Alex Shaw.

And it was Alex Shaw himself who was now stepping out from behind the wheel with curious slow movements, as if his nerves were drawn taut against his will. He spoke out of the corner of his mouth to the other man on the seat—it was Dutch Pete. Dutch Pete nodded and remained in the car, a great sprawling relaxed figure, with one leg hung over the door.

Alex Shaw stepped forward three or four paces, his hands over his head. Here, evidently assuming that they were apprised of his intent, he dropped his hands and called out to the invisible defenders. His sheriff's badge showed ostentatiously on his vest, an unaccustomed ornament.

"Can you hear me, Major?"

"I hear you, all right."

"Is Stephen Sessions in there?"

"Do you think we're fools?" Major answered equivocally.

"Well, his car's out here!"

"I supposed you'd have found out by this time," Major called, "that we sent a party over the Gunsight during the night."

Alex Shaw hesitated. "Mr. Sessions," he shouted, "if you're in there, sing out."

They saw Sessions fill his lungs to answer, but Bart Holt's gun prodded the prisoner's stomach. Sessions glanced at the hard blaze in the old cattleman's eyes, smiled dryly, and closed his mouth.

"Well, that's all right," said the Adobe Wells leader after a few moments of waiting. "The men we want are in there just the same. I saw them as I come up, by God! I'm asking for the turnover of Dick Major and Clay Hughes!"

"Go to hell!" said Major.

The new-made sheriff shrugged his shoulders. "I'll tell you plain out," he said, "we aren't going to fool

252

with you!" He stopped to pick up a blade of grass, and chewed it reflectively as he went on. "Right now you're in the best position you'll ever be in: you got a chance to give yourselves up in peace. If we have to rout you out of there, it's going to cost us some men. What good will that do you? You'll be liable for the murder of every man killed in routing you out. In the end we'll get you, all right! You know that as well as me."

"To hell with you," answered Major again. "And to hell with your brother that thinks for you, and the gunmen he's hired to do the work! Back out o' here, before I get sore and throw down!"

"That's final, is it?" They could make out the twisty grin that crossed the face of Alex Shaw.

"Until hell freezes and splits!"

Without another word Shaw turned on his high stockman's heel, stepping back to his car.

Bob Macumber clapped Hughes upon the shoulder. "Well, so long, Clay. Take care of yourself."

"What the— Bob, what you doing?" Startled, Clay Hughes made a snatch at Macumber's wrist, as Bob flung open the door; but Bob freed himself with an impatient twist of his arm. He was walking out, toward the car of Alex Shaw.

"Bob—you damn fool—" Hughes sprang forward to catch Macumber, drag him back; but Bart Holt, unexpectedly seizing Clay's gun belt, jerked him backward with all his strength. Bart Holt snapped, "Help me, Chris!" and Gustafson's enormous arms closed about him, swinging him clear of the ground. He heard Bob growl, "Just a minute, Shaw!" Then he was dragged backward through the door.

"What's the matter with you?" Clay's voice rose in angry protest. "Can't you see—"

"What's the mater with *you?*" demanded Major, glaring into Clay's face so savagely that he was checked. "If you go out there the shooting will start, because they're set to get you, and you'll both be killed. They've got nothing against Bob. Let him speak them if he's set on it. Maybe he'll get away with it. Anyway, we can't stop him."

The heavy door banged shut, and the bar fell.

"You can at least give him the cover of the guns," Hughes raved.

"Well, we're doing it, ain't we?" growled Dick Major. He had taken a station at one of the two high, small windows on that side.

"If you'll sit tight, we'll let go of you," said Bart Holt.

"All right."

Gustafson released his terrific bear-like grip, and Hughes took his place at the shoe-box-sized window.

Beside the car Alex Shaw waited; and Macumber advanced upon him slowly, with that rolling gait of his, head forward, like a bear. Sally Major called out once, "Bob, come back!" Macumber appeared to falter in his stride, but he did not obey.

Up at the main house a shutter banged; the gray shadowless light of the early morning struck no gleams from steel, but Hughes thought he saw movement at one window of the house, then at a second

254

window, and a third. Shaw's deputies were swarming into the house from the far side, taking positions from which they could rake the pump house from excellent cover.

Ten feet in front of Alex Shaw, Bob Macumber had stopped, and the two stood facing each other, their thumbs hooked lightly in their belts in that deceptive nonchalant position of ready men. The two were speaking, low-voiced, so that those in the pump house could not make out what they said. Alex Shaw's mouth twisted in that ugly one-sided smile. Then they saw Bob Macumber's right hand move slowly away from his side, the fingers stiff and extended, and they heard the growl of his voice as he spoke an indistinguishable command.

Bob Macumber, the man who forever blamed himself, was paying off his imaginary debt to Sally Major.

What happened then was instantaneous, over with in the flash of a second. Alex Shaw's hand traveled only a few inches as it brought the gun from the holster at the front of his thigh; it seemed that the weapon spoke almost as it came out of its leather. Bob Macumber's holster was too far to the side, behind him almost; his right hand clutched, fumbled, and brought the gun up late. As Shaw's gun spoke Macumber jerked violently, then caved forward to his knees. Shaw whirled and leaped for the cover of his car as Dick Major fired twice, both shots going wild. Then Macumber's gun spoke once from the ground; Alex Shaw's hands flew up, and he pitched full length forward upon his face.

From the house burst a ragged fire and little gouts of dust began to jump around the now motionless body of Bob Macumber. Clay Hughes, at the window, whirled to find Sally Major close beside him.

"Down! Get down, and stay down!" He seized her shoulders roughly and forced her to her knees close against the adobe wall beneath the window. As he stood up to look out again the old wood of the window frame splintered six inches from his face; there was a thud in the adobe of the inner wall opposite, and little clods fell to the floor, rattling and whispering, as the bullet struck.

And now Dutch Pete fired from behind Shaw's car. At the first whip of action Dutch Pete had removed himself from his vulnerable position with an extraordinary agility, and taken cover behind the machine. They could not see his position because of the unfavorable slope of the land to the bed of the Buckhorn; but as his gun spoke three times, Macumber's body jerked, and they knew that Dutch Pete must have fired under the car itself, between the wheels. A whimpered imprecation burst from Clay Hughes, and he sprang to the door. Chris Gustafson jumped to intercept him, and once more the powerful arms of the big Norwegian clamped him, this time about his throat from behind, as Clay's fist knocked the bar out of its slot.

Hughes fought savagely, but Bart Holt and Dick Major, corning to Gustafson's aid, helped Chris bear him down.

"Let me go!" Hughes raged. "He's down, and

they're letting drive at him still! If you think I'm going to stay here and—"

"What good can you do? Sit on him, Chris."

Outside the firing had ceased abruptly. From the little high window Oliver Major said, "Old Doc Hodges is coming out. He'll do anything that's to be done."

"Let me see if he is," demanded Hughes. "If there's a doctor going to him, I give you my word I won't go out." They let him stand up to peer out of the little window again, Chris Gustafson keeping a heavy hand upon Clay's belt. A hatless man in rumpled street clothes was walking across the open toward the car beside which lay Alex Shaw and Bob Macumber. It was Hodges, the Adobe Wells medico—perhaps the only man in the Buckhorn who took no sides.

Hodges went directly to Bob Macumber, and for a moment stooped in examination. Then he stood up, facing the pump house, and made a gesture of utter finality. Hughes turned away.

Watching his face to read the verdict, Sally Major suddenly hid her face in her hands. Her shoulders shook uncontrollably, and between her fingers trickled slow irrepressible tears.

CHAPTER EIGHTEEN

It was dusk; the fifth dusk that they had seen from within the now bullet-spattered adobe walls of the old pump house. In all those age-long five days of the siege nothing had ever happened at just this hour. And now an unaccustomed quiet was upon the Lazy M; not the quiet of something ended, but of something about to begin.

In the five days of their siege they had withstood no less than eleven attacks, and of these eleven only two had been made by daylight. Night was the time for everlasting alertness, long strained waitings, whispered councils, all of which forever came to but one end: the shock and the roar of the guns as the people of the Lazy M once more drove the attackers back.

They knew now that Earl Shaw himself was directing the siege. Even had they not caught a distant glimpse of him as he arrived, the Lazy M people would have known that he was there by the changed tactics with which they were harassed. Before the arrival of Earl Shaw, Dutch Pete, taking the place of the fallen Alex Shaw, had twice rushed the adobe in an attempt to crash the door with a battering ram. The Lazy M defenders could have killed their besiegers by the dozen then.

But the great weakness of their position lay in the fact that so long as the Bar S faction held legal authority, the Lazy M men dared not shoot to kill, even in their own defense. Oliver Major had a stubborn faith that as word of their situation spread, such a storm of protest would rise from the cattlemen of the southwest as would force Theron Replogle to take the law from the hands of the Shaws, to whom he had given it, and secure a neutral enforcement. This hoped-for intercession—if it ever came—would be worthless to them if they had complicated the case against them by the killing of men who were acting technically in the support of the law. The defenders must shoot only to disable and drive off those who now sought to dig them out of their stubborn redoubt.

The firing from the adobe had therefore been more warning than lethal through the first day of the siege. Dutch Pete had lost eight men in wounded at his first attempt to ram the door. The second attack broke up more quickly, and only three disabled men were dragged away with the attackers when they dropped their log ram and took cover. After that Dutch Pete had settled back to await the arrival of more brains.

With the advent of Earl Shaw the siege took on a different color. Shaw had begun by planting long-range snipers in positions so secure that their disablement, except by complete destruction, was out of the question. These sharpshooter nests brought an accurate and searching fire to bear upon the loop-holes of the defenders. Those within the adobe could keep watch during the day only by peering through minute cracks; to uncover so much as a knot-hole was to court an instant splatter of lead. The diminished accuracy of the snipers after dark was all that made defense possible at all. Even at night, the long range rifles were a constant hazard.

And this fire had taken effect. A bullet which tore through the muscles at the side of Bart Holt's neck had been almost their first warning that the hour for careless exposure was past. Holt lived and would recover; but, as far as this fight was concerned, the old tracker could help them no more.

Chris Gustafson had a hand smashed when a bullet came the wrong way of the rifle he was sighting, turning him instantly into a one-sided man. He was still in the fight, unfevered and stoic, but he was reduced to the revolver now.

Dick Major, before the fight was done, promised to fare the worst of all. A spent ricochet had broken his collar bone close to the throat; he had been shot through the left forearm, and a third shot had chucked a ragged splinter of wood into the side of his face with such effect that it was now bandaged from eye to jaw. Yet these injuries had impressed no one less than Dick Major. Twice he had opened the door recklessly to fire into the night, oblivious to lead which splattered into the planks beside him like thrown gravel; and he could not always be restrained from jerking down the defensive planking of a whole window to get a shot he wanted. Three times wounded, he remained the wild reckless kid he had always been, his incautious eagerness making him one of the primary hazards of defense.

Twice, and sometimes three times in a night, Earl Shaw sent his men to storm the adobe in his own way. Under the covering fire of his sharpshooters, his men crept forward through shadow seeking means to break the stubborn defense. Standing flat against the adobe of the outer wall of the pump house, they attacked the timbered defenses of doors and windows with axes; until Hughes and Major, partly opening the door, met them with such a storm of fire that only one or two were able to retire without help. Again they attacked the adobe itself with mattock and pick. Oliver Major and Clay Hughes, now the only two unwounded men within the defense, ripped a hole in the sod and timber roof. Defended by the walls, which extended several feet above the line of the roof, these two blasted the ambitious work party from above. Once Shaw's men came with fire, hoping to find the roof inflammable, but this was of sod; and again they attacked the wooden doors and windows of the defense with gasoline and fire, but failed again.

Thus every night brought some new mode of attack, sometimes stubborn and violent, sometimes merely clever and ingenious, designed to cause the defenders to expose themselves to the fire of the planted rifles. Yet, violent though some of the attacks might be, and expensive to the attackers in wounded men, those within had the feeling that Earl Shaw staked but little upon success by these means. They had the feeling that the boss of the Bar S was only amusing himself, playing with them as a lion plays with a hurt rabbit, while he waited for the sheer endurance of his siege to take effect.

How many men the attackers had lost in wounded and disabled the defenders could not know: they were more than a dozen, certainly; perhaps many more. Whether or not anyone had been killed in the tumult of night fighting they could not guess. They did not even know whether Alex Shaw had survived the wound he had received in his shoot-out with Bob Macumber.

One man they knew was dead: it was Art French. Now that they were fully apprised of his treachery, as well as of his almost certain connection with the death of Hugo Donnan, they could not be sorry that he was rubbed out, complicate their position though it might. Yet the gunning of Art French had all but cost the life of the man who had downed him. No one had supposed Walk Ross would attempt to take up a gun. Since he had been moved to the pump house he had laid very still, hardly the flicker of an eyelash disturbing the stillness of his bloodless face. And they had not seen him stagger to a window, and bring up a gun with the one hand which he could still use. How long Ross stood at the window, accurately locating his mark and making good his rested aim, they did not know; but when Walk Ross fired at last, it was Art French who pitched forward with a galvanic jerk, to hang head-downward, suspended from the waist, from the loft of a barn.

That had been four days ago, when the fight was young. Tonight, with their rations running very low, and no sign without of slackening or intercession, it seemed they must be very near the end—some kind of end.

Hughes went into the adobe's smaller room, where the ponies were being kept. The animals stood head down, logy from five days' standing. One of the defenders always had to stay in this room to watch developments at that end of the building. Two or three people were enough to keep an eye out all around most of the time, but with only four of the men still on their feet, and but two of these unwounded, Sally Major was carrying her full share of guard. It was she who was watching in the dusky stable room now. The horses moved slowly in the awkward hip-lurching way of horses close confined, as Hughes made his way through them to Sally's side.

"Anything doing?"

"No." She lowered her voice to a whisper, leaning close to his ear as he stooped to peer out through a crack between the planks. "I want to talk to you about something, Clay. Did you notice something funny just now, just before dark closed down?"

"What kind of funny, Sally? In here or outside?"

"Outside, way outside."

"You mean—?"

He couldn't see her, but he could feel her presence very close. Her shoulder momentarily swayed against his arm as he stooped to peer out; the warm soft touch carried the deep electric thrill of vitality he had always received from any manifestation of the nearness of this girl. Her whisper came to him so near and quiet that he could feel the warmth of her breath upon his cheek, yet could hardly hear it at all.

"A little while ago," she said, "did you hear Dick say he could make out somebody driving stock, down to southward?"

263

"Yes."

"Did you look to see what he saw?"

"We all looked, I guess."

His hand, as he laid it upon the deep recessed window ledge came in contact with one of hers, and he was startled to find how cold and tremulous her fingers were. Searching in the dark, he found her other hand also, moving gently and slowly for fear she would jerk them away. They seemed very small and slender; soft fingered, yet delicately strong. The tremor went out of them as he closed them in his own, and she did not take them away.

"So did I," she said. "Clay, that didn't look to me like anybody driving stock!"

"Could you see anything but the dust?" he asked. "I couldn't."

"No; but the dust different things raise is just about as different as the shadows of things. That dust was too steady, too business-like. It wasn't like the dust you make driving loose stock at all. At first I thought it was a car; but it was too slow, and too long, and too much."

"I noticed that," he agreed.

"Clay, that dust was made by ridden horses—a lot of them, an awful lot of them—sixty, eighty, a hundred head! I haven't lived all my life in a country where you can see a hundred miles, without learning to read dust."

He hesitated before he answered. "I've been thinking the same thing."

"Oh, Clay, are you—" There came into her whisper the half-fearful, half-exultant tremor of the hope that is afraid to hope—"are you thinking what I am?"

Slowly he said, "I'm afraid I'm not."

"But what can it be? It certainly can't be more posse—they come in cars. And heaven knows they've got enough posse now against—against just two unwounded men."

"They've found this old pump house an awfully tough nut to crack," he said grimly.

"Don't you see what it may be?" she urged. "The whole southwest must know about this terrible thing, by now. Dad has friends everywhere, old cattlemen, old trail-drivers, men of the old fighting ways that aren't afraid of the law, or the world, or the devil. They'll come! Somehow, in the bottom of my heart, I've known it all along. Clay, it must be they; the cattlemen, the old-timers, gathering to stand by their own. They're the men that whipped the Apache and the Comanche. How could they sit back now?"

"Honey child—" he said hesitantly, "honey child—"

"Clay, what's the matter?"

"Don't you stake too much," he said slowly. "Don't you set your heart on it, Sally girl, until we know."

"Then you don't think—"

"If I could keep myself from thinking at all," he said softly, "I reckon I would."

"But, Clay, have you been watching *him?*" He knew that she meant her father. "He saw it too. I know he did; and he thinks as I do. I can see it in his eyes.

265

There's a new life come into him, Clay, a new hope. I believe it was what he was playing for all along; he knew they wouldn't fail him, and they're not going to, all those grand old men!"

He tried to speak, but found that there was nothing he could say. Impulsively he bent his head and pressed his lips to the palm of her hand, wondering what the expression of her face was, so near to his, yet invisible behind the thin screen of the dark. . . .

Oliver Major and Stephen Sessions were arguing again when Clay Hughes returned to the other room. A lantern in the middle of the floor, protected by an improvised cone of sheet iron, cast a thin plane of the dimmest yellow light along the floor alone; it showed the stirrup of a saddle, a rifle butt, Oliver Major's high heeled boots, and the corner of a bale of straw. Everything above was shrouded in heaviest shadow.

The voice of Stephen Sessions was thin and dry, seeming to have lost a great deal of body in the five days during which he had been a prisoner with the besieged; and it seemed strange to hear him speak, he had spoken so seldom since he had been their prisoner here. The presence of that silver-haired, dominant, and somehow unctuous old man had been an anomaly from the start. Once he could have turned aside the on-rushing avalanche of disaster. To Oliver Major, his presence here now was a grim joke, and a just one. To Bart Holt at least, who had never favored holding him here at all, that silent, inappropriate, and sphinx-like presence had seemed a Jonah, a constant reminder that

266

their battle was against forces which could draw upon the resources of the commonwealth itself.

Sessions had taken his situation silently, stoically even; and though the ruddy unctuousness of the man drained out of him, that stubborn look of square-cut granite remained, nothing shaken by the gun roar, nor swayed in opinion by the nerve-racking tedium of the siege. He might have been an aged and weary traveler, waiting interminably in a way station for a train.

In the face of Sessions' weary stoicism, some of that exasperation he had inspired ebbed away; as if, very close to the end as they were, it became more apparent that each man is what he is, as helpless between his own character and his fate as a bronc rounded for breaking.

"It's going on three hours since dusk," Sessions said. "They'll be coming on again soon."

Something new, perhaps that newly strengthened hope which Sally had seen in his eyes, was subtly resonant in the voice of Oliver Major as he answered. "It may be they're not coming on tonight," he said.

"You planned to fight three days," said Sessions, dryly. "You thought the posse would dwindle and fade. Instead they're stronger, and in a stronger position, now than ever before. Instead of three days, it's been five. The grub is almost gone."

"I'm thinking of something else," said Oliver Major. His voice was very hard, but edged with that faintly vibrant note of a new hope.

There was no question in Stephen Sessions' voice,

but only a wondering, ironic statement. "You still hope, then, that Theron Replogle will reverse himself!"

"I think," said Oliver Major, "that Replogle knows what's best for Replogle."

There was a silence. If in the darkness Stephen Sessions smiled with a weary dry contempt, the smothered gleam of the lantern did not disclose it. Oliver Major's boots moved out of the flat circle of dim light, as for a few minutes he engaged himself in a tour of the lookout.

"How long," said Stephen Sessions after a little pause, "do you think you can go on with this?"

"Go on?" repeated Oliver Major. His voice was curiously without emotion. "We can't go on."

"You've made a good fight," said Stephen Sessions with the finality of a man who speaks of a thing that is done. "I never would have believed that you people could have made a stand of it like you've done."

No one answered him. They knew that what he said was so. That thick old adobe that Oliver Major and his brother had built with their own hands so long ago had, with the improvised planking shields at its openings, stood immune to fire, impregnable to lead. The scathing rake of the enemy fire had held them down very tightly; not so much as a knot hole was safe from the searching guns. Yet, over and over again the defenders had proved that in the pinches their own guns could lash out murderously, withering short range attack. The defense was an extraordinary thing—certainly they knew it must be a singularly baffling thing to the heavily manned, and heavily armed army-like posse without. Yet it could not last forever.

"No, Oliver," said Stephen Sessions, "like you said, you can't go on. God knows I tried to make you see what the end would be when you began. It had to come. But, Oliver, I want to say this: from the bottom of my heart, from the bottom of my soul, I'm sorry! I can't say more than that."

If it occurred to Oliver Major that this man, now expressing his purely futile regret, could have, at one time, changed the whole circumstance with a word, he found no reason for bringing it up again now. They had threshed that matter to the bottom, and at the bottom they had been deadlocked still.

In the oppressive silence the dim mumblings of the delirious Walk Ross fumbled vaguely. "Three head more . . . before we quit . . . It's darker than all blue hell. . . ." Beyond the walls Hughes made out the thin threading cry of a coyote, far off.

"So you see," said Stephen Sessions, as if he could bear the silence no more, "Oliver, you have to give up."

"Give up?" said Major, very softly. "We can't give up."

"But," said Sessions, the impatience of overwrought nerves coming to the surface, "you just admitted that it can't go on."

"I know you never believed me, Steve," said Oliver

wearily, "but if I know anything in the world, I know this one thing for truth: if we'd given Clay Hughes and my boy over into their hands they never would have been seen alive again. The same old story—'shot trying to escape'—like it was with Grasshopper Tanner, like it's been with others before. I know Earl Shaw, and I know this feud, root, trunk, and branch. God knows I have reason to know it well! You can't believe that, Steve; partly it's because you don't want to believe. But I can't very well give the boys up—just to prove my point."

"I don't see the alternative," Sessions said.

"There's been two other ways," said Major. His boots had moved back into the low plane of light from the masked lantern, but his voice came from utter darkness, like a voice detached, thin, weary, and very old. "Right along there's been two other ways. No; three. One was that Theron Replogle would see the light in time. Almost it looked as if he wasn't going to; but Steve, his hand has been forced, I think!"

"Forced?" said Sessions.

"Just before dusk," said Oliver Major, "there was that long dust, like driven stock to southward. It seemed to me that that dust didn't come from no driven stock. I didn't say nothing. I was almost afeared to believe. But the silence that's come over Earl Shaw's gang out there tells me now that it was so!"

"Tells you what?" demanded Sessions.

"That dust," said Major, "was kicked up by ridden

270

stock. The horses that made it are picketed out there now, maybe a half a mile off—between sixty and ninety head that came up under the saddle. Did you think the old-timers of the west would stand by and watch this thing with idle hands? Did you think the news wouldn't run and spread that a rustling, gun-throwing gang had laid hands on the government, and was using the law itself to saw-whip an honest brand? Do you think the old cattlemen forget the men that rode with 'em, ever, while they live? If you think that, you've forgot the day that you was one of 'em, and swung a rope with the rest."

"But Theron Replogle—" began Sessions.

"Earl Shaw knows tonight that a state isn't made up of politics, nor technicalities in books. By God, the southwest is still made up of men! What Earl Shaw knows tonight, Governor Replogle will know tomorrow. Do you think he imagines he can fight the cowmen of the southwest, once they rise up and take the saddle? They made him, and they can bust him, and well he knows it. Let this be a lesson to the world, never to throw in a poker hand till the last card is down! Sessions, you ought to thank me for a swell ringside seat to the saving of the Buckhorn water!"

There was a brief silence, then Sessions said: "What was that third chance, Oliver?" The words came very thick and slow. If anything could have put a pall upon the exultant dead certainty of Oliver Major's voice, it must certainly have been Stephen Sessions' tone, for it was the tone of a man who looked ahead into things from which he would rather turn his face.

But the grim, indomitable faith of Oliver Major bent to no one, and to this man least of all. "Thank God," he said, "it will never come to that third chance."

"Are you sure?" said Sessions slowly.

"Wait and see!"

Sessions repeated, "Wait."

Slowly the minutes dragged by; fifteen minutes, twenty-five. They had been under strain there a long time, too long to relax now before hearing the final word that would confirm Oliver Major's faith. In their weariness they could not exult in, or perhaps wholly comprehend, the deliverance in which Oliver Major so firmly believed.

The end of uncertainty came in an unexpected way.

Across the night, thin and far, but clear and recognizable beyond any possibility of misinterpretation, came the notes of a bugle.

There was utter silence in the besieged adobe. The far bugle, distinct and sweet in the still night, was blowing taps, the slow sad call which the army uses in all circumstances denoting finality. "When your last . . . day is past . . . from afar, some bright star, o'er your grave . . ."

It was the hour of the night which had fixed that call; but to those who waited in the close, little-broken darkness of the ancient adobe, the notes of that familiar call seemed to bear another meaning, as if, of all possible messages, this one carried the deepest, the most inevadable meaning.

No one moved, nor spoke, while the far call played slowly through to the end: "Watch will keep . . . while you sleep . . . with the brave . . ."

When the last long note had died away there was still a moment's silence more. It was Stephen Sessions who spoke then. His voice was shaking and queer, as if his throat was very dry and constricted; yet the words seemed to tumble from him. Too long that man of many words had maintained his stoic silence. There was almost a touch of hysteria in the words that poured from him now.

"You see—see, there's your answer. There's your answer from the cattlemen you looked to—the cattlemen that didn't come! There's your answer from the government, from Theron Replogle! You thought the governor would reverse himself? You thought the old west would rise up against the law to save your brand? There's your answer to both—all the answer you could ever expect, and more! Ridden horses under that dust? By God, you know now what was under that dust. It was cavalry rode there! You hear me? That's National Guard Cavalry called out by the governor to guarantee that first, last, and always, your old-time gun-throwers will keep their hands off the law. You heard their bugle—and by God, you know it for what it was!"

He paused for an instant, and Hughes could hear his hoarse breathing before the words welled up out of him again. Stephen Sessions had been an orator once, who could sway a multitude with the deep resonance of his voice, but that voice was thin, high, and shaky as he cried out in that constricted adobe now. "You know what it is now, not to listen to a man that deals in facts! You know now what friendship is worth, or old associations, like God knows I have reason to know myself. Where are your cattlemen? Where's the old west that was going into the saddle to pull you out of the hole? I'll tell you where they are! They're every man of them laying low, each thinking of himself, and hoping he's beyond trouble's reach. It's the day of the law, I tell you! And the day of the guns is gone!"

As he stopped a complete silence fell, so heavy, so curiously complete that Sessions must have felt that he was alone, unheard. It could only have been a few seconds, though it seemed vastly longer, before the apparent emptiness of the dark about him seemed to become too much for the old man of legalities and words. Abruptly he reached for the lantern upon the floor, and raised it above his head. As the dim flame of the lantern's shielded light lifted, the figures in the room became suddenly visible, figures motionless as the walls. Old Oliver Major was sitting with his rifle across his knees, his hands locked upon the stock; and his face was like brown wax, its hard carved lineaments sagged and wilted, as if the wax had turned soft in the heat. It was the face of a man stunned, a man forsaken, not so much by the world as by the sudden demolition of hallucinations which he had held as solid and as real as the rock of the living rim.

But it was the face of Stephen Sessions to which

Clay whipped his eyes, narrowed in an estimating scrutiny. And this face too had changed. All of that profound, unctuous surety was gone, and something of the granite too; it was no longer ruddy, but a dirty grey, and Hughes thought he had never seen such desolate and haggard eyes in living face.

Swiftly, as if his arm had suddenly weakened with the weight of the lantern, Sessions lowered the light to the floor again. The room's motionless figures disappeared abruptly, leaving in the faint small circle of remaining light only the stirrup of a saddle, a. bit of ragged hay, and a glimmer of polished walnut where rested a rifle stock.

CHAPTER NINETEEN

There was the catch of a breath in the darkness near Hughes, and someone moving near him stumbled. Without seeing the figure as anything but a shadow in shadows, Clay knew that it was Sally Major. He drew her down beside him, and gathered her in his arms. In the brief span of days that they had known each other, he had never told her that he loved her, had hardly so much as touched her hand; but now she turned her face into the hollow of his shoulder and her tears were hot against his throat. It was as if they had both always known that Sally Major in tears belonged in the arms of Clay Hughes. In the stress that circumstance had put upon them they were pressed together by an individualized law of gravity, tacit and accepted. Without knowing exactly when or how, they had recognized one another, turned to each other across silences, understanding unspoken things.

It was Clay Hughes to whom Sally's eyes had turned when Sessions had raised the lantern; and if he could have seen himself as she saw him then, he would have wondered that she recognized him at all. The lantern light had shown a big gaunted, tangle-haired figure, with bloodshot blue eyes, very hard-edged as they turned upon the face of Stephen Sessions. Most of the buttons had got torn out of his shirt in one of his sorties to the roof, so that the dilapidated remainder hung ripped open to the belt; and a bristly five-day growth of sandy beard robbed his face of resemblance to itself. Few border ruffians have ever looked tougher than Hughes did that night. Yet, as his arms found her, her quick nervous vitality relaxed and she rested all her slight weight against him, hiding her wet eyes in the curve of his throat. He kissed her hair; and finding one of her hands, he put it inside his shirt against his ribs and held it tight against his side with his arm.

Dick Major called out from his post in the room where the ponies stood. "Well, do you hear him or not? Dutch Pete has hailed you three times, Dad! Do you want to talk to him, or shall I give him a shot?"

Oliver Major said in a dead voice, "To hell with him! Give him a——"

"Tell him," Hughes ordered sharply, "to come up and talk if he wants!"

Dick Major raised his voice to a hail. "All right, all

276

right! Come on and talk, if you've got something to say this time!"

There was a moment or two of shouting back and forth. Dutch Pete did not like his job of envoy, but it was evident that powers outside himself had stuck him at it. In a little while more the thick-syllabled, inertly brutal voice of Earl Shaw's chief killer was heard from a short distance outside.

"I'm standing twenty paces out in front," it said, "which is as close as I aim to come. If you fellers want to take a shot at me—I ain't armed; but twenty rifles will take a slam at the flash of your gun."

Bart Holt called out in an unexpectedly strong voice from where he lay, "Quit worrying, you big yellow streak! As soon as you turn and run for it, I'm going to get up and salt you plenty!"

"Shut up, Bart," said Hughes. Gently he released himself from Sally's arms and went to a cigar-box sized window. He swung aside the shield. His right hand brought his six gun to the sill of the window before his face, and lay there, relaxed and ready, as he spoke again. "Speak your piece," he ordered Dutch Pete.

The voice of Dutch Pete was dogged. He was a man performing an act in a way not his own. "I'm giving you your last chance," he said. "The county's wasted enough time and money, and there's enough good men hurt on account of you hellions. If you think you've got a chance, why, that was a squadron of cavalry you seen come in tonight. What do you think about that, huh?"

277

"Oh, did you need help?" said Hughes. "Just exactly what is the cavalry going to do for you boys?"

Dutch Pete's voice raised in exasperation. "The cavalry ain't going to do nothing—that's what they're going to do!" he snarled back. "I'm telling you because it shows where the state stands, that's all! That's state troops, you hear?"

"If you came down here to ask my advice," said Hughes, "I say, send back for four more squadrons, and a field piece!"

"I came down here to give you your chance," Dutch Pete shouted back doggedly, carrying out his instructions against his preferences. "I'm telling you, I mean to stand for no more nonsense. You've run your little old bluff long enough, and you're through. I've sent to Adobe Wells, and I've got a case of dynamite. I'm giving you an hour to make up your mind. Either you'll come out with all hands reaching, or by God, I'll blast you out! And if I have to blow you to hell to do it, that's all right with me!"

"Where do you figure in this?" Hughes taunted him. "Go back and tell Earl Shaw that if he wants to talk to me he can come up here himself, and not be hiding behind the oversize chaps of a big square-head. Go back and tell your boss that you must have got the message all balled up; we couldn't understand it!" He slammed the shield shut.

"Gun him, Ol'ver!" said Bart Holt in a dry croak. "Throw down on him, and it'll be one less of 'em, anyway . . ."

278

There was a silence. "Well, you heard him," said Hughes.

"It's the last notch, Oliver," said Stephen Sessions, his voice very deep and low, but harsh with strain.

The voice of Walk Ross interrupted him, coming thin and bodyless from where he lay. The blur of delirium was gone from his tongue for almost the first time since his second wound. "I've got it," he said suddenly. "I know now! Just a little bit ago I was starting to tell you something. I've been tryin' to remember what it was. I remember now. Listen, listen—get this! This—this is good!"

"Yes, Walk?" There was movement in the close dark as some of them moved closer to him. His story came out in ragged phrases.

"I know now how word got to Earl Shaw that Grasshopper Tanner knew something. I took the word in myself, though I was too dumb to know. You might say I took it in on my clothes. When I told Art French I was bound to go to town, he told me that Bill Finley, the bartender in the Red Dog Saloon, owed him a piece of money. Art says to me, 'Grasshopper knows all about it and can dicker with him for me. Give Bill Finley this note.' Art showed me the note. I don't know why he showed it to me; unless it was because he couldn't keep me from reading it anyway, if I got suspicious and set out to. So he showed it to me. It said something like this: 'Grasshopper knows all about it. Better give it to Grasshopper for me. Art French.'"

There was a silence. "So that was how it was," said Oliver Major slowly at last. "You hear that, Steve? That clinches the case against Art French."

"Art French is dead."

Walk Ross closed his eyes. His face looked very white and drawn. In spite of the blankets piled upon him he had shaken with repeated chills. "I'm a fool," he said in a loud distinct voice. Then, more faintly, "I been resting here, saving my strength. I'll be all right when I get up. I got Art French. I'm going to get a couple more. That's all I want."

"Be quiet, Walk," said Sally.

"You see," said Major, "you see, there's another that they would never dare let live to tell his story in court." He seemed to be speaking to himself; the fruitless argument with Stephen Sessions he had abandoned long ago, hardly later than the hour in which the convincing of Sessions had ceased to be of use. "Now that we know the truth about Tanner, I suppose there isn't a man here that they can afford to bring to trial or leave an the loose."

"Oliver," said Stephen Sessions, "even so, it's the only chance."

Hughes noticed that he no longer was prepared to scoff at Oliver Major's theory that Shaw and his men would take execution into their own hands without legal procedure. It was the first time that he had admitted by phrasing or tone that there was any sane objection to complete submission to the law.

"Never in the world," said Oliver Major with utter

conviction. "Anything but that!"

"What else can you do?" cried Stephen Sessions, something very like panic creeping into his voice.

It was Sally Major's voice which answered Sessions. It rang clear and cool, fearless and defiant.

"Fight," she said, "first, last and always! We can always do that."

Dick Major said, "We can at least have a whack at shooting our way out—"

"And leave Walk Ross and Dusty Rivers behind? They can't be moved."

Clay Hughes lifted the lantern once more; now, at the last, it seemed that it offered no extra hazard. He hung it on a hook in a beam overhead.

"But the girl?" plead Stephen Sessions.

"What of the girl?" Sally blazed at him. Her face was white, proud, and her eyes were clearer and more keen than those of any of the men. "Do you think there is anything in the world for me with my men rubbed out?"

"But—" Sessions tried.

"The trouble with you," said Sally, her low voice an icy whip, "is that you're fat, and soft, and a coward. You can't bear to face facts in your mind. Even yet, you're trying to smooth things over and let yourself down easy; twisting the facts around, because it isn't in you to look them in the eye!"

"Speaking of me—" said Sessions. He tried to put a light twist to his approach to this last and nearest subject of all, and the effect was ghastly—"speaking of me, what about me? If you still mean to hold me here—"

A crazy laugh cracked Oliver Major's voice. "Speaking of you—speaking of you—"

"Just a minute," Clay Hughes cut in. "Mr. Major, I haven't asked a favor yet. I want one now." They waited in silence. "I've stood this thing through with you," said Hughes, "and I'm with you yet. I'm entitled to this one thing. Will you give it to me?"

"Anything you say," said Oliver Major, as if nothing could make any difference in this world.

"Then," said Hughes, "give me this man."

"Sessions? What do you want with him?"

"What do you care what I want with him? I'm asking for him. Give me this man!"

"Take him," said Major. "Do what you like."

Hughes turned to Sessions, his voice even and cold. "Your race is run," he said. "You want to go, don't you? You want to save your hide. Well, I'm going to let you go . . . Not yet! Wait a minute more.

"Before you go, I want you to understand why I'm letting you go. It's because shooting is too good for you. I want you to live and take the gaff. Your race is run. Ask yourself why the National Guard Cavalry has been called out by the governor. To squash us, with fifty men against us already?

"You know why! It's because public opinion is already so strong that Theron Replogle is afraid. Afraid that enough cowmen will rise up to ride over this posse of fifty men like they'd ride down sheep!

Ask yourself what Theron Replogle knew before he called out the National Guard—as the defense for a posse of fifty men! Theron Replogle hasn't quite as much savvy as you have, I should judge. You wouldn't have done it in his place. You'd have known better than to do it. And you know now, already, that he's through, and you with him. And that's not all.

"You been trying to believe what you wanted to believe. Almost you made it stick, didn't you? But you, couldn't quite do it, for I've watched you. How deep are you in the Silverado project, Sessions? I don't know, but I'm betting it's plenty deep. What I do know is that Shaw is a part of your organization. Ask yourself what becomes of the organization when it gets in so deep that it has to kill man after man just to keep one jump ahead of the rope! You know the answer to that. One stone out of the arch, and the whole tower falls.

"You know that; you know what's ahead of you. That's why I'm kicking you out, to save your hide now. But there's just one thing more. You're going to remember this the day you die. You've got a good memory, haven't you? But you never thought that you'd remember anything like you're going to remember what I'm going to tell you now! . . . Wait a minute; don't be in a hurry. You're going to get it all right."

He got out a cigarette paper and a pencil with which he had tallied calves on more ranges than one. "Sally," he said, "I promised you that when I was ready to tell what Hugo Donnan said, before he died in Crazy Mule Canyon, I'd tell you first of all. Well, I'm ready now."

He hesitated an instant, then on the cigarette paper he wrote these words: *"Donnan said nothing. I am going to lie."*

Then he went on, aloud. "Hugo Donnan died in my hands, Sessions, as you know. Until this moment I've never told a soul what he said to me before he died. It hasn't been understood very well why I held it back. You'll see when I tell you now. I held it back because I couldn't see what possible connection the name he used could have. Well, I was thinking of it from the wrong angle, as you'll see.

"Hugo Donnan pulled me down close to him and he said, *'Get Stephen Sessions.'* Then he died.

"Naturally, I couldn't see how Stephen Sessions could have any connection. You can see where I looked at it wrong. I thought he meant he was trying to name the man that was to blame. He couldn't have been, of course. You were too high up, Sessions, and in a different part of the state. And—you didn't have the guts. So I said nothing. So long as I thought Donnan meant to point you out as guilty in some way, I couldn't see what he meant. But I see it now. You all see it.

"*'Get Stephen Sessions.'* That was what old man Major here said, when trouble come down on him and his brand. That's what every honest, hard-fighting man has said in this part of the country when crooked-

284

ness got him tangled up in an unfair way, and he had to have help from higher up to get out. 'Get Stephen Sessions.' I reckon that's been said many and many a time!

"Me being new here, I didn't know about that then. I didn't know about what getting Stephen Sessions meant, when I heard Donnan say it as he died. I didn't know he was telling me to get help to straighten out this awful mess. I didn't know he was just repeating at his very end, and in the worst trouble he could be in, what maybe he heard his father say once, way back in the earlies when this country was new.

"Now you all know what Donnan said when he died. You all know what he meant—and what those words meant that he didn't know—'Get Stephen Sessions.' And I guess maybe that last half-cocked send-out for help has turned out to be an accusation after all. Maybe that dead sheriff was making the most terrible accusation that was ever made by any man, just when he asked for help in a place where God knows there was no help to be had.

"I reckon we're lucky here. I reckon I'd rather be the man that's at the bottom of all the Buckhorn trouble, and caused every killing the Buckhorn's ever seen, than be the man that people turn to—'Get Stephen Sessions'—and then found out what we all know now.

"You can get out now. Take a good look at a couple of these people first—you ain't going to see 'em again, but you'll remember them often enough. And I don't have to tell you to remember those words that

Donnan said. You can't ever forget 'em now. You'll hear 'em like the drum of hoofs, and in the wind, and in the rain, and in the blow of the sand; and they'll ring in your ears when it's dead quiet, and that'll be worst of all. You'll hear 'em until some night you'll get out your six-gun, that you haven't used for so long, and you'll put it up to your head; but you won't pull the trigger, not you! Because you haven't the guts, any more. So you'll just have to go on with it, for by that time you won't even be half way. And I've got no doubt that pretty soon you'll be asking God to help you with it, and you already know the answer to that one too. No, I reckon it'd be a right smart injustice, old Steve, to let you get killed now!

"Now—get out! Stick your tail between your legs, and run!"

There was silence in the room when Clay Hughes had finished that long halting speech. He had used more words than he had ever used in his life, or ever would again; and they were also more words than these people were accustomed to listening to. Mostly their minds had wandered off before he was done, turning off to what was ahead of them, and perhaps also a little bit to things behind that they were not going to see or experience again, by the look of things now. But one man there listened because he couldn't help but listen; and it was not the ears, but the infallible memory Stephen Sessions owned that was listening to Clay Hughes.

To Hughes that halting indictment was perhaps the

286

supreme effort of his life; but it was not the low-voiced stumbling phrases of the cowboy that Stephen Sessions was unable to shut out or to evade. Of all men in the world, he was the one who could see, clear and distinct in the half light of that boasted memory of his, the face of every man or woman who had ever said, 'Send for Stephen Sessions': and Lord knew that they were legion. They were scattered over mountain and desert and plain, all the length and breadth of the southwest. He remembered their voices, and their troubles, and their names, effortlessly, against his will. And he knew why he had chosen to fail them all, and what had been the price of each. Without that deep-mottled background of faces, and of memories sharper than those of face or name, the others could not feel the thrust of those slow halting words; but this one old man—

There was a silence again; and the face of Stephen Sessions was an ugly thing. The granite was out of it, so that it looked like something shapeless and pallid in which the bones had swiftly gone bad. And the hard-set line of the mouth was strictly a thing of the past by now, for the lower lip hung pendulous, and jerked.

Yet he did not speak; and as the moments passed Hughes was forced to the slow conclusion that he had failed. Ever since Hugo Donnan had died in his arms in Crazy Mule Canyon, Hughes had nursed the scant thin hope that in the end he would be able to conceive a bluff which would somehow pull the fortunes of the Lazy M out of the fire. The opportunity had never come.

It had seemed to him for a moment that he had a chance. Stephen Sessions was an old man, and weary in his years; the terrific strain of the past five days might well have brought him near the cracking point. That Stephen Sessions was allied with Earl Shaw in the Silverado project was now obvious. And without seeing the memories that stood ready to flood the mind of Stephen Sessions, Hughes yet knew that there must be hidden there a heavy weight of guilt.

Perhaps, he was considering now, Stephen Sessions after all had not had the power and authority which they had believed rested in him. Perhaps it was only that with every other moral resource cracked away, nothing but the aged stubbornness of Stephen Sessions remained, of no value to himself or to them.

Little time remained. Soon now Dutch Pete would come for his final word. Old Oliver Major, Hughes knew, would not wait for that. Whether Major would wish to rush the house, in an attempt to break through the security behind which Earl Shaw directed operations, and confront his enemy face to face at the last, Hughes did not know; but the old man would certainly walk out fighting, to face the guns. And the rest would go with him, those that could walk, ending the long fight over the Buckhorn water in a final blaze. Oliver Major was looking slowly about the room, gazing at the walls, at the beams, and Hughes knew that he must be seeing things that other eyes could not see. Here were the courses of adobe which Oliver and his brother Sol had laid with their own hands, back in the days when they and the range were young. There was the old fireplace, the old shelves; in this little two room adobe, lonely then in the broad valley, Sally Major and her brother had been born, in the days when Major's dream of the Buckhorn water was filled with young hopes. Now the Lazy M was ending where it had begun. In the dim lantern-light the air was heavy with the odor of horses, of leather, and the smoke of guns. The scene was one which might have taken place in the days when that adobe was new; only the iron pump engine in the middle of the room bore witness that there were years of great change between.

Oliver Major spoke. "You boys ready?" he said. "My idea of it is this: We'll—"

The smash of lead upon the wooden shields of one of the windows broke in like an interruption upon his low voice. Someone, seeing the light of the raised lantern at some crevice, had been unable to abide by the hour's armistice which Dutch Pete had declared. It had become almost a familiar sound to them in the last five days, that thud and shatter of bullets; but Oliver Major paused a moment, listening by habit. Four times the lead smashed into the wood of the barricade at brief, regularly spaced intervals. There was something singularly vicious in that deliberate searching fire, the message of a rifle rested and well aimed. There was a moment's pause, and once more Oliver Major opened his mouth to speak. Then—

The fifth and last shot found the lighted crack in the planking that it sought. There was a smash of splin-

tered wood and the short growl of the smothered ricochet. A jagged bit of plank half the size of a man's
hand spun the length of the room like a bat. As the
fragment passed, the thin cloth of Sally's dress was
torn open at the shoulder as if by the stroke of a knife,
revealing white flesh that instantly covered itself with
a swift run of red.

Hughes and Dick Major sprang to support her, one
on each side, but after an instant she pushed them
away, rigidly, ashamed to yield to pain.

"It isn't anything," she said, her voice small and
shaky. For a moment as she stood apart from them,
very thin and still, she looked like a little girl, trying
to hide the fact that her fingers were brushing away
tears.

Stephen Sessions' voice broke out unexpectedly, a
voice that no one would recognize as coming from
this man. "It isn't worth it! Nothing's worth it! By
God, I'm through!" He jerked to his feet and moved
lurching toward the door. "It's too much! It's gone too
far! Let me out of this!"

"I told you to get out," said Clay Hughes, his voice
low and cold.

"I can stop it yet! I will stop it!" Stephen Sessions'
hands were shaking, ineffectual claws as they fumbled
at the bar of the door. "Replogle will acknowledge
what I do in his name. That Colonel of Cavalry will do
what I say. I gambled two-thirds of my fortune in the
Silverado, but this—this is too much!"

"Wait!" said Hughes, jumping to the door.

"Let me out, I say! I can turn the cavalry against them, and call the posse off!"

"It's too late," said Oliver Major. "No man can get out of here unless we all go out with our hands up; and if we do, you know what will happen then."

"They must let me pass!" gibbered Stephen Sessions.

"Sing out to them, then!" said Hughes. "Flatten yourself to the wall, and I'll open the door a crack." He unbarred the door, and opened it an inch or two. "You, out there!" he hailed. "We'll talk to Dutch Pete!"

They could hear voices beyond in the dark, calling Dutch Pete's name; but moments passed, and Hughes called out twice more, before they heard the voice of Dutch Pete himself answering them across the darkness from the house.

"Talk loud if you want to talk to me," came the words, thick and heavy, but made small by the distance. "I'm not coming down there no more."

"Yell across to him," said Hughes to Sessions.

Stephen Sessions' voice rang big and powerful, the voice that had once harangued crowds and rounded votes. "This is Stephen Sessions speaking! I represent Governor Replogle here! Hold your fire while I come out!"

There was a brief silence.

"Who?" called Dutch Pete at last.

"Stephen Sessions, I say! I demand safe conduct while I come out!"

"You lie," Dutch Pete answered after a moment. "Steve Sessions skedaddled over the Pass with the women, before the fight began."

"But I'm here, I tell you!"

In the silence they could hear dimly the heavy booming chuckle of Dutch Pete as he said something they could not understand.

"Good lord!" Sessions burst out. "Don't you recognize my voice?"

"Sure I do," Dutch Pete shouted back. "Old man Major's who *you* are!"

"Then let me talk to Earl Shaw!"

"Earl Shaw's gone back to town."

"Do you suppose," said Stephen Sessions huskily to those within the adobe, "that that's true?"

Oliver Major spat. "It's like him," he decided. "If they're coming on with dynamite, he'd rather leave the finish in the hands of Dutch Pete, so as to be clear of it if the investigation bears down too hard afterward. Yes, I suppose he's gone back all right—or more like, he's laying low and given out that he's gone back."

Stephen Sessions' face was ghastly. The flesh sagged away from his eyes so that they stared fishily. "They can't shoot me," he mumbled. "They can't shoot me . . . I'm going out."

"Stand where you are," said Hughes.

Before he could be restrained, Stephen Sessions threw up the bar of the door and flung it wide. He was stumping out into the night as Hughes seized him by the belt, jerking him back with all his strength. Outside, with the opening of the door, a ragged salvo of gunnery wakened to life, dusting the outer adobe of the wall, sending a scatter of bullets scudding, by the handful it seemed, into the timbers of the open door. Hughes dragged Sessions in bodily; the door was slammed shut, and once more barred.

"They can't shoot you, huh?" said Hughes. Sessions staggered backward, caught his balance, and stood swaying; he was staring unbelievingly at one of his hands. A bullet had just nicked the side of it; it was his only wound. "They were firing on me," he said idiotically, as he watched the slow trickle of blood run down his little finger and drip to the floor.

"Oh, were they?" said Hughes.

"But I can stop this," Sessions persisted dimly. "I can call this off. I can change the sheriff; I can get a change of venue. If only I can reach that cavalry camp I can stop this whole damn—"

"You could have once," said Oliver Major. "You had your chance when you were the only hope we had. It's gone now. They can put forty guns on the man who tries to make the break. It's all over, Steve."

Hughes stepped forward and jerked Sessions to faze him by the front of his shirt. "Look here," he demanded. "Can you write a message to the Cavalry Colonel that will do the work?"

"You mean—"

"Does the officer in charge of the Cavalry out there know your signature?"

"Of course he does. It'll be Bob Everett; I've known him since— If it isn't Everett, it'll be one of the others. Yes! If we can get a message—"

"Then write your message." He snatched a tally book from a shelf and thrust it with a pencil into Sessions' hand. "Write it, and write it quick, and make it full and complete. There mustn't be any mistake or misunderstanding now."

"But—"

"Write it, I say. What are you waiting for?"

"We can get no message out!"

"The hell we can't. I'll get the message out."

CHAPTER TWENTY

"It can't be done," said Oliver Major. "No man could do it in this world."

"What can't be done?"

"No man could get out of here with a message to the cavalry or anybody else. Any one of a dozen men that Earl Shaw's got out there can shoot so as to stop a man the minute he steps out. Just one of those men could do it—you hear? And instead of one man, I suppose they've got forty!"

"Sessions just showed himself, and he's alive," said Hughes.

"He showed himself for half a second; it come as a surprise to them, and he was only partly exposed anyway. Do you think he'd have lived to move three strides?"

Hughes made an impatient gesture and turned on Sessions. "Put down what I say. Write—"

"I know what to write," said Sessions. Slowly, in a ragged vibrant script, he began to write on a blank page of the tally.

"It's suicide," insisted Major. "It's quick death if anything ever was."

"Give me your gun, Dick," said Hughes.

Dick Major obeyed, and Hughes thrust the gun into the left side of his belt.

Sessions was writing rapidly now, his hand overcoming the shock of its slight wound. He had wrapped his handkerchief around it, yet here and there his script was emphasized by little smudges of red. There was silence while the swift pencil covered a page, started on the next. "Are you going to write all night?" said Hughes.

"I must make sure," said Sessions. "There mustn't be any mistake."

"What are you going to try to do?" Dick Major demanded.

Sessions answered slowly as he wrote. "Everett must take full charge. All prisoners under his protection. He must declare an emergency of martial law until the Shaws are removed and replaced . . . It'll mean the discrediting of Shaw, instead of Major. It's the end of the Silverado project; nothing can save it."

"But Everett and his cavalry— Will he do as you say? Will he dare do as you say?"

"He won't dare not to. They know which side their

checks have been buttered on these many years. After all, all that is needed is a delay, as far as he is concerned. I am telling him in detail what he must do."

"You can save your pencil," said Oliver Major. "The message will never reach!"

"It's got to reach."

There was silence through a long minute, and another, while the hurrying pencil of Stephen Sessions scribbled, blackening the sheet. Watching over his shoulder, Hughes saw that he ended his message with a few words of code.

"What's that last?"

"It proves the signature, is all. Everett, or whoever is in command there, will know that to disobey this is to disobey the government of the state." The old man paused a minute, and one hand gripped his writing wrist, as if to steady it. Then bearing down hard in a firm sweep, he signed his name, "Stephen Sessions, by authority of Theron Replogle."

He tore out the sheets and handed them to Hughes, who folded them lengthwise and wrapped the strip around his belt. Clay pulled off his boots and flung them into a corner.

"Follow the Buckhorn bed," Stephen Sessions was saying. "The cavalry will be camped close by the water, and just beyond the range of guns. As you come into their camp you'll be picked up by the guard, and taken to whatever officer is in charge. In God's name, tell them to be quick!"

"Put out the light," said Hughes, "and get back from the door."

Sally Major cried out sharply, "No—no! You mustn't go; you mustn't try it."

He turned his eyes to her slowly, almost reluctantly, then smiled queerly on one side of his mouth. "I'm afraid there's no time to talk it over much," he said, and turned to go.

"Are you going to let him go?" she cried. "He won't get ten paces, he won't get five! It's certain death to go out there now!"

Oliver Major said slowly, "What is it for us all, if we stay? . . . You'd better go out the window on the far side. The door is towards the stream, and it's from there that most of their guns have been sweeping us three sides. But on the west you're only covered by the guns from the house."

"No," said Hughes, "there's nothing to be gained there. I'm going to rush the Buckhorn bed. Once across, and I'll lose them in the willow brakes."

"Good-bye, boy," said Oliver Major. He shook Hughes' hand, gravely.

"Then take a horse," urged Dick, "and—"

Hughes shook his head. "A horse makes a fine noisy mark on a job like this. Well, I'll be seeing you before long." He stooped, lifted the lantern, and blew it out.

Sally Major flung herself upon him. As her arms clamped about his neck he felt the jerk of the sob which she sought to smother in her throat. He thought she was going to urge him once more to stay, but she did not. She pulled his face down to hers; and her tears were salty upon his lips as he kissed her mouth. Then she let him go.

"Keep out of line now," he said. He took Dick's gun in his left hand and brought it to the cock, then slowly and soundlessly unbarred the door. He opened it inch by inch, so that its movement might not be heard. "Close it quiet behind me," he whispered; and sidelong, silent on his bootless feet, he slid out into the night.

For a moment he flattened himself against the adobe wall, out of line with the door, and eased his own gun into his right hand. After the utter darkness of the interior, the starlight seemed very bright. There was no moon, but the big near stars of the desert country leaned close, flooding the empty ground before him with a faintly blue, unwelcome light. For a moment he waited, accustoming his eyes to that light; locating the exact point of the streambed which he would try to make.

The curve of the Buckhorn gave him his cue. Once he had reached the point between the streambed of the Buckhorn and the house, a part of the enemy fire would perhaps be confused, for he would be between two fires, and the guns that searched for him from one side would discommode those upon the other. He picked out the exact spot for which he would try. The streambed was narrow here, and he could make out the black brake of the willow thicket, low in the far side of the cut beyond. Beside him he heard the very gentle closing and barring of the door.

It was a long fifty yards to the wall of the Buckhorn cut at the point he would try to make; and those fifty yards were open, flat as a table top, and as bare of cover. The starlight seemed to become plainer as his eyes accustomed themselves. A moving object in those fifty yards would be a mark almost impossible for trained guns to miss, and the range would shorten as he rushed the streambed. For all he knew, the point at which he aimed was itself a nest of snipers. There was no point along that streambed for a hundred yards from what the Shaw men had not fired upon the pump house.

There was a chance in a thousand that a man could make it through, one chance in a thousand to bring rescue to those within the adobe; one chance in a thousand to go out living, one chance for the Buckhorn water. He took a deep breath and crouched low.

After the dense air of the adobe, heavy with burning kerosene and the reek of engine oil, with powder smoke and the thick warm odor of horses, the outer air was cool and clean, like starlight, or clear water. Never before in his life had he consciously realized that life was very sweet. Now, in a sudden rush of awareness he realized that he loved life, and everything in it, from the smell of spring grass and wood smoke to the thunder of the hoofs of cattle, and the sharp tang of cold nights under the stars. He loved the harsh burn of raw whiskey, and winter cakes and sausage, and the battling of a bucking horse, and the voices of wolves singing the moon on long prairies; and many others were somehow in his mind for one sharp moment in which the world and the flesh seemed infinitely precious; and the hot pressure of Sally's lips was sweet upon his mouth. . . . He stepped forward, crouching very low, chest near the ground.

Three steps forward he moved, four, very quietly and slow. He had intended to try to gain six paces before staking everything on his rush of the cut; but as he counted four a gun spoke from the house, and dust as sharp as salt jumped into his face. Hughes sprang forward, every nerve exploding into action as he sprinted for the cut, running with everything that was in him.

And now abruptly the world awoke in a roar of guns; a ragged staccato rattle at first, instantly rising to a drumming thunder. The precarious silence of deceptive peace had split wide open on an instant's notice. From half a dozen windows of the main house the Bar S rifles lashed out, and from the bed of the Buckhorn itself others answered from a dozen places, the red stab of their explosions converging upon the runner. Under the crash of the guns the air was filled with the droning hum of bullets. It seemed to him that in the cleared space across which he ran nothing could live, that even a gopher would have died there, shot to rags in an instant. He moved within a cone of droning lead from which no living thing could escape.

Ahead of him, at the exact point for which he was making, and on either side of it, new guns now woke, meeting him head-on with a rapid fire. These his own guns now answered, as Hughes fired with both hands as he ran, dodging and twisting like a rabbit struck at by the unseen.

What would happen when he flung himself head-long upon the guns in front of him—if he lived that long—he could not foresee, but there was no choice now. Behind him the defenders of the pump house had gone into action, covering his rush as best they could with a steady stream of answering fire. Every opening in the pump house seemed to roar and blaze with the fury of the defenders' guns. If the pump house fire and his own could confuse and hasten the fire of those immediately in front of him for an instant more—

As Hughes started his dash across the open ground, the watchers at the pump house loop holes tore down the heavy window shields, flinging them aside into the dark, careless of whether they would ever be wanted again. There were two of those little pigeonhole windows on the streambed side; Chris Gustafson and Dick Major each took one of these. An array of extra weapons lay ready to their hands. At the end of the pump house, toward the main ranch house, was a single window. Oliver Major stationed himself here.

By the time the shields were ripped clear, the siege had already taken Hughes under its withering fire. Considering that many of the besiegers must have been caught unready, it was unlikely that more than twenty guns were in action; but that converging fire, its many voices melting into a drumming roar, with the Shaw men firing as fast as they could pull—faster perhaps than some of them could aim—seemed the concentration of at least a hundred. The empty space across which Hughes sprinted was an arena surrounded by watchers, and every spectator was a gun. Death poured itself into that dusty ground like storm-driven rain. It seemed to fill the air with invisible striking wings; and low to the ground there rose a knee-deep unnatural mist of dust that jerked and shifted as new gouts and puffs were struck up by the storm of lead.

No one there had ever before seen so vicious a concentration of power close upon a single man. It was a burst of unbelievable nightmare, so sudden and overwhelming in its violence that the watchers, prepared for it as they were, seemed half stunned, unable to think or feel.

Not stunned past action though. Oliver Major was training his spitting rifle upon the main house, at the windows of which the flash of a dozen muzzles could be seen. Major's rifle was a five-shot clip-loader, extra long of barrel, but beautifully balanced, made to his order. It was said that he could shoot the head off a partridge with that gun, at seventy yards.

Swiftly, with inspired hands, shooting as he perhaps would never shoot again, Major was putting his accurate shots into one window after another of the house. The opposing windows continued to spit flame; it seemed that if he was finding his marks at all, the silenced guns were instantly replaced. He fired swiftly and grimly, his long legs bracing him hard against the wall. And if any could have seen his face then, they would have seen that tears—tears of wrath and frustration and hate—were wetting the polished walnut of the rifle stock. Dick Major wept also, but in a different way, whimpering bitter oaths as he wildly emptied a six-shooter, and a second, and a third at the entrenched line of guns in the streambed.

Of the three men fit to stand to action there, only Chris Gustafson fired cool and slow, aiming carefully with rested gun at the flashes as they showed, intent on making each shot count. But it was only in comparison to the others that Gustafson's shots were slow, for the big impassive cowboy was shooting as he had never shot before. Three times he fired at the flicker of a single gun, shooting as close past Hughes as only a man who knew the steadiness of his hand could dare. Only when the flash upon which he fired ceased altogether did he pats on to a second mark; yet he had time to get his second man.

And that time was brief; only the time in which it takes a man to sprint fifty yards, running as a man runs into the face of fire—a brief span of seconds, hardly more than a finger-snap in the face of time. Yet in that roar of guns the passage of time seemed to hang suspended forever. To those who brought their guns into play to cover Clay's rush with the pitifully weak defending fire that they could command, it seemed that the running man lingered forever, vulnerable and defenseless in that open ground. The race took on the agonizing slow motion of a fever-dream. Hughes had sustained the first burst of fire and was still alive . . . He was half way, and he was still alive. . . . He was almost within reach of the streambed. Both his guns were speaking now as he rushed, crouched low, directly into the face of the enemy guns.

But the three men fit to stand to their weapons were not alone in bringing guns to the support of Hughes' rush. Those that stood to their guns at the windows did not know then in that turmoil of action that Sally had flung wide the door. With the heavy rifle that she had caught up in the dark she was firing past the figure of Clay Hughes, even more narrowly than Chris Gustafson, cool-nerved and steady, as she tried to pick off the Shaw men directly ahead of Hughes.

And to her side came two others, lurching unsteady figures out of the shadows. One, a stooped and twisted figure, was Bart Holt; he held his six-gun hard against the jamb of the door with his left hand, firing with his right. And the other, the tall shadow that swayed on wide-braced legs, firing a rifle from the hip like a six-gun, as if it were too heavy to raise, was Dusty Rivers.

One more was in that fight. Walk Ross lurched against Dick Major, begging for room, and raised his six-gun to the sill. For a long time—or what must have seemed so to him—he tried to steady his almost invisible sight upon a fitful flash far to his left. He fired once, clung to the sill long enough to see that the man he had chosen fired no more; then lost his grip and slipped to his knees.

All that was simultaneous, while those few brief seconds dragged into eternity; and still they knew that Clay Hughes was alive. Clay's crouching rush, incredibly threading the maze of singing lead, had cut the distance almost to nothing when at last they saw him go down.

It seemed to the watchers that Hughes turned in midair, as if in running his knee had struck a fixed post. The dimness of the starlight confused their straining eyes, but they knew that as he went down he rolled like a rabbit shot on the run. A gasp that was half a sob was torn from Sally Major, and the rifle slipped from her hands. She flung herself forward blindly into the starlight. It was Bart Holt who caught her wrist, clamping it in fingers hard and cold as iron. The jerk of her weight wrenched a gasp from the wounded man, but he held on, and threw his weight backward to drag her in. Bart Holt's knees buckled under him, but still he held on, restraining her with his dead weight.

Then Sally cried out, "He's up! Clay's up!" She stood rigid in the doorway's shadow as Bart Holt's fingers relaxed slowly, losing their grip. Clay Hughes was somehow on his feet again. They saw him lurch forward three paces, and both his guns spoke once more. A gun lashed out in front of him, almost in his face, and they could not tell whether he sprang or fell as he drove over the lip of the cut, and was lost to view.

Within the adobe the firing ceased, leaving a silence that still seemed to ring with the explosions of the guns. The air was thick with the heavy reek of powder. Dusty Rivers was down in a crumpled tangle in the doorway, coughing as if he would cough out his life. Bart Holt, however, had dragged himself away; and though Walk Ross was down somewhere in the dark interior, no one knew exactly what had happened to him nor took tithe now to find out. Oliver Major picked up Dusty Rivers bodily and laid him upon a bunk. Dick Major was blubbering, "They got him—they got him—the damned—"

They heard Bart Holt's voice, low and harsh, "It's the end of the rope."

Oliver Major's voice rose unnaturally. "Now, out, and fight. There's nothing left but to rush the guns."

Sally cried out, her voice clear and sharp. "No! Are you crazy? Not now, not yet!" She snatched for the heavy door, slammed it and threw the bar.

Oliver Major's voice droned dimly. "There's nothing left. . . ."

"You've got to give him his chance!" Sally Major's hands found her father in the dark, and twisted the gun from his hands. "He's got to have his chance; he's going to have it!"

"He's dead," said Oliver Major, his voice toneless and uncomprehending.

"How do you know he is? He got up and went on!"

"He dove square in the flash of a gun."

"If they've got him—at least—at least they don't

know it," Sally insisted. "Hear them? There's still firing going on in the Buckhorn bed."

A weird dry chuckle came from Bart Holt. "They'll be shooting each other by mistake out there," he said.

"Dick, Chris!" Sally Major ordered. "Light the lantern! Do you hear me? Are you there?"

"Yeah, Miss Major," came Gustafson's measured voice through the dark.

"Then do as I tell you."

"I'm doin' it."

Oliver Major's voice was low and shaky as he spoke again, as if all the life, all the fighting spirit had burned out of him in those few incredible seconds of gun work. "What are you trying to do?" he demanded dully.

"We have to see who's hurt here, don't we?"

Chris Gustafson's match flared at last. Yellow light welled into the room again, then immediately diminished as he covered it with the cone that permitted only that little circle of light on the floor.

"Now get that planking up again," Sally ordered them. "Hurry it up—have you forgotten how to move? Dad, are you going to stand there like a dummy?" Gustafson, Dick Major, and her father moved to shoulder the heavy shields back into place, and Stephen Sessions materialized, out of nobody knew what corner, to help them shakily in their work. Sally raised the lantern for a quick look about her.

Bart Holt had propped himself up in the back of a bunk, motionless as a clothed skeleton, saving his strength. Walk Ross, too, was sitting up against the wall in the spot where his legs had failed him. His haggard face was no longer dark enough to give contrast to those eyes which had seemed so curiously light, like bits of shell. The man was colorless, curiously suggesting that he was no longer anything but a place where a man had been; yet he managed to smile at her wanly, and his lips formed almost silent words. "I certainly am a big flop," he apologized.

It was Dusty Rivers who seemed to be in the worst case. He lay in the awkward position in which Oliver Major had put him down in the dark, one arm flung out awkwardly into the room. His eyes were open, but as unseeing as glass, and his heavy breathing had brought a bit of red-flecked foam to the corner of his mouth. Setting the lantern down, Sally went to him, straightened his limbs, and wiped his face with her handkerchief.

Working dully, in the manner of men who have outlived the over-keyed energy of battle, and with only Major and Sessions unwounded, it took them a long time, it seemed, to get the shields back into place.

"Do you suppose," Oliver Major said when they were done, "do you suppose that there's a chance that he got through?"

"No," said Holt.

"They're firing still," Dick offered.

"They're all balled up out there in the dark," said Holt contemptuously.

"He got up and went on."

"Yeah, he got up," Bart Holt admitted. "It was the gamest thing I ever saw a man do. You could tell by the way he spun when they got him that they got him good and final. And after that he dove right square into the last shot on the bank. I seen his hands throw up as he fell."

"Looked to me like he jumped in," said Dick.

"Jumped hell," said Bart Holt dogmatically. "He throwed up his hands and fell. They finished him with that first hit. Only he just wouldn't give in, that's all."

"I never saw his hands throwed up," said Chris Gustafson.

"Sally," said Major, "you've got keener eyes than the rest. What did you see?"

There was no answer, and after a moment Major, lifting the shielded lantern, saw that she was no longer in the room. Dick Major, searching, presently found her in the stable room, huddled limply in a corner pile of hay, under the ponies' low swung heads. Kneeling beside her, her brother gathered her against him with his unwounded arm; and she clung to him, weeping convulsively. . . .

Outside the firing had fallen away to ragged bursts here and there in the stream bed itself. It had a random desultory sound, but continued persistently.

Clay Hughes had almost reached his objective—the defended streambed of the Buckhorn—when the enemy's first hit caught him as he ran. A shock like the impact of an axe smashed one leg from under him, so that he was spun in his stride and went down, rolling with his own momentum. He knew as he went down, the bared teeth of his open mouth grubbing up earth, that he was through and would never get up; yet somehow, without knowing how he accomplished it, he was instantly up, rushing the streambed once more. One leg was as numb as if it no longer existed. Its stumbling irregular action, over which he had no authority, gave his rush an uncontrollable lurch and stagger, as if the legs which carried him forward were not his own.

Then a gun blazed in his face, so close below and ahead of him that he took the blinding sting in his cheek to be the burn of powder. Both of his own guns answered from the hip as he stumbled and plunged headlong into the streambed itself. The crash of his fall brought a flash of light into his head, but he twisted as he hit, coming to his feet again like a spilled halfback.

A voice cried, "Frank, don't shoot!" Dark looming figures were closing upon him like falling rock, so close about him that they could not fire without landing each other. An insane battle craze came into him, the desperation of one man alone, swarmed over by enemies; he fought like a wounded animal, or a man inspired. Clay fired once with his left hand, and a man went down almost under his feet, but his right gun clicked empty. A gun muzzle, swung viciously downward at his head from behind, streaked his scalp; he whirled and smashed down a man with the barrel of his right-hand gun, then hurled the empty weapon into the face of another who in that instant fired at point blank range without effect.

For a moment he was clear of the hornets' nest in which he had landed. Two paces away, as he turned to the stream, a shadowy figure struggled to its knees; he could see it against the stars reflected in the Buckhorn water. He fired once more with his left hand, and the figure toppled and splashed in the shallows.

Behind them they were firing again as he splashed through the shallow Buckhorn, running with a stumbling lurch. He had almost reached the black cover of the willows on the far side when the next smashing hit knocked him headlong into the edge of the cover; his right arm crumpled useless under him as he fell. Turning on his side, he fired once more with his left hand; then that gun too was empty, and he let it fall.

He wormed his way forward on his stomach deeper into the black shadow of the willows. A great driftwood log offered momentary protection; a bullet threw rotted wood in his face as he rolled over it. Dragging himself silently, tight to the ground, he worked downstream through the willows. More Shaw guns were searching for him now, clipping twigs behind him, above him, as they beat the willows.

Men were calling out with excited angry voices, questioning voices, voices uncertain in the dark. "We got him—he's down somewhere in this damn brake!"

"Somebody get a light!"

"To hell with your light—you want to die?"

"For God's sake be careful; he got Smoky square in the teeth."

"Who was it?"

"It's that damn Wyoming gun fighter."

"He dodges like a rabbit, and he throws two guns like a fool. . . ."

The searching bullets became less accurate as he worked his way yard by yard downstream. He had gained a rod, two rods; three. No one seemed anxious to beat the brakes for him by hand. They supposed that he was dead, and if so, he could wait; but if he was not, no one wanted to stumble onto his guns in the black shadow. Well downstream where an angling irrigation trench raised the Johnson grass stirrup high, he left the thinning rift of the willow thicket. The ditch led him to a lateral that turned southward; and by the time he was out of the irrigated ground he knew that he was probably far enough south to have distanced the search. He rolled under a fence, checked his direction, and began running steadily southward, twisting between clumps of cactus and sage.

The craze of battle that had sustained him in the streambed was out of him now. In its place was the necessity of swiftly covering the ground. He did not know how much time he might have before Dutch Pete closed upon the pump house for the last time. His escape in itself might have precipitated the one last attack that could not be withstood.

He clutched his wounded arm to his chest with his

left hand, and put everything he had left into steady running. A racking pain had come into his wounded leg, but it seemed to be working more smoothly now, on the level ground. He forced himself to greater speed. His breath labored as he drove himself, until his windpipe turned raw, and the starlight dimmed. He tasted copper.

He was almost done, and it seemed that he must have passed the cavalry station long ago, when the dark low shadows of the picket line loomed ahead, and a voice called out sharply, "Halt! Who's there?"

"Friend, you damn fool," gasped Hughes; and barged head-long against the rifle of the guard.

CHAPTER TWENTY-ONE

"I don't suppose," said Oliver Major, "that I ever seen anything like that before. I misdoubt if anybody's ever seen anything like that before."

Once more he sat in his office, sidewise, at that ornate Victorian desk, as he loved to sit, now that he was old; he sucked fragrant clouds of smoke from his pipe, and a tall whiskey toddy stood beside him on the desk. His haggard face, gleaming silver with the unshaved stubble of its beard, looked older than they had ever seen it, even in those worst hours in the pump house adobe; but though the long siege and the fight was over, and those slim youngsters in the O. D. of Replogle's cavalry were noticeable all over the Lazy M as an assurance of returned peace, Oliver Major did not seem ready for sleep. Outside the dawn was bringing a cool lucid light to the corrals and adobe buildings; Sally had been sent to bed an hour ago, and the rest of the defenders of the pump house—there was not an unhurt man among them now—had been glad to turn in. But the old range-wolf, the iron man of the saddle, seemed ready to stay up and carry on.

Clay Hughes, who had now been carried up from the cavalry camp, lay on the couch in old Oliver Major's office while Doc Hodges redressed his wounds in a more professional manner than had been his fortune in the hands of the cavalry. Hughes, Hodges now found, had been wounded no less than five times; but though he was weak from loss of blood, none of the hits had found a vital mark. It was as if he, like Oliver Major, who was the one man untouched, had been defended by the unseen. It was the sort of miracle that had made the Indians believe in mystical medicine in the old days, medicine that could make a man indestructible, immune to rifle fire.

"I'd swear," Oliver Major said, talking to Doc Hodges, "an undersized coyote couldn't have got across that space. The Bar S people churned up that dust like pouring a quart of buckshot in the bottom of a pail."

"It was a fluke," said Hughes faintly.

"Fluke hell," said Oliver Major. "For one thing, you're the most durable feller I ever see. Your hide would certainly be great for saddle leather. But that ain't all. That message was got through by means of a

314

cool head and cast-iron guts. Dutch Pete said you got three men as you shot your way through."

"A fluke just the same," said Hughes.

"As for me," said Oliver Major, "I'm beginning to believe that there's something takes care of people that's got sufficient guts."

"Nothing took care of Bob Macumber," Hughes mumbled.

"No. And we're lucky if we don't lose Dusty Rivers and Walk Ross. They're alive; and that's about all you can say."

"Dusty Rivers especially," said Doc Hodges. "Now hold steady, boy. This is going to hurt for just a minute. . . ."

There was a light, almost furtive tap upon the door, and Steve Sessions came in. He had spruced himself up somewhat, evidently in the habitual effort to make himself look like what he was supposed to be. Yet, he was no more like the Sessions who had arrived in the Buckhorn a week before, dominant and assured, than a gunnysack is like a saddle.

"I couldn't sleep," he apologized, his voice husky and unconfident, "so I got up and shaved. What I'm wondering now is can a man get hold of a drink?"

"I sure guess you're entitled to one, Steve," said Major. "You turned the trick for us, in the end."

Stephen Sessions shook his head. "It was too late," he said, "it was way too late. God knows how Hughes made it through."

"Looks to me," said Hughes, ignoring Hodges'

effort to keep him quiet, "like we may be in worse trouble than we were before. We'll still be under suspicion in the killing of Hugo Donnan; and on top of that, who's going to be responsible for the fight we made against Shaw's sheriff and his men? We stood 'em off as harmless as we could, but heaven knows we must have finished some of 'em in the course of the five days."

"They lost eight men," said Hodges, "not counting the wounded that I'm liable to pull through. Now, if you'll—"

"We'll still be held responsible for that. Mr. Major, we're a long ways from home."

Stephen Sessions accepted the glass that Oliver Major offered him, and drank deep. "Hagh!" he ejaculated; then slowly shook his head. "No; the Buckhorn war is over with, Hughes. You'll see this whole thing dissolve and blow away."

"But how?" Hughes insisted.

"Because we made a stubborn rightful stand," said Major.

"No," said Sessions slowly. "It isn't exactly that. It's more like what Hughes said last night. You knock just one stone out of an arch, and the whole tower comes tumbling down. As far as the Hugo Donnan killing goes, you've got circumstantial evidence against a man who is dead. I mean Art French. The testimony of Walk Ross shows that Art French was desperately afraid to have the truth come out about that killing; afraid enough so that he sent word to Adobe Wells that

Tanner must die. And in Walk Ross' testimony as to how Tanner died, you too have a terrible indictment against the Shaw outfit, who then had the sheriff's office in their hands. The stone is out of the arch, and the tower is down. It's Theron Replogle's worry now how he will smooth over the fact that he put that sheriff's office in the hands of killers and thieves."

"But can we prove that Art French killed Hugo Donnan?"

"What use to prove a murder on a man that's dead?"

"But Tanner's testimony was that there were two killers."

"You've never had any doubt, have you," said Sessions, "that the other man in that killing was from Adobe Wells?"

"Never," said Oliver Major, "in our own minds; but when it comes to proof—"

"Ask yourself what will happen now, with the tide turned against Shaw? What always happens when a corrupt organization begins to crack? The rats will begin to break for cover, first a few, and then all, every one for himself; and when state's evidence begins to turn, there'll be half of them across the border, and the other half— You'll have the other killer of Donnan all right. Only I'm thinking that when you do, you'll have caught another dead man in the net."

"The rats will run for cover, all right," Hodges said. "One of the supervisors told me—I don't want to say which one—that he was going on French leave to Laredo, and that if once things broke against Earl

Shaw he was going over the border, and it'd be hell ever getting him back."

"What did you mean," Oliver Major demanded of Stephen Sessions, "when you said that when we got the other killer of Hugo Donnan, we'd have caught another dead man in the net?"

"Give me another drink, Oliver. I'm afraid," said Sessions, "I'm not sure enough to answer that."

There was a silence, then Hughes said, his voice husky and faint, "Is Alex Shaw alive?"

"Just," said Hodges. "During the night he's been better; that's the first encouragement I've had that I can save him. Lord knows how he's hung on!"

"Is that what you meant, Steve?" said Major.

Sessions hesitated. "I can't answer that, Oliver."

Oliver Major bore in upon him. "You won't deny that it's in your mind, as you sit there, that Alex Shaw himself was the man who killed Donnan?"

A heavy voice came from the door, "What if he did?"

The door, left unlatched by Stephen Sessions, had drifted open with the draft; and now in the doorway a tall stooped figure stood. Hughes tried to sit up, and Doc Hodges forced him back, as those in the room saw that the man in the doorway was Earl Shaw.

Oliver Major had blown out the lamp, and the early morning was not so advanced as to show the man in the doorway in a strong light. Working always in his chosen background shadows, he was a man who had seldom confronted his enemies face to face. To many of them he had remained no more than a menacing name, half tradition and half myth. And he was a shadowy figure still, as he stood in the doorway facing the old boss of the Buckhorn water across the width of the room.

Then as Earl Shaw took one slow step into the room, the light from the window caught him square, so that he was a shadow and a name no more, but a reality as solid and as hard as rock. Once more Hughes felt the stubborn strength that lay in the mass and set of the bulldog head, in the wide heavy jaws, in the blunt and bony nose. The man's face was as grey as granite, and no less hard; and the harsh humor was gone from the eyes, which were bloodshot now.

Oliver Major got to his feet with a slow noiseless motion, like an old dog who catches the wolf scent, and rises from his rest.

"What if Alex killed Donnan?" said Earl Shaw. A taunting note crept into his voice, bitter-hard and husky as it was. "What if I sent Alex to kill him because he knew too much, and was trying to quit my gang? What then?"

"You admit it then?" Oliver Major demanded.

"Certainly not, you old fool," said Earl Shaw. "But you think you know it's true, don't you? I'm asking you, what then?"

"I guess you know what then," said Oliver Major.

"Oh, do I? Where's your proof? Art French is dead. What passed between Alex and Donnan and me isn't known by another soul. He's slipped on through the loop of your rope, you hear? I wanted you to know that. I wanted to see you chew on that, before we go on."

"Slipped hell! So he's guilty, is he? My answer is that I'll see him swing!"

"No," said Earl Shaw. "He'll never swing, Alex won't."

"I promise you—" Oliver Major began.

"My brother," said Earl Shaw, "died ten minutes ago."

There was a silence in the room. Then Oliver Major, looking square and hard into the bloodshot eyes of Earl Shaw, said, "That's good." Just the two words, spoken very low, but so inhumanly cool and hard that a shiver ran down the spine of Clay Hughes.

"You'd better be wishing," said Oliver Major after a moment, "that it had been you. You're at the end of your rope, Shaw. This is once too often that you've come after the Buckhorn water. I've got you this time, and I've got you to keep. I've got you in the death of Donnan, and Tanner; and through Art French I've got you for the gunning of Walk Ross and Dusty Rivers, if they die. You've got a few too many wanted men in that gang of yours to expect them to stand by you now. I thought I'd taught you. I smeared you when you come with cattle, and I smeared you when you come with sheep, but you had to come again, like a wolf coming back to strychnine—and you got it again, didn't you? Yes, you got it now!"

"That's as may be," said Earl Shaw. His voice was so low it was almost dead. "You'll never live to see it, Major, I'm promising you that."

"You think I won't?"

"I know you won't. I'm calling you out."

Clay's eyes were on Oliver Major's face; and he saw incomprehension change to a slow incredulous hope. "You mean—" he said, as if he could not believe, "you're calling—you're calling me—"

"I'm calling you out," said Earl Shaw again. "You heard me, I guess; but maybe you've forgot what that used to mean."

"No, I ain't forgot. Only—I never believed you'd dast face me with a gun on. You've got no gun on now."

"It's here all right," said Shaw. He jerked open his vest to show the shoulder holster beneath, swung well to the front. "Strap on your gun, old water hog, and come out where there's light."

Oliver Major did not reply, but Hughes saw a slow inward smile cross his face, half closing his deep-set eyes, as he turned, reached for his gun belt and strapped it about his lean hips once more.

Earl Shaw stood aside as Oliver Major led the way out. The door closed behind them.

"Wait!" shouted Stephen Sessions. "Wait! You can't do this! I tell you—" His voice died away, and he stood sagging, a helpless and pouchy old man, tugging at a pendulous lip and staring at the door.

Hughes struggled up and swung his feet to the floor. "No—lie down," Doc Hodges urged him, forcing him back.

"No! By God, I'm going out!"

The tumbling arguments of Doc Hodges checked themselves as Hughes fought furiously in his weakness to get up. Abruptly Hodges gave it up and helped Hughes to his feet. "You'll pay for this," Hodges was insisting, "as sure as—"

"I've got to get out there!"

Stephen Sessions was trailing behind them as if drawn against his will, as they came out into the first rays of the early sun. Shaw and Major had drawn a few paces away. They were speaking together, but the others could not hear what was said. In the offing a little group of those slim swaggering kids that made up the National Guard Unit turned to watch curiously, unaware of what was happening, but sensing that something was queer.

What arrangement was made between Major and Shaw the watchers could not know. Hughes, half supported by Doc Hodges, was within a few paces of the two old men as they separated and walked away from each other, not in opposite directions, but divergently, as along the arms of a Y. Oliver Major's strides were clean and sure; Earl Shaw's steady, but very slow.

Behind him, Hughes heard Stephen Sessions say in an incredulous, almost silly voice, as if he could scarcely conceive of what was happening, "Why, they're going to shoot it out! Why, there's a man going to be killed!"

"Shut up, you fool," said Hughes.

What happened then only Hughes apparently understood in time. At what point the two old men had agreed to stop and face each other, the watchers did not know, nor by what signal they had agreed to draw and fire. But as the two walked their divergent ways there was a moment in which the back of Oliver Major was turned to his lagging enemy.

Perhaps something broke within Earl Shaw with the strain of a personal war that was older than the trees under which they stood, so that the nursed hatred of the years suddenly became too much. Or perhaps the man who all his life had worked in shadows learned suddenly that to face death in open sunlight was to discover fear. Hughes saw Earl Shaw check his stride, and turn suddenly tense as a cat, tall and stiff on his toes. Shaw's right hand whipped to the hidden holster where he carried his gun.

Sometimes in the split second flash of necessity a man can make a decision instantaneously, without thought, making a choice which later proves the only possible choice which could have been made. If Hughes had shouted to Oliver Major the warning would have come too late. Instead he shouted with all his strength the one word, *"Shaw!"* and with his left hand snatched for Hodges' gun.

The very over-keyed tensity of Earl Shaw saved Oliver Major then. In the instant of drawing his gun, Shaw whirled, and his gun swung upon Clay Hughes at a range of twenty feet.

To the watchers it seemed that both guns spoke together—Shaw's weapon and the gun Hughes had snatched from the holster of Doc Hodges. Actually,

Earl Shaw's gun must have come a split second late. Dust jumped at Clay's feet and the ricochet snarled past his knees. Earl Shaw toppled forward and fell heavily, limp to the fingertips, face down in the dust.

It hardly seemed that the watchers needed the word of Doc Hodges, who left Hughes to rush forward to the fallen man, to tell them that Earl Shaw was dead.

For a few moments there were shoutings back and forth, and hurried inquiries, and running O. D. clad figures, coming up from all portions of the Lazy M. Perhaps twenty had gathered there, almost before the smoke of the guns had drifted down the breeze. Yet, perhaps, no one there but Clay Hughes remembered the story of the Buckhorn water well enough to understand the single comment of Oliver Major. It was a long time since Sol Major, Oliver's brother, had been a living force in Buckhorn Valley.

Oliver Major spoke low and quietly, as if to some one unseen, close by his side. "It's finished, Sol," he said; then turned and walked away.

Hughes stood swaying on his one good leg, trying to keep the weight off the one that was stiff and bound. "Mr. Major," he called out, "are you all right?"

"He's all right, and he's walked away. Can't you see that?"

"Not very good," said Hughes. "I'm sleepy, I guess." They saw him raise one hand to his eyes, then turn and walk stiffly toward the house. Sessions and Hodges hurried forward to assist him. At first he tried to push them away; but a moment later he was glad of their support, as he realized that otherwise he would not have made the house on his own legs.

CHAPTER TWENTY-TWO

It was hard for Hughes to believe that anything could put him entirely out of commission, holding him down in a bed which he quickly learned to hate. But as his wounds stiffened and bound, he was forced to admit that time must pass before he could get up and ride. The days had dragged into weeks before he sat in the patio again, one of his arms still stiff and ineffectual as he tried to haze the old rhythms from the banjo.

"De la Sierra Moreno,
Cielito Lindo, vienen bajando . . ."

A number of things had changed while he had been held down. Even Dusty Rivers was far along the road to recovery by then. Except for Walk Ross, the others had mended rapidly. Walk's great effort, in which he had struggled up to fire a single shot that got his man, had been too much for him. For a few days he held on, seeming to rally; then one night, unexpectedly, he had turned his face to the wall and died.

With Earl Shaw dead, the Adobe Wells organization had blown apart like a started covey of partridges. Smoky Walters and Frank Muldoon, ace gunfighters of the Bar S, were dead; Dutch Pete was in Mexico; Judge Greer, the heart of the Walkerton branch of the organization, had sailed for the Orient for unclear reasons best known to himself, with no definite date set for his return. Theron Replogle, his political throne tottering in the blast of furious opinion that had arisen from cattlemen throughout the state, promptly steadied himself by throwing the collapsed Silverado project to the wolves; soon no one would hear anything more about the ambitious steal which had threatened the Buckhorn. And already the state's official investigation of the Lazy M's armed stand against the law was, under the guidance of Sessions and Replogle, drifting off into obscure vague channels, becoming neglected and forgotten by the daily press.

Almost from the moment in which Clay Hughes had stumbled into the cavalry camp with the message from Stephen Sessions which lifted the pump house siege, the luck of the Lazy M had changed. The last battering which adversity owed the fortunes of Oliver Major seemed to have spent itself; soon, apparently, only the bullet-splashed adobe walls would bear visible witness to the war which had threatened to reduce the Buckhorn itself to a waste.

Yet, there was verity in the mournful note of the song which the crippled banjo accompanied:

"Ay, ay, ay, ay!
Canta y no llores . . ."

It was the fifth day in which he had been allowed on his feet. Today, for the first time, he had saddled a

326

quiet, well-worked-out horse, and begun to work himself into saddle shape again. He had been surprised and angry to find that the saddle had turned into an instrument of torture. It seemed a long time since he had struck out at a high lope, his disreputable hat jerked any old way on his head, one foot swinging free of its stirrup, rolling a cigarette as he rode any old pace, any old ground. But all that would come back.

One thing, though, seemed lost. Since he had shot his way out of the pump house siege Sally had changed.

It seemed to him that she seldom met his eyes, and even when she did he found he could no longer see into their depths. Somehow, without reason or explanation, she had retreated beyond the gulf, and he seemed unable to call her back.

Just at first, while for a day or two he had been too weak to lift a hand, she had nursed him constantly and tenderly. It was when he had begun to mend a little that he noticed the change. He had tried to hold her hand then, no more; and she had drawn away.

He jerked bolt upright, startled by the unexpected. The fever blazed in his head, dizzying him so that her beloved face swam hazily before his eyes. He reached out to her with the one hand he could move. "Here—look here—you can't do that—look here—"

His whole soul was making love to her, but the words were not in his head. They seemed to have been shot out of him, like his songs, like his strength. His hand dropped limp upon the blanket as he suddenly realized that the emotion which swept her face was alarm. For a moment he had stared at her dizzily, shocked by an overwhelming sense of loss.

She forced him to lie down again. He tried to resist her, but the strength was out of him, as if his muscles would not obey his will. He heard her say, "You mustn't do that. Be quiet. Don't you want to get on your feet again, ever?"

Perhaps her voice was gentle, but his anger at his own weakness deafened him to everything but the general drift of her words. He turned his face to the wall, fighting the savagery of his resentment. That night the fever came back into him, and the next day when he broke all rules by getting up, hunting out his clothes, and trying to dress himself, he collapsed upon the tiles. After that everything seemed out of step. He fumed and fretted, delaying his recovery. Once he grasped Sally's arm as she brought him a glass of water, and pulled her close. "What is it, Sally? What's the matter?"

"What do you mean?"

"I thought we understood each other," he tried to explain. His mind was skip-stopping on him again. "Now something's wrong; something's changed."

"Nothing's changed, Clay."

"In the pump house I took you in my arms. You were different then. I thought—"

He saw the red flush come into her tanned face, the face that he was always seeing wherever he looked, awake or in his dreams. "Oh, that," she said. "I don't think we'd better talk about that now."

He stared at her for a moment, and the treacherous fever rushed into his head again. Dark anger smothered him, and as he raised himself on his elbow that mysterious weakness which he was unable to accept or understand was dragging back upon his shoulders, bringing a touch of madness. The combination was suddenly unendurable, and he burst out at her furiously.

"You're like everybody else," he raved senselessly. "When I was one more gun to the defense of the brand, I was all right, wasn't I? Oh, sure, I was a good boy then, a top hand! But now the shooting's over, and my gun isn't needed, it's different, isn't it?"

Suddenly his eyes had cleared, and he saw that she was watching him wide-eyed. Instantly he was swept with remorse. "I'm sorry," he said brokenly, "I didn't mean it. I don't know what's the matter with me."

She made him lie down again. "It's all right," she said. "It makes no difference."

"No difference—no difference." The words kept repeating themselves to him after she had gone.

He decided that he must make love to her no more until he was on his feet again, and could see how things stood. This self-imposed restraint made him cool and short of speech. When she was away from him he remembered her as more desirable than everything else in life put together; but when he saw her again, he realized that he had forgotten how essential to him she had become. The wave of her hair and the

329

curve of her throat, the quick glance of her eyes, made the distance between them intolerable; and the least touch of her fingers was cool flame.

This was torture. More than once when she was with him, he turned away his face.

Now, as he tried to make the banjo speak as it used to, he was realizing that it was past time for him to leave. The old call of the trail that had drawn him all up and down the west was in his ears again, but this time in a new way. The trail no longer beckoned with any point or meaning. He thought of the endless wandering horse trails with weariness, for he no longer believed in any mysterious benefit at the end of any of them.

There was a smell of early frost in the air, forecasting the bleak rigidity of winter upon the barren granite of the high divide; and the end of all trails seemed emptiness, an emptiness haunted by the remembered face of a girl. It seemed to him that he would never again hear the wind in the timber without imagining that he heard her voice; and he would be seeing her eyes—not aloof as they had lately been, but warm and deep, speaking to his own—when he broke his soogans on the long prairies.

It was time to move on.

He bent over the banjo, and with an impact of effort ended the fumbling of the strings. The wrench of pain that twisted his lamed arm went unregarded as the banjo woke to life again, singing once more in the old syncopating way. A beat like that of loping hoofs came back into the strings, and to it he crooned his song very low, singing only to the banjo, to himself, and to the girl whom he knew was not listening. And low and quiet though the song was, he had never sung it as he sung it now, with all his heart in it, and all the accumulated passion of the long trails.

"Pues qué he de hacer, si yo say el abandonado?
Pues qué he de hacer, será por el amor de Dios . . ."

The last chord blundered into disorder, as the lame arm refused to go on. He laid the banjo aside and wearily covered his face with his hands, as once more there crept through him, fainter now, but very real, the sickening physical weakness that was his temporary heritage from the guns. Yet he recognized that it was now less definite than before. In a little while it would return no more, and he would know himself again.

Then, somehow, he became aware that Sally Major had come across the patio and was standing in front of him, and he raised his face.

She was wearing the white lawn dress which was the first dress he had ever seen her wear. From behind her the treacherous desert sunlight struck through the light lawn as if it were thinly frosted glass, revealing the clean slim curves of her body so clearly that Clay caught his breath. There was no beauty in the world like the half-hidden, half-revealed beauty of Sally Major; in it lay a power that could destroy a man, a magic urgent and impelling: irresistible as the world thrust that had built the rim, more subtle than the war lust that ran hidden in the Buckhorn water. Hughes wished to look away, but could not.

"Come here," he said unsteadily. "Come here and sit down."

She obeyed him, but he saw that she was faintly hesitant, uncertain. He regarded her with the beginnings of a new comprehension, and the loneliness of trails was forgotten. She returned his gaze; and it seemed to him for a brief moment that her eyes were warm and deep, and answered his, as he remembered them in the time before the Bar S guns had brought him down. Then she dropped her eyes.

He said, "That's better."

"What's better? I don't know what you mean."

"Don't you?" Suddenly there went out of him all that unaccustomed sense of uncertainty which his wounds had left him. The old buoyant vitality came back into him with a rush, so he knew that his trail held for him what he demanded of it, no more—and no less. Sally no longer seemed distant, but very near.

"For a while around here," he said, "it seemed like you were a million miles away; sometimes I thought you weren't going to get back at all."

"Away?" she said, puzzled. But she was looking at him curiously as if just becoming aware that he too had returned from a far place.

"Maybe it was because I wasn't seeing very good," he said. "I don't know what's been the matter with me the last couple of weeks."

"You don't know what's been the matter with you? Why, silly, do you think you're a grizzly bear? An ordinary man would have been rubbed out by the gunning you took!"

"Oh, shush," he said. "Anyway, it seemed to me that you'd changed considerable, in ways I hadn't allowed for."

Her face was averted, but she answered him deliberately. "Because of that day when you wanted to hold my hand?"

"Things like that."

"Did you think," she said queerly, looking at him squarely, "that after I'd kissed you, I didn't want you to so much as hold my hand?"

"I guess maybe it seemed like that, right then."

"They said that you were to be kept quiet; that you were not to be excited in the least, in any way. Later it seemed like—" her voice was an even drawl— "maybe I'd flattered myself."

"Flattered yourself?"

"By thinking," she said, still in that soft drawl, "that maybe I was exciting to you. So often, when I went into your room—you—turned away your face."

"Good lord," he said. He moved closer to her, and commandeered both her hands. She sat motionless, watching him with unreadable eyes. "Listen," he said. "In a few days, I'm heading up into the Nevadas. Up there—"

"But I thought—" she exclaimed. "Why, didn't Dad tell you that you're welcome here always, as long as the Lazy M runs beef? I thought—"

"Listen," he commanded. "Some people I know up there run a mine. It's in a bad place, and the ore has to be packed out with mules. In winter time it's mighty hard to get packers to contract the work. I can have that contract if I want. It's hard, mean work, but it pays high. You see, I couldn't very well hang on around here as a worthless hand that was owed something for some gun fighting once. I can make my stake, and I will make it, and when it's made, maybe sometime I can come back and throw in with the Lazy M again, in a small way. But now—"

She suddenly sprang up, white-faced and defiant, and tried to free her hands, prisoned in his grip. "Let me go! What do I care where you go, or when? Go saddle and ride, and don't come back!"

"I thought you'd be right interested in what place I had in mind," he said.

"Why should I?"

"Because," he said, "you're going with me."

She stared at him a long moment, as if uncomprehending. Then she said in a small voice, "What makes you think I will? If you're asking me—"

"Asking you?" he repeated. "No, I'm not asking you. I'm telling you, child."

"Well, I won't—" Her voice faltered, and she suddenly sat down on the bench, her face away from him. He gathered her into his arms, gently, coaxingly; and after a moment she hid her eyes as she had hidden them once before, in the curve of his throat.

334

He lifted her chin and kissed her lips; and a medicine that ran deeper than the Buckhorn water came into The Valley of No-Peace.

Center Point Publishing
600 Brooks Road ● PO Box 1
Thorndike ME 04986-0001 USA

(207) 568-3717

US & Canada:
1 800 929-9108